I0672677

Grab Bag

13

www.barbarianspy.com

WARNING: This book is for sale to **ADULT AUDIENCES ONLY**. Contains graphic gay male sex, multiple partners, anal sex, interracial sex, and gay love all of which may be considered offensive by some readers.

All sexually active characters in this work are at least 18 years of age.

This book is copyright © habu 2017
habu asserts his right to be known as the author of this work.
Published by BarbarianSpy in 2017
Cover design © S Bush 2017
Cover images: manipulated: | © Wrangel | Dreamstime.com
ISBN: E-Book: 978-1-925568-25-7
Paperback: 978-1-925568-26-4
All rights reserved

No part of this book may be reproduced in any form, except for the inclusion of brief quotations in a review or article, without written permission from the author or publisher.

All characters in this book are the product of the author's imagination and no resemblance to real people, or implication of events occurring in actual places, is intended.

BarbarianSpy
Toronto, Australia

Grab Bag 13

Habu

Table of Contents

Introduction   7

Great Smokies Relay Riding System   11

Caribbean Christmas Cruise   27

Addicted to Dick   45

The Jacket   63

Snow Crash   81

Strangers Off the Street   93

Avoiding the Inevitable   109

On a Snowy Afternoon   124

Sugar-Coated Hot Pepper   140

Close-Up   164

And I Will Be Yours   186

Shared Crisps   189

Honey Tom   198

Indisposed   218

Final Turn of the Wheel   236

About the Author   241

BarbarianSpy Books   242

Introduction

"Thirteen" is a lucky number for the readers of habu's eclectic gay male erotica Grab Bag collections with the launching of *Grab Bag 13*. This collection of fifteen short stories, written during the winter of 2016–17, offers a large variety of themes, fetishes, and settings. As with past Grab Bag collections, the stories are laid out in the order in which they were written and represent inspirations that hit habu during a relatively warm and snowless winter in his region when more severe weather surrounded him.

In contrast to earlier collections, which included several historical pieces, *Grab Bag 13* stays close to the present in time period, and although habu ventured out for one Caribbean cruise and a visit to his beloved Key West in this period (inspiring "Caribbean Christmas Cruise" and "Sugar-Coated Hot Pepper"), the local Blue Ridge Mountains figured heavily in this season's writing ("Great Smokies Relay Riding System," "Addicted to Dick," "Snow Crash," and "Honey Tom"). His writing of international locales is covered, as he takes the reader to Paris ("The Jacket"), Spain ("Strangers Off the Street"), Guatemala ("Avoiding the Inevitable"), Switzerland ("On a Snowy Afternoon"), England ("Shared Crisps"), and Cyprus ("Indisposed").

Habu has signature topics, which are represented in this collection, as usual. Espionage is represented in "On a Snowy Afternoon" and "Sugar-Coated Hot Pepper" (which brings back Sam Winterbury's CIA Candy Store unit). The hunky Greek and Turkish men of Cyprus, as well as Cyprus' convoluted and sensitive political situation, are depicted in "Indisposed." The glories of being gay in Key West can be found in "Caribbean Christmas Cruise" and "Sugar-Coated Hot Pepper." Habu's unabashed vignettes written in sexual heat are reflected here in "And I Will Be Yours," and the danger of letting opportunity pass you by is fittingly treated as the last story in the collection ("Final Turn of the Wheel").

The anthology opens up with a bang—a series of gang bangs and tag teaming, in "Great Smokies Relay Riding System" as a pole dancer is handed from one "helper" to the next as he travels down the Blue Ridge Parkway en route to a cruise ship gig in Florida. The cruise ship theme comes more to the front in "Caribbean Christmas Cruise," when two Colorado guys escape the snow to hook up with paying swingers on a cruise to Key West that takes a turn back to the snow. In the third story in the collection, with a tertiary connection to the Caribbean (where habu was cruising when writing this section of stories), a young convict's boyfriend has absconded to the Caribbean, leaving the young convict to take the wrap and prison term for a drugs crime. Entitled "Addicted to Dick," the story depicts the difficulty of getting out of the prison system once you've been entangled in it.

"The Jacket," which takes the reader to Paris, is one of those stories that comes directly from one of habu's mundane life experiences. One day he pulled an intricately designed wool jacket, acquired in Norway and passed down to habu, that he had rarely worn but that seemed perfect for the weather conditions, out of the closet and wore it out to get a haircut. Coming out of the barber shop he suddenly wondered if the coat he wore and wasn't familiar with really was his jacket, or not, and if he'd perhaps taken the wrong one from the barber shop. What if he'd gotten the wrong jacket? What if the man who got his jacket was a hunk? What if they went to the same café and recognized that the other one had their jacket? Habu went home and wove this jacket story from very basic material.

It was still winter of 2016–17 when habu wrote "Snow Crash," and some of the subsequent stories still to come up in this anthology, but this winter saw little snow in the Virginia Piedmont, where habu is based. He was invited up to the Wintergreen ski resort on the Blue Ridge Mountains, where snow had been artificially created on the ski slopes. He went and thought back to the first time he'd been invited up to this house, near the end of a dead end road and around a nasty curve, when the snow was deep, when he stood at the window and saw the figure of a magnificently built black man in a window of the neighboring house—and when the black man was invited over by habu's host to provide company on a snowy night and the electricity went off as they were watching a film.

In the high heat "Strangers Off the Street," written after viewing a Spanish sex video, a young, high-class London male prostitute goes to Barcelona to enjoy a busman's holiday with strangers.

An Army officer and enlisted man continue a "sometimes" affair of passion and deception across the years and continents in "Avoiding the Inevitable" that is brought to a head by the revenge of the officer's son. A son also comes into play in "Close-Up," set in Beaufort, South Carolina, where an author of young adult books has come to mix pleasure with photography and sex with a particular sort of man, both younger and older.

"And I Will Be Yours," is just a little flash "come and get it" vignette, written in high heat from the submissive's perspective. Habu then moves to whimsy and humor in "Shared Crisps," an England-based story that makes the most of a simple misunderstanding.

"Honey Tom," written as an April 1st story, is the only story written for this collection that could be seen as set in a past historical period. This story, inspired by a book habu was reading at the time about hard times in mountain coal mining areas in the last century, goes up into the "hollars" of the Blue Ridge mountains, where a charismatic bee charmer and hive provider dispenses his honey in more ways than one. Going abroad for another April 1st story, habu includes one of his Cyprus-based stories in "Indisposed," the story of jockeying for position in the UN Secretariat via unification negotiations in Cyprus, and losing out hinging on an official's sexual libido.

Having written through a nearly snowless and warm winter, habu wraps up this thirteenth Grab Bag anthology with a sad story, "Final Turn of the Wheel," of two men having nearly waited too long to enjoy a relationship. It shouldn't be too long, however, before *Grab Bag 14*, composed of stories written by habu in the spring and summer of 2017 will be released to the marketplace.

~

Great Smokies Relay Riding System

I wasn't sleeping—I was dozing really—when he rolled over on top of me in the sleeping bag. I reached down for him and, not surprisingly found him hard again. He had fucked me every two hours through the night. He was in great shape, coming, I guess, from working in the woods on the mountain tops. I dutifully spread my legs, rolled my pelvis up to give him a straight shot, and hooked my heels on the meat of his calves. He let me fiddle with a condom disk, roll it on him, and guide his bulb to my entrance as he held my head cupped between his hands and looked intently into my face. I knew he wanted to watch my facial expressions when he spiked me. He wanted to know he was big enough to belabor a rent-boy.

He was big enough. When he thrust inside me, deep, my body jerked involuntarily and a look of satisfaction flashed across his eyes. I screwed up my face in shock and momentary pain and let out a deep groan. Liking this, especially coming from a pro rent-boy, he smiled and lowered his face to mine, taking my mouth in a possessive, tongue-swabbing-throat kiss.

He started a strong, steady pump immediately. It was getting lighter in the tent. He'd been inside me three times already—every two hours since he'd entered the tent. I was totally open for him, but I made sure to cause the muscles of my channel to grab him and ripple over his cock as he fucked me to give him the feel of a tight shafting. I'd learned some time ago that this was what men liked.

He was heavy, though—a football player physique and all muscle, very little fat, nothing really to hang on to at his waist as he plowed me, so I reached down and palmed his buttocks, squeezing

11

his cheeks at the moment of each thrust, letting him know I was with him in the fuck. He thrust hard enough to jerk my body each time. There was no drifting of attention away from the fuck at hand with this guy.

Involuntarily groaning and searching for his name, which I'd been told, but I only could come up with Schwartz, I managed a, "Hey, guy, you're too heavy. You're crushing the breath out of me."

"Sorry, Rob," he said and lifted his chest off mine, supporting much of his torso weight on his forearms. He went enough onto his knees between my spread thighs to take some of his lower weight off me too. But he didn't miss a beat in his long-slide fuck. Being lifted off my chest allowed his teeth to go to my nipples. Probably knowing this was his last go at me, he power fucked me to an ejaculation, with me releasing myself with a hand stroking my own dick. He helped me explode by getting one of his hands down there, entering me with three fingers, which he used to spread me wide, and pumping his cock between them. As if he wasn't big enough already.

He satisfied me more each successive time he screwed me. This last time, he was inside me forever, the fuck beginning languidly and building up to a frenzy of him pounding me deep and me arching my back, thrusting my pelvis up into him on each of his rhythmic dives. Clutching his buttocks and his shoulder blades with my fingers, digging my claws in, as he pumped me hard, mercilessly, diving deep, varying his rhythm so that I gasped and clutched at him. Finally, he exhausted me, continuing to ravish me, and I surrendered totally to him, going docile, fully open to him, lying there, panting and vulnerable, and whimpering the mastery of his cocking.

He allowed as he liked this a lot, seeing that I was a rent-boy and had had it all. I praised his prowess and didn't have to lie about it. Most of the time in the club, the fuck was quick. This man was taking me to the heights again and again, demanding all, taking all.

Afterward he remained in position, licking my nipples and up into my throat and kissing me on the mouth as we cooled down and listened for the birds to come into song at the camp ground off

12

the Appalachian Trail along the top of the Great Smoky Mountains east of Knoxville, Tennessee. He'd taken me inside the sleeping bag in four different positions, plastered to each other with our legs around the other's hips yoga style, a doggie fuck, and a side split before he did me in a missionary. He was young and strong, fit and virile. I didn't object to him covering me in the least.

"I'll get the bathhouse unlocked, and you can slip in there before the other campers wake," he said, as he rose off of me, pulled on his park ranger uniform, and rolled out of the tent. There weren't that many campers at the Newfound Gap camp grounds on the Blue Ridge Parkway that night, and I'd pitched my camp away from any of the others. The two of us had eyed each other when I'd first walked into camp. I'd figured he'd be visiting my tent that night.

The ranger—his last name Schwartz, I was pretty sure, and the first name a short one, starting with a T; maybe Tom—had made the rounds of the campers, arriving at my tent close to dark. I was cooking over the campfire and offered him some, which he turned down, but he offered me some beer from the satchel he was carrying, saying it was against the rules to have liquor up here, but if I didn't tell, he wouldn't.

That's all it took to disarm me, I'm sure he thought. I'd known when I walked into camp that he'd fuck me if he wanted to. It didn't hurt that he was a real hunk. He was probably a few years older than I was, but I hadn't reached twenty yet, so he could still be classified as young. He wore the uniform well, and it didn't take long, as he settled in, propped up by a boulder, just within the light of the fire, for us to reach an understanding.

I'd been walking the trail and the edge of the parkway from Gatlinburg for two days without having talked to anyone, so I was ready for the company—and, of course, he was easy to look at and was giving me the eye in the way I well understood.

I opened up to him, responding to his easy way of talking and his show of interest rather than judgment. I was on my way to take up a contract with Royal Caribbean in Tampa, Florida, to be in one of their cruise ship dance troops, I told him. He'd said something about everyone knowing what all male stage dancers were, and I didn't contradict him. I just let that lay there for him to think about.

He said that a dancer must be incredibly flexible and sort of leered at me, and I didn't contradict either the statement or the leer. I knew then that I'd let him fuck me if he wanted to. He seemed to be working up to wanting to.

I told him I wanted to toughen up more before appearing for work and that I had decided to hike the mountain tops from Gatlinburg to north of Atlanta and then bum rides the rest of the way. Two days out, though, I was beginning to realize how tough walking was going to be.

He showed interest in the cruise ship dancing gigs but really lit up when I told him what club I'd been working in in Gatlinburg. He knew it, I could tell, and I'd mentioned it to check out his preferences in case I was misjudging the looks he was giving me. It was a gay men's club and I had been riding both the pole and the clientele there for money. It became increasingly obvious that he knew of the place because he'd been there. He knew young guys rode the poles because he'd watched them. And he knew the pole riders rode the patrons because he'd been ridden. He told me this last bit just before we went into the clutches out there by the fire, when we both knew that he was a driver and I was going to be driven.

As we worked up to this, the gathering night and the campfire and the beer and the discussion were free flowing and he was a hunk. I opened to him in conversation and honesty about who and what I was. I even told him that I was becoming disenchanted with the idea of walking all of the way to Atlanta now that I'd been on the trail a couple of days. He wanted to talk about what I did at the men's club in Gatlinburg and how far I'd go with a patron. I could tell that excited him as he was rubbing his crotch. He asked how much I usually got for a fuck and I told him. He pulled out a wad of cash, peeled off five twenties, and laid it on a log beside where I was sitting. He gave me a questioning look and I smiled and slightly nodded my head.

"You want to fuck me?" I asked.

"Yes. If you haven't been playing me, I think you want me to fuck you."

"That covers more than once at the discounted rate for hunks like you," I said.

"I was hoping for a deep discount and at least a three rounder," he said.

I laughed, assuming he was shitting me about his stamina. He laughed too, apparently knowing how long he could keep it up and keep pounding better than I did.

"Let me see you naked," he said.

And so I stripped off in front of him, making a performance of it, and then said it was unfair for me to be the only one out in the woods in the raw.

Then I wasn't the only one naked, and I gasped, not just because his cash was laying on the log, but also at the muscularity of his body and that he was hung.

Then, as we went into the clinches and lay out by the fire and sixty-nined for a while, I opened my legs to him and that's when he fucked me yoga style, him sitting in the moss with his legs encircling my hips and his arms encircling my waist and me sitting on his thighs, with my legs encircling his hips and my hands cupping the back of his head. He was inside me, me gasping and arching my back as he invaded me deep and thick, and the two of us rocking back and forth against each other in the light of the campfire, concentrating on the resulting movement of his cock inside me until we'd both come.

He provided the condom. While we were still hooked up, he reached over for his trousers, ferreted around in a pocket and came up with a handful of condom packets.

"You know it can get cold at night here. It's really best to sleep with other body heat. Some people travel with a dog."

"I'm going on cruises," I said, with a laugh. "No dogs allowed on cruise ships."

"It's a pity. You'll probably get cold tonight."

"Where are you sleeping? Going back down the mountain or do you pick out a camper every night."

"I pick out a camper every night," he answered. I thought he was joking. Later I wasn't so sure.

"Luckily, when I bought my sleeping bag, they only had doubles for sale."

"Yes, lucky," he said. "If I stay with you tonight, though, you won't get much sleep."

"I'll manage," I answered. I didn't believe him then. I thought he was just bragging. Before first light the next morning I had found out he hadn't been shitting me. He was going at me most of the night.

He reached into his trouser's pocket, presumably to pull out more money when there was some question how long he'd be in the tent with me, but I moved my hand to his and whispered, "That's not needed. Just keep me warm and be good to me."

"I'll fuck you all night," he warned. "What that be good for you?"

"I'll let you if you can," I answered, "and, yes, that would be good for me."

He kept me warm and was very good to me. I didn't get much sleep, and I managed, but what I managed was a cock that could go hard every two hours and could plow me for much of the next hour before shooting off.

When I came out of the shower room he'd opened for me, he had made us breakfast over the campfire. He was all decked out in his ranger uniform, though, more neatly squared away than before he'd opened the shower room, and I'd heard him talking with other campers outside the building. He was all business now. He was finishing a call when I came for breakfast, and, giving me a salute and a smile, he'd wished me a good ongoing journey and left with just a Styrofoam cup of coffee in his hand.

No "thanks for the lays" or anything like that. Now all park ranger business. But I'd known he was having as good a time as I was last night. He certainly didn't seem as tired as the two-hour-interval couplings had made me.

All he said was, "I suggest you hike the parkway rather than the trail for the next day. It's easier going and shorter in distance."

He must have seen that I was walking somewhat bowlegged from his attentions in the night and not exactly in a straight line. Thanks, Mr. Park Ranger.

＊ ＊ ＊ ＊

I had walked south on the verge of the parkway for two hours. With each step I took I was increasingly sorry there was so much in my backpack—including that double sleeping bag that had seemed so useful the night before. A double-cab park truck passed me slowly, moving south as well, and pulled over on the side of the road ahead of me. It remained stationary while I walked up to it, and I had just about reached it when a young black guy opened the front passenger door, got out of the truck, and then opened the back passenger door.

"Need a lift for a while?" he asked. "You look like you are dragging."

"I look that bad?" I asked as I came up to him.

"No, actually you look quite good. Ranger Tim called us. He described you and said you'd probably appreciate being given a lift down the road. He also said you gave a great ride." The black guy was grinning. The great-looking, young, muscular black guy in a park maintenance uniform was grinning. "He said you were from Nathan's Den up in Gatlinburg and would give favors for a favor. Sam here and I would be happy to do you the favor of giving you a ride in exchange for you giving us rides. How about it? Interested?"

Tim. That was it. Now I remembered what was on the park ranger's nametag. It was Tim Schwartz. And I'll bet that was what the call was that he was making this morning. He was setting up a tag team.

"You look fine. What about your friend?" I asked. I leaned into the backseat and got a look at another young hunk, a blond, in the driver's seat. The black guy wasn't waiting for approval. He was taking the pack off my back and taking it around to throw into the bed of the truck. I would have let him fuck me just for relieving me of my backpack. As it was, he held close behind me as I was leaning into the backseat and he gave me a feel. I wiggled my ass for him, letting him know that Ranger Tim wasn't setting them up for a cruel joke.

It turned out the black guy wanted a blow job first, which I gave him in the backset of the truck while, his friend, Sam, drove us down the road. The black guy's name was Duane, and they were polite enough to show me the money before they used my body.

While Duane was pawing me in the backseat, Sam took a wad of money from somewhere and fanned the twenty-dollar bills out. "Ranger Tim said you'd do a couple of party rounds for $100. So, here, on the dashboard, I'm putting $200. And there's another $100 if you'll let us photograph it. You'll have to sound out if you won't go with the photography."

I didn't really have time to consider that, let alone object to it. Duane already had a very nice black cock out of his fly and was pushing my head down into his lap. For the next pretty long time I had my head below the window line, giving him a blow job. It wasn't until he came and I came up for air that I noticed that we were turning off the parkway at the sign for a picnic area. The sign also said the picnic area was closed and there was a bar across the main road. Sam just drove the truck around the side of that and into an area where there were picnic tables strewn around beyond sight from the road. He drove to one that was far into the interior of the area, stopped, and we all got out, stripped by the truck, and walked over to a wood picnic table. I was dressed in nothing. They each were dressed in just a video camera. The $300 was already in the pocket of my shorts back in the bed of the truck.

Sam sat on the bench of the picnic table, his arms stretched out on either side of him along the surface of the table. I knelt between his spread thighs and sucked his cock, while Duane filmed us. Then I was on my back on the top of the table, my legs spread, feet on the bench, and Sam knelt between my thighs and sucked my cock. When I had come for him, he came up onto the bench on his knees, hung my legs over his shoulders, and did me with a long, thin cock in a missionary fuck, while Duane recorded it all.

When he was done, he coaxed me over onto my belly on the table top, with my knees on the bench, and he took a turn filming, while Duane came up on the bench, with his feet on the outside of my knees, crouched over me, mounted me with more channel stretch than Sam had done with a much thicker, black cock, and pounded me in a doggie fuck while Sam filmed it.

Midway in the fuck, Sam came around to the other side of the picnic table, grabbed me by the hair, pulled my head up, and presented his cock for sucking. I obliged. I did more than this back at Nathan's Den in Gatlinburg—and for less money than they were giving me. Money was always nice to have. As I'd shown with Ranger Tim, I wasn't averse to doing it for free either, if the guy was a hunk. Ranger Tim had been a hunk. These two guys were hunks too. Working outside for the park service obviously was good for body building.

I discovered that we still were being filmed, though. I hadn't heard the other truck drive up, but now I could see it. It wasn't a park service truck. And the guy filming us now wasn't in any sort of park service uniform either. He was older than the three I'd already coupled with. His hair was gray and he was gaunt and sinewy. He was well muscled, but in a stringy way, and his face was gaunt-looking too, although he was good looking enough. He had to be in his late forties or early fifties and came across as a man of the area—a mountain man. The park service guys all seemed like they'd come off a college football field.

Duane had stamina. He rode me like a jockey trying to win a long-distance race and not caring if his horse finished with him. I enjoyed the ride, going soft at the core for him—and he could reach the core and filled and stretched it to the limit. His cock was a cruel gift, but a gift it was, and I gave him full value for his money.

And speaking of money, before Duane was finished, the older guy, the new arrival, slapped his $100 down next to me on the table top and, as Sam and Duane withdrew, he climbed up on the table, turned me lengthwise on the boards, put me into a full nelson as he stretched out over me, and, pressing my thighs together with his knees, drove a hard cock up into my now-tight channel. His was the cruelest fuck of the three. He also was the most experienced of the three and didn't miss a trick in taking what he wanted from me. But I'd managed worse before and this outdoor sex was pretty kicky. The money was also good.

He lasted almost as long as Duane had and was a power driver. When they were done, they sat around on the bench, with me, still panting, lying full length on the table top, and drank beer and chatted. It was evident that, just as they were called by Ranger Tim, they had called this guy, named Chuck, and that I was going to be relayed to him at this point if I didn't want to get back to hoofing it down the road.

I'd figured out that if I stuck with the relay, I was going to be stuck with a whole bunch of cocks along the road.

They put a beer on the table for me too, but I didn't get into the mood to drink it before they got into the mood to do me again, which each of them did.

As Sam and Duane were dressing by their truck and preparing to leave, Chuck patted me on the rump and said, "If you're tired of walking for a while, I can drive you down into Robbinsville for a day or two and provide a comfortable bed, hot showers, and your meals. I have a bookstore down there. You might like the books I have in the back room. I put together photo books too. I'd pay you for letting me use stills from this afternoon and doing some other photo shoots. Interested in taking a breather from the trail?"

Well, sure, who wouldn't be? Duane hauled my backpack from the back of the park service truck to the back of Chuck's red Dodge Ram, waved at us, and then he and Sam were gone. Chuck hauled me off the picnic table and threw me over his shoulder like a I just a sack of feed. He walked us over to his truck, pulled open the driver's door, jumped up into the cab, sitting, facing the side, put me on my knees between his thighs on the running board, and pulled my face down into his crotch. He took his turn of getting a blow job from me, before he drove me farther south on the parkway and then off onto highway 74 and into Robbinsville.

It turned out that Chuck had a film studio behind the dirty book room that was behind the regular bookstore in his shop in Robbinsville. For three days he filmed me by day and fucked me by night. Most of the photos were stills in provocative poses with various backdrops. He paid me $20 for each photo and he turned out high-quality shots. He put a portfolio together for me and I knew I'd be able to use it somehow for future job possibilities. He said they'd come out in a book and he showed me other books of photos of hunky hikers he'd enticed down from the Appalachian Trail for a few days. I wondered then if this was some sort of racket, starting with Ranger Tim, going through Sam and Duane, and ending with the young guy in Chuck's bed and in photo shoots in Robbinsville.

I didn't wonder for long, though. It turns out that several days of walking on the Blue Ridge Parkway through Tennessee didn't cover much ground in the valley. We hadn't left Ranger Tim, Sam, and Duane behind. They appeared the first evening at the bookstore, and I starred in a couple of gang bang porn films. Chuck ran a subscription Web site too, and he paid me $300 for each film I appeared in.

It was all good with me. They all were hunks, and I got paid.

The fourth morning Chuck put me back up on the parkway, on my feet, the backpack on my back. I hadn't walked more than a half hour before a big SUV pulled over in front of me at the edge of the road. The driver's door opened, and a middle-aged bald guy, who later told me his name was Nick and that he was a football coach at a private school down near Robbinsville and who was in great shape, popped out, extended an arm across the roof of the vehicle and called out, "Chuck down in Robbinsville told me a guy looking like you needed a ride down the road in exchange for a good ride. I'm going down to where 76 crosses the parkway. I can give you a lift that far, if you want."

When I climbed into the vehicle, he fanned five twenty-dollar bills out on the dashboard in front of me. "I understand you'll give a good time for a hundred," he said.

He fucked me in the backseat of his SUV, sitting in the seat and holding me in his lap, both facing him and then away from him and slamming my passage up and down brutally but gloriously on a steel rod of a thick cock. I was beginning to think that these guys were all members of a club where having a thick cock was a membership requirement.

At the intersection of the parkway and Route 76, Nick relayed me to Fire Watch Ranger Aaron, who rode me at the top of a fire tower on Blood Mountain.

"Let me take you up to the fire watch platform," he said when I was getting out of the coach's SUV. "You can see into both Tennessee and Georgia from there."

I can't attest to what how far beyond the platform you can see from on top of Blood Mountain, because all I could see most of the time was the puffed up face of the short, hairy guy named

Aaron, as he worked hard over me, me flat on my back on an old mattress in the center of the platform, my legs bent and spread and my pelvis rolled up, as he worked his stubby cock inside me in a missionary fuck and vigorously pumped. This was where my "thick come as a membership requirement" theory went bust. He couldn't reach much beyond the prostate, but he gave that a fantastic beating and I came for him twice, my hands running into the dark curls of the pelting on his pectorals and my head turned to the side, tongue hanging out and panting with every sensation centered on that thick bulb beating on my prostate and my eyes glued to the scattered twenty-dollar bills on the boards beside my head.

He was something different—not intimidatingly huge—and he was a short, squat Jewish guy covered with curly black hair and with something of a pot belly, but his cock bulb bulged and he could put it right on the money and do a tattoo on the spot. God could he pull the cum out of me.

* * * *

Ranger Aaron drove me right up to the base of yet another fire watch tower, this time on Springer Mountain, thirty miles to the south on the parkway and nearly outside of the southern end of the park. Atlanta was about fifty miles away and thus far I'd walked little farther than from one paid fuck to another.

An older man, tall but very thin and sinewy, with a grizzled appearance, salt-and-pepper hair, bushy eyebrows, and two day's growth of beard, was coming down the stairs. He had a uniform on, but it was a different style from that of a park ranger.

"Juan's a game warden," Ranger Aaron explained. "He's a senior ranger in the park. He's over nine inches."

On the basis of that last comment, I looked at the man again, with a little more regard this time and with slight trepidation. He was Hispanic and probably in his fifties, but if he could get it up, I was going to be taxed. I could see that he had a wad of cash in his hand. When the man hit the dirt, he stood up ramrod straight, gave me a piercing look, that told me he was in command and would dominate me, and said, "This the male whore fucking his way south then?"

"Yes, his name's Rob, and he's a great lay."

"Was it a hundred, did you say, and a ride out of the park for all night?"

"Yeah, that's been the going rate," Ranger Aaron said.

They were talking about me like I was a piece of meat that was just hanging on a rack next to them, which I guess I, in fact, was. I might have said something, but I was afraid it would come out as a moan if I tried, because he'd reached out with a strong hand, with long fingers and was fingering my crotch, getting under my balls and weighing them with his hand and then tracing the line of my dick in the loose shorts. My cock reacted by engorging.

"A real looker, ain't he?"

"He's got a great body too," Aaron said, "and he's real flexible—a dancer, you know." I wasn't sure I could live up to his testimonials—or that I really wanted to. The words "more than nine inches" came to mind. And then "a cruel master" flowed into my thoughts as his hand closed over my balls through the thin material, and he squeezed. My eyes began to water and he gave me a sharp look. I wasn't about to show weakness, so I just stared back at him, producing a bit of a smile.

"He's a pretty boy. You sure he can take it?"

"From what I hear, he's taken in almost constantly all the way from just south of Gatlinburg. He didn't have any trouble taking me. And you should of seen the positions I put him in to bury it."

Ranger Juan gave Ranger Aaron a somewhat disdainful look, like he knew Aaron was kind of stubby, but he must have been satisfied, because he stuffed the wad of money in the hand he wasn't squeezing my crotch with in my pocket, turned, and said, "Well, come on up then and let's get it on."

The fire watch platform was much the same as the one on Blood Mountain, down to the bare mattress laying in the center of the covered space. The platform was open on all four sides, with strong railings all around. And it was a good thing they were strong. I still worried about the one that Ranger Aaron was leaning his back into as he crouched, facing the interior of the tower, and put me on his crouched thighs, facing him, both of us naked, and him

23

embracing me around my waist as I leaned back, skewered on his cock, his bulb pressing at my prostate and rubbing it languidly.

Ranger Juan watched us a while. He too was naked, and I couldn't take my eyes off him—and off his cock, which kept growing and hardening, and curving upward as he watched me rise and fall on Aaron's cock, using the leverage of my feet pushing off on the log slats of the platform railing. Fuck nine inches. My experienced eye measured him at ten or more before I lost sight of Juan as he moved behind us, straddled Aaron's thighs, and, after positioning his cock head at my hole above where Aaron was dug in, moved my legs so that my ankles were hooked on the top of the railing on either side of Aaron, grabbed my waist between his hands, and started the long journey up into my channel.

My passageway measured him out as more than ten hard inches too.

Between them, they fucked the shit out of me, Ranger Aaron worrying my prostate mercilessly and Ranger Juan pounding me hard, fast, and deep. After Aaron had gone, Juan put me on all fours on the mattress, mounted me, and fucked the shit out of me again.

He gave me a bit of rest and a beer and then, as twilight was setting in, put me back on all fours, mounted me, and fucked the shit out of me again. He fed me dinner and then fucked the shit out of me. He took me down from the tower and to his nearby cabin, tied my wrists to his headboard, and fucked the shit out of me, missionary style, through the night.

I lost count of how many times he came and how many times I came. I just know that he was perpetually hard, well over the advertized nine inches, and my balls ached from being pumped dry. In the morning, he untied me, turned on to his back, put me, straddling his pelvis, on his hard ten inches, and I rode him one last time.

I was glad to do it. I now knew I could outlast someone as long, virile, and vigorous as he was.

Over breakfast, he said, "I can take you down to where 5 meets Interstate 575. You'll still be forty miles north of Atlanta. I can take you today, or I can hook you up with a ride from there the day after tomorrow. If you stay, I won't pay you, but I'll fuck the stuffing out of you. You're a good lay and you can keep up with me. Which will it be?"

He banged me for two more glorious days and turned me over at the 575 interchange to a group of Hispanic seasonal workers he knew were headed south in a beat-up old bus.

A good week earlier than I had programmed my hike for, since I'd thought I'd be walking the whole way, I was coming south into Atlanta in the back of an old bus loaded with toned-up and boisterous Hispanic seasonal workers who gang banged me on my sleeping bag in the aisle on the floor of the rear of the bus all the way. If it was only forty miles to Atlanta as Ranger Juan had said it was from that point, they must have gone off on slow-route back roads. I couldn't verify that, as I was on my back on the floor of the bus, with my legs spread and my ankles propped up on seats on either side of the aisles, my backpack under the small of my back to elevate my buttocks, and my eyes counting the dried-up wads of bubblegum stuck to the underside of bus seats, while a succession of muscular, berry-brown men fucked me.

The fact is that I liked being fucked and having guys want to fuck me, and I was seasoned to lay there and take it all day.

They couldn't pay me, but they certainly could show me a good time and I didn't have to do any more relay hitching into Atlanta. They were willing to drive me all the way down to Florida, but I didn't think my body could take them that far. Also, I didn't need their money and I didn't need to hitch anymore. I had more than enough money to fly from Atlanta to Tampa in style. I gave them all of the camping stuff from my backpack, including that double sleeping bag, which made what was left a quite manageable weight, and had them drop me off at the Atlanta airport.

I could hardly walk as I entered the departure lounge. Still, I think I would have been hobbling just as much if I'd had to hike the whole way on my feet rather than ride south through the park on men's cocks.

I highly recommend the Great Smokies Relay Riding System for anyone whose channel can take the beating and upwards of ten inches of cock; who likes to fuck in the outdoors and in the back of cars, trucks, and buses; who looks good enough

and is experienced enough to command $100 a fuck session; and
who appreciates variety in his men.

If you go and start where I did, tell Ranger Tim hi for me.

~

Caribbean Christmas Cruise

"Look, there it is again," Jerrod said, turning his tablet around so that Kyle could see the screen. "It's the same cruise. And, look, it says they are prepared to be very generous, based on performance. I wonder what generous means."

"I wonder what performance would mean," Kyle said, unwrapping the cashmere scarf from around his neck, rolling it up, and laying it on the bench seat next to him. He was only now beginning to thaw out from the early December cold and snow in downtown Denver. They were sitting in the Edge bar of the Denver Four Seasons Hotel, waiting for their potential hookup. Jerrod, older and more experienced than Kyle, was borderline excited; Kyle was downright nervous. He hadn't done this before. There'd been a few before his professor at the University of Colorado in Boulder, where they'd driven here from in more than a foot of snow, but until now it had all been one on one. It had been Jerrod who had told Kyle that he'd like couples and that couples would love him.

"You know what it means. And, trust me, maintain your aura of innocence and your 'aw shucks' boyish looks and this could pay off big—maybe even enough to cover the cruise to Yucatan. You know I've got to get out of this snow at least this Christmas season or I'll scream. For the first time I have time off to allow me to escape."

"I can do Christmas here without any problem. Snow is part of Christmas," Kyle answered, but he didn't think Jerrod was even listening to him. There were times with Jerrod just steamed right through him. Kyle was a submissive. He knew it, and Jerrod knew it—and took advantage of it. And Jerrod was giving that tablet more attention now he was giving Kyle.

"Snow sucks big," Jerrod said with a big sigh.

"Whatever," Kyle muttered. Then, looking at Jerrod fingering his tablet, he asked, "So, what are you doing now?"

"I'm responding," Jerrod said, working the keys on his tablet. "This is the third place I've seen this guy say he and his wife are taking a Royal Caribbean Christmas cruise from Miami, around the western Caribbean, and to the Yucatan Peninsula and wonders if any player male bisexuals will be on the *Empress of the Seas* cruise. There are. That's us."

"You can't set anything up, Jerrod. I haven't decided yet. You may be bi, but I don't know if I can be. You're moving too fast."

"You've fucked a woman before. You've told me you fucked girls in College."

"Yeah, because my fraternity brothers were there, we all were doing it, and I didn't want to admit what really turns me on. You got pointed to and razzed if you didn't do it too."

"Did you get hard with them and come?"

"Yes. My fraternity brothers would have noticed if I hadn't."

"Trust me, you can be bi then. As long as they want your body—and you've got a great body—and can get it up, you are good to go with a woman." He turned his focus back to the tablet screen. "It doesn't hurt to open a conversation. We don't have to give any particulars. It's a big ship. We probably won't even know who they are if we don't go any farther. But don't be nervous. You'll do just fine with couples. And this Chinese pair . . . ah, this must be them now."

Jerrod stood up from the banquette behind the cocktail table and Kyle looked up. His first impression was the difference in their heights and their stature. The Chinese woman was small, delicate, like a porcelain doll, with alabaster skin. She was gorgeous. She wasn't young, but she was holding her age well. She was wearing a cobalt blue Thai silk suit that fit her trim body with a shimmer that gave the impression it was flowing on the curves of her body. Her long, cobalt-blue painted nails arrested attention as her hands fluttered around. In contrast, the man was taller and bulkier than Kyle thought of Chinese men being. He looked austere. He was a good-looking man in a camel-tan sports coat that was cut to look casual but also to make clear it was very expensive, but he had piercing black eyes that constantly seemed to be assessing the value—to him—of whatever he looked at. He looked like he'd pick your pocket while you were lying in the street crying out for a medic.

He was looking past Jerrod at Kyle and his mouth went into a tight little smile. His eyes remained cold and assessing, and Kyle had the sensation that he was being undressed with the eyes and assessed for his physical attributes—which exuded blond, sensual, fresh, underaverage stature, and yielding.

Jerrod introduced Kyle and himself to Tessa and Bernard Chin, a cocktail waitress appeared for drink orders before the Chins had a chance to sit down, and the couple sat—he warily, like a vigilant panther, and she like flowing water—in chairs on the other side of the cocktail table from the banquette.

As they sipped their cocktails, they engaged in small talk, each side of the table scrutinizing the other. The Chins claimed they were in Denver temporarily. She was a movie actress in Taiwan and he an international financier based in Hong Kong and Chicago. There were a couple of board meetings in Denver and that's what they were—bored. They belonged to an on-line sex club that Jerrod belonged to as well. They had time this weekend and interest—specific interest in Jerrod's listing on the Web site.

Jerrod Hastings had been a star player on the university's basketball team He was of robust Nordic aspect and had just stayed on at the university a decade after graduating. What kept him in Colorado was being hired as an assistant coach and Communications Department assistant professor at the University of Colorado in Boulder. Kyle Toliver, who was one of his students, was a part-time clothing model and was training to be a news reporter. Tessa and Bernard were going by those names, but Jerrod and Kyle weren't going by their given names, of course. Jerrod was Sven and Kyle was Craig for the purpose of this meeting.

Yes, it was lucky the four of them were in Denver for the weekend, Jerrod said. He didn't reveal that he and Kyle were only here because the sum of a $1,000 for a two-hour session had been mentioned in their Web site exchange.

Yes, Jerrod had participated in these arrangements before, but, no, Kyle hadn't. Jerrod poked Kyle's thigh under the cocktail table and Kyle turned his innocent boy look on the couple across the table. "Would that be a problem?" Jerrod asked, knowing that, as long as Kyle was willing and Jerrod was there to help with the tryst, it would be a delight for the Chins.

"Not in the least," Bernard Chin answered, turning eyes on Kyle that already had him naked and on a rack. "I would pay $200 extra for that and if he was totally submissive. $500 extra if your friend here is a virgin."

"Alas, he's not," Jerrod admitted. ". . . a virgin, that is."

The man still looked very interested, but his eyes dulled down just a tad. Tessa's eyes were alive with excitement, but she was more democratic, moving her gaze from Jerrod to Kyle and back to Jerrod. She reached across the table and let her fingers play in the fuzz of hair on the back of the hand Jerrod had resting there.

As he answered, Chin, extended his hand on the surface of the table as well, but he didn't take anyone's hand. He was just placing a wad of folded bills on the table, wrapped around a hotel room access card.

"Room 1417," he said, as he stood up, drained his drink, and then turned his eyes on Tessa. She nodded at him and stood and the two slowly walked out of the bar and across the lobby to the bank of elevators in the fifteen-story downtown all-glass skyscraper.

Kyle sucked in his breath when he walked into the dimly lit hotel room. It was, of course, sumptuously furnished, with a king-sized bed dominating the room. But what took one's attention from the doorway was the full wall of glass that looked out on the snow-covered Rocky Mountain range to the west that seemed close enough to touch. Kyle immediately felt tingly; he loved the snow on the mountains. This was his favorite time of year in Colorado. It was something he and Jerrod didn't agree on.

The room had a fireplace, which was crackling happily and providing most of the light in the room. It also had a bar at one side. Bernard was leaning on the bar, naked except for an open-at-the-front silk robe. He had a Buddha belly but was otherwise muscular. He was in erection, but that didn't seem to bother him. He had a drink in his hand and his eyes were darting everywhere

Kyle followed the line of Bernard's sight to the bed, where Tessa perched, wearing only a bustier, which started below her full breasts with rouged nipples and ended above the black, curly hair of her snatch. Her labia were plump, as if they'd been surgically enhanced, and had been rouged. She wore black net stockings and red high heels. Bernard next looked at Jerrod and he nodded. Jerrod began to strip. At last he looked at Kyle and growled, "Come here."

Bernard slowly undressed Kyle, taking time to explore and fondle until Kyle was panting and putty in the man's grasp. Kyle had worried if he could go hard in a bi situation, with a woman watching him being undressed, but his cock didn't mind it at all—it went to full staff. The man dominated him. He had correctly assessed Kyle as a total submissive. Kyle went docile at the first showing of domination, and Bernard was taking full advantage of that.

After having stripped Kyle bare and buried his face in Kyle's crack as the young man bent over and grasped his ankles, Bernard rose up as he leaned against the bar, grasped Kyle's hips, slowly pulled Kyle's channel back onto his cock, and fucked Kyle from behind, as the young man remained bent over, holding his ankles. Kyle turned his face up to look beyond the room, to the snow-clad mountains in the near distance. While languidly manipulating Kyle's submissive body, Bernard looked over the young man's head to the bed, where Tessa was on her back on the bed, buttocks on the footboard edge of the bed, legs spread, and Jerrod hovered over her between her legs, squeezed her breasts with his hands, and slowly fucked her. She was scraping her long fingernails over Jerrod's back, curling them into claws and digging them into Jerrod's back and emitting a little cry on every third thrust.

The background music was some sort of floaty Oriental tune, played on stringed instruments, but it was the bare mention of music. The main music in the room was panting, groaning, and low moaning. Occasionally Bernard, in a whispery voice, said, "Yes, open to me. Take it. Open. Clutch it and pull it in. Ah, yes, like that." From across the room, Tessa murmured. "Baby, baby, baby."

After several minutes of this, Bernard pulled out of Kyle and shuffled him over to the bed, growling for Jerrod to make way. He put Kyle were Tessa had been; Tessa on her feet at the base of the bed, leaning over Kyle and sucking his cock; and Jerrod fucking Tessa from behind. Then Bernard mounted Jerrod from behind and fucked him. It ended with Bernard pushing both Jerrod and Tessa aside to continue on the bed beside him and him moving in between Kyle's spread legs, thrusting inside him again and pounding him hard to an ejaculation.

Kyle lay there, docilely staring out of the window wall, mesmerized by the play of the full moon's rays on the Rocky Mountains, the only indication he was being fucked his deep moans, light panting, and the almost imperceptible rise and tightening of his buttocks to cushion the savage thrust to Bernard's cock and release as the cock drew back, only to thrust again.

Later, with Jerrod and Kyle back in the hotel's Edge bar and Kyle trembling a bit and having to hold his drink with both hands to keep it steady, Jerrod said, "There, now, that wasn't too bad, was it? Certainly worth the twelve hundred dollars he gave us. If you could have feigned being a virgin, we could have earned more. I didn't want to expect that from you this time, though. But you did good."

"He didn't wear a condom," Kyle said with a shaky voice.

"Neither did I. We'll get checked when we get back to Boulder. But you've done it once. This dude we're on the cruise with and is interested in . . . ah, yes, he's answered my message." Jerrod was concentrating on reading the screen of his tablet. Kyle reached out for the tablet, but then withdrew his hand again. Jerrod punched out a message on his tablet. "There."

"There what?" Kyle asked.

"We've got a date. He's given me a cabin number. The $500 per session offer is firm. Not what the Chinese guy gave, but you don't get a high roller like that every day."

Kyle sat back in his chair and sulked. Jerrod had asked him what he thought about the bi swinger experience, but he hadn't even waited to discuss it with Kyle before signing him up for another one. Kyle felt screwed—and not just by the demanding Chinese guy. And it was weird being blown by the woman. Kyle hadn't gotten a blow job from a woman before—and as nice as it was, it wasn't the same as getting from another guy. But she'd gotten him hard—and off, scraping her long, cobalt blue-painted fingernails on the sides of his cock while she was sucking on the bulb. He wasn't sure what he thought about that, and Jerrod certainly hadn't told him he was bi before they got involved.

* * * *

Kyle held his resentment through boarding the *Empress of the Seas* on 19 December in Miami for an eight-day cruise to Key West, Honduras, Belize, Mexico, and back. They wouldn't get back to Miami until two days after Christmas and then they'd go on down to Key West to party for New Year's. The ship would dock at Key West two days after leaving Miami for most of a day. Maybe Kyle would get a sense of why Jerrod was so excited about being on the key for New Year's. All Kyle knew was that it would be as warm as a Colorado summer, which he could get in the right season without traveling to the Caribbean. It was the season for snow now—"white Christmas" and all that.

The tension between them continued when they got to Miami—not that Jerrod seemed to realize that Kyle was pouting—but Jerrod had gone out for cigarettes after dinner in the hotel they'd booked for the night before boarding on the cruise, and he hadn't come back until 3:00 a.m. When he'd entered the bed, he pulled Kyle to him, embraced him, and fucked him, but still. . . . If he'd showered first maybe he'd have gotten the smell of another man off him. The total submissive, Kyle of course had just opened his legs to Jerrod, taken him inside, and concentrated on the shaft filling and working him. But separated from him the next morning had let the feelings of resentment flow back in.

Getting on the ship was a hassle and then Jerrod's suitcase arrived late and he was running around in a snit about that. The ship was putting out to sea when their time to appear in the main dining room came up. They had a table set for four but assigned to just the two of them. Jerrod had made that arrangement so they could haul in big fish and work them at the table as they got the chance. They spent their time at dinner that night ogling the other diners and wondering who the Anges were—the couple they were to meet and swing with if they'd appeared to be compatible. The next day was a full day at sea and they'd arranged to meet on neutral ground at the Bolero Lounge at 9:00 p.m. to look each other over.

There were some good-looking men to look at on the ship. Most were older and had a woman in tow, but there were some unattached men, or men attached to men, like Jerrod and Kyle were, of Jerrod's age bracket, the early thirties. There were fewer in Kyle's age bracket, the early twenties. Jerrod got as many looks as he did looking, but Kyle got even more. Women—and many men—couldn't take their eyes from him.

A group of three, a forties-bracket man and woman, both looking well-heeled and well-preserved came in with a younger man, in his thirties, and went to a table for three in the center of the dining room. The man and woman were dressed to the nines and expensively so. The younger man with them was dressed more Western style, with a fringed deer-skin jacket, well-pressed jeans, and cowboy boots. He didn't look cheap; he just looked Western, which was distinctive on a Caribbean cruise.

"Wouldn't mind if that was our couple. Even sort of looks like their photos," Jerrod said. "But it looks like they already have their male bi candy in tow."

Kyle was looking at the cowboy, who was looking back at him.

They went to the casino after dinner and Jerrod got snappish, both because he lost at cards and because he was tired, having stayed out, "looking for cigarettes," until 3:00 that morning and then having had a grueling afternoon getting checked onto the ship and tracking his luggage down.

He also drank too much in the casino, and neither man was in the mood for sex when they returned to the cabin. The next morning, the ship being at sea and the cabin rolling a bit, Jerrod wasn't even interested in getting up for breakfast. After a quick breakfast in the Windjammer Café, Kyle pulled on a Speedo and a T-shirt and headed to the pool with a book—a gay male Western he'd gotten off Amazon with the provocative title of *Ridden West*, by a Dirk Hessian—and a bottle of suntan lotion. He couldn't do anything about the Caribbean being sunny and warm rather than snowing with sleigh bells in the background, so he decided he might as well take advantage of the sun and work on a tan.

He laughed when he arrived at the ship-top swimming pool. Christmas carols were playing over the loudspeaker. The lounge chairs were beginning to fill it and he found one of two that a family with toddlers was vacating. They were set very close together. He settled down on the lounge bed, pulling his T-shirt off and dropping his sunglasses, paperback novel, and bottle of suntan lotion on a side table at one side. A lounge bed was nudged right up against his bed on the other side. When he looked up at the pool, a fringed deerskin jacket hanging off the end of a lounge bed across the pool caught his attention. The cowboy from dinner the previous night was stretched out in the bed in a Speedo and was watching him and smiling at him over the top of sunglasses pulled down to the tip of his nose.

Pretending he wasn't looking at the guy, but looking as much as he could to assure himself that the man was a hunk, which he was, Kyle walked to the side of the pool, dove in, and swam laps. There were far more people lying around on the lounge beds than there were in the pool.

When he came out of the water and tossed his head back and forth to jettison some of the water he was soaked with, his eyes went to his lounge bed. The one up against it was occupied now. A fringed deerskin jacket hung down from the foot of the lounge bed.

He sat down on the side of his bed with the side table, his back to the other lounge bed, and toweled his torso off.

"The sun burns fast in the Caribbean," a rich baritone voice came at him from behind. "I'll trade. I'll spread the lotion on your back if you'll do mine."

"OK," Kyle said, turning and looking at the hunk, who was still a hunk despite Kyle's feeble attempts not to notice that. As they said, tall, dark, and handsome. Also sultry and muscular and, yes, there was a nice bulge in the Speedo. Kyle could see the line of the man's cock inside the material. He was thick and long, especially since he was at least half hard. "I'll do you first. Sit up, turned away from me."

"Do me?" the man asked, an amused smile on his face.

"Apply the suntan lotion," Kyle said, deadpan. "Turn away from me."

The man complied, and Kyle went up on his knees behind him and started applying lotion.

"Because I usually do the doing," the man said. Then, before Kyle could respond, he continued. "I'm Roger. This could do double service. A shoulder massage would be mighty fine."

"Sure," Kyle said, digging his fingers in deeper and being rewarded with a satisfied grunt. "I'm Kyle."

"From the Florida area?" Roger asked.

"No, out West. Boulder, Colorado. You too maybe? That's a nice deerskin jacket."

"Yeah, we're nearly neighbors. I'm from Jackson Hole, Wyoming. Own a Western shop there. I guess you could say I'm a walking model. I sell a line of these deerskin jackets. Lots of people ask me where I got it, and I make a sale. I just happen to have a rack of them in my cabin. I have a share deal with the cruise line."

"You could be a model," Kyle said, and as an afterthought. "I model clothes part time myself."

"I would have guessed that. You should come on up to Jackson Hole and model for my store. Is that what you do in Boulder?"

"I'm a student—at the University of Colorado there."

"You on this cruise with your boyfriend?"

Kyle's hands stopped from the shock of the question. Roger turned his head. "Hope I'm not being forward. I saw the book you're reading. I've read Dirk Hessian myself before—cover to cover gay sex. I've seen you checking me out. I saw you with a man older than you last night, but not old enough to be your father."

"Oh."

"I've read that too—the book. Pretty steamy. No, very steamy. Some positions that even I haven't tried and I'm known to be pretty athletic in bed. I'm gay, in case you wondered. A top. A power top."

"Oh," Kyle said again. "Yeah, I guess I'm on the cruise with my boyfriend. He's an assistant basketball coach and an assistant professor at UC."

"So, you like older men?"

"He's not that old. Early thirties."

"I'm in my early thirties," Roger said. They suddenly didn't have anything to say in that progression of conversation, but Roger was the first to speak. Kyle had returned to rubbing his back and shoulders, but in a rather desultory manner.

"I think I'm done. My turn. Stretch out on your stomach. I'll do you."

Kyle decided not even to touch that line. He rolled over on his stomach and Roger started giving him what was more of a back massage than a lotion application. It went to Kyle's legs, and, when Roger ran his hands up the inside of Kyle's thighs, up high, without thinking about it Kyle widened the stance of his legs. He also emitted a low moan. Roger gave a low laugh.

Roger leaned down and whispered in Kyle's ear, "I'd love to do you."

The hands went back to massaging the meat of Kyle's thighs and calves, but they returned to run up the inside of Kyle's thighs, this time going higher, fingers almost reaching Kyle's perineum. The moan was deeper now and, again without realizing he was doing it, Kyle raised himself slightly on his knees, presenting his ass.

Roger gave another low laugh and leaned over and whispered in Kyle's ear, "You have the reactions of a submissive. You take a man inside you, don't you? All a man like me needs to do is take it and you'll give it, won't you?"

"Yes," Kyle answered with a whimper.

"Are you hard for me?" He surreptitiously ran his hand up between Kyle's thighs, cupped the young man's basket, and found his own answer.

"Yes," Kyle murmured.

"Will you let me fuck you?"

"Yes. Take me someplace. Fuck me. Ride me."

"Come into the pool with me."

"There are people here."

"Come into the pool with me for just a few minutes and then come back to my cabin with me. There's no one in the cabin but me. You don't have to decide right now. Come into the pool with me and decide then. I want you to feel what I have for you."

"Yes," Kyle whimpered.

"You first," Roger growled. "Go into the pool."

Shaking, Kyle pulled himself off the lounge bed, struggled over to the side of the pool, and dove in. Roger dove in behind him and pulled him over into one of the curves of the pool by where a peninsula of walkway went out in the water. No other swimmers were coming into this area and it was difficult to see anything but heads from the pool deck lounge beds.

They were facing each other close, but, by all appearances, only close enough to be carrying on a conversation. They, in fact, did make small talk—about college and marketing and clothes modeling and about how each of them had been dragged out of the Christmastime snow that they loved to go on this cruise—Kyle by his professor boyfriend and Roger by his brother from Las Vegas and his brother's wife. As they talked, their hands were busy inside the Speedo of the other, feeling and fondling each other, stroking and engorging each other's cocks.

As long as Roger was taking command, Kyle was docilely submitting to him.

"I don't think I can wait to go back to the room," Roger whispered. "I want to fuck you now."

"Yes," Kyle answered.

"Right here," Roger said.

"Yes, if we could manage without being discovered, but of course we—"

"Yes, we can. Even if we're seen, you'll do it for me, won't you? I want to know if you will submit to me completely, no matter what the risk."

"Yes. Do it. Fuck me."

"Push your suit down, but keep it on one ankle and that foot on the bottom of the pool. Lean back into the side of the pool, but jut your pelvis toward me. Hook your other leg on my hip."

"You've done this before, haven't you?" Kyle asked.

"I've done everything before. If you go with me, I'll do everything with you, to you. I'll use you like you've never been used before."

"I don't know. I—"

"Do it, let me in," Roger hissed, reaching out and palming Kyle's buttocks and squeezing and separating them, pulling Kyle's pelvis toward him. He was in command and was insistent.'

"Oh shit, oh fuck," Kyle muttered, as Roger pushed his cock head inside Kyle's hole. "Oh shit."

"Don't stop talking. Take it. stretch your arms out on the pool deck, talk to me, smile at people passing by, and take it. We'll do deep later, in my room. Take it. Yes, good, like that. Don't stop talking. Doesn't it give you a thrill that we're doing it here in front of everyone and no one knows it? Take it. Oh, god, you're sweet. Take it. Take it."

Kyle stretched his arms out across the top of the lip of the pool, picked out a hunk on a lounge bed across the pool who was looking at him intently, shared a smile with him, and took it—and took it and took it. He was being fucked shallowly, but well. It wasn't just Roger who was fucking him. In his imagination, it also was the hunk sharing a smile with him and all the other randy hunks on the cruise who were fucking him.

The hunk knew exactly what they were doing—what Roger was doing to Kyle—and it gave Kyle a little thrill that he did.

When they returned to their pool beds, there was a note, with a cabin number on it, laying on his pool bed. Kyle had little trouble figuring out it was from the hunk who had watched him and the cowboy in the pool. Kyle had no real intention taking up with the guy, but he was flattered that the man was seeking a hookup.

Later they did it on the double bed in Roger's ninth-deck junior suite, where Roger gave it to him deep. Kyle was stretched out on his stomach on the bed, his buttocks raised as he had unconsciously done on the lounge bed, Roger on his knees between Kyle's thighs, trapping Kyle's arms folded across his back, and riding his ass hard. And then they did it on the balcony, with Roger sitting in a chair, facing the ocean, and Kyle in his lap, facing him, and riding the cock by leveraging off his bare feet on deck.

A couple of hours after arriving there, Kyle was leaving Roger's cabin to go down the corridor to the stern area of the ship where Jerrod and his ninth-deck junior suite was. Roger understood that they couldn't meet again openly—that Kyle didn't want Jerrod to know they were fucking—but they had agreed to try to find time for themselves on the cruise. Both thought it very fortuitous that Roger had his own cabin, 9124. His brother and his brother's wife had the one beside his.

"We must try not to look at each other during dinner," Kyle said. "Jerrod's no dummy. He'll know something is going on."

"I can only try," Roger answered.

It must have worked, because, although Jerrod, who was in a better mood from having spent most of the day in bed with the cabin curtains pulled, rated all of the men—and some of the women—who passed their table, he made no mention of Roger, sitting five tables over, fortuitously having taken a chair with its back turned to their table.

Jerrod didn't even react much when the hunk from the pool, who had watched Roger fucking Kyle, drifted by the table and gave Kyle and knowing smile.

At 9:00 p.m. sharp Jerrod and Kyle were entering the Bolero Lounge, arriving for their rendezvous with the Anges, the swinger couple they were going to hook up with for $500 a session if all were amenable to it after they'd met. Jerrod had gotten good looks at the photos they'd sent. Kyle had hardly glanced at them.

He went into shock as they approached a table Jerrod walked a direct path to, sure of the identification made possible by the brighter light of the bar over that of the dining room. The man, elegantly dressed, trim, and dapper, stood as they approach, obviously recognizing them as well. Kyle couldn't take his eyes off the other man sitting with them. Roger just returned his gaze with an amused look on his face.

They ordered drinks, engaged in a bit of chit chat, and, eventually, Jerrod said, "Well, where from here?"

Edward Ange turned and shared a look with his wife, Janine, who said, "Yes, I can hardly wait. They're beautiful." Edward reached into his coat pocket and took out a roll of bills and a room key card. "Cabin 9122, ninth deck," he said. Jerrod put his hand over the wad of money.

Kyle wasn't surprised by the cabin number. He knew that Roger's cabin number was 9124.

Roger, who hadn't been saying much during the conversation, more sitting off to the side, not part of the transaction, cleared his throat.

"I want in. I'll pay $300 to have Kyle alone first before anyone else uses him."

"Kyle?" Jerrod asked, turning his face to his young boyfriend. The look on Jerrod's face indicated he wanted Kyle to say no. Jealousy at the competition from another man his age perhaps?

"Yes, fine with me," Kyle answered.

"Janine? Ed?" Jerrod asked, turning his head toward them this time.

"You can take care of us yourself?" Edward asked.

"I can take very good care of you. And you can have a hundred back this time. We'll be cruising for several days. You like what you get and want Kyle too, there can be other sessions."

"Other sessions sound good to me," Janine quickly chimed in, her eyes betraying her need. "I want Kyle too."

"So do I," Edward agreed.

"Next time," Roger said, giving his brother and his wife a challenging look. "I want him alone the first time."

Roger took Kyle to his cabin and fucked him all night long. They competed with the neighboring cabin on how loud their sounds of sex were. He used challenging positions that Jerrod had never even hinted that he knew about, and Jerrod was always good for declaring that he knew everything. What Jerrod did experience that night before he dragged back to their cabin as the ship was pulling into Key West that Kyle, who dragged into their cabin fifteen minutes later didn't, was that Jerrod's torso, buttocks, and legs were covered with welts.

"He bound and fucked me and she whipped me," Jerrod said, as Kyle applied the salve. "How about you?"

Kyle just hummed, not about to tell Jerrod how much better Roger was at taking care of him than Jerrod ever had been.

"One thing is for sure," Jerrod said. "I won't be going into Key West today. If you want to go, you'll have to go alone."

No, I won't, Kyle thought. He and Roger had already agreed to meet at a gay bar Roger knew off Duval Street, if they could shake Jerrod. Now they didn't have to worry about shaking Jerrod.

* * * *

"This is the bar you had to take me to?" Kyle asked. They hadn't walked far from the dock at the Mallory Square pier in Key West when Roger ducked into what looked like an alley and opened the door of a cinder-block-fronted storefront.

"It isn't what is in the front at the bar, but what's behind it," he said and, nodding to the man behind the bar, he continued to the back and guided Kyle through a doorway covered with a beaded curtain. They were in a dimly lit corridor with doors off each side.

"You've been here before?" Kyle asked.

"Many times," Roger answered.

Kyle shuddered at the thought of the experience this man must have and of his own weakness in the face of the man's decisiveness and commands. "Why come here at all? We could have done it on the ship."

"The ship doesn't have the special equipment they have here," Roger said. Kyle shuddered again.

Roger entered one of the rooms. It was small. The walls, ceiling, and floor were all painted black. There was a black straight chair where Roger said they could fold and place their clothes, and, in the center of the room, there was a black vinyl version of a fuck platform called a cube—essentially a cube of pliable plastic with restraints attached to it.

Kyle moaned and turned back toward the door, but Roger pulled him in for a deep kiss. Still holding him close, Roger murmured, "I need to have you under my control totally. I need to know you trust me—will trust me and will give me everything. I'll pay you $500 for this, but then you will lay under me only if you want to be with me. You'll give me everything, free. I'll give you

42

the money whether you let me do you bound or not. Giving up everything to me will be because you want to and are willing to. You'll have to trust that I will take care of you. That's why you have to be bound and completely at my mercy."

"I don't think I can," Kyle whined. "I saw how Jerrod came back from your brother this morning. I can't take being beaten . . . whipped." Submissiveness had its limits. Kyle was afraid of cruelty and pain.

"I'm not my brother," Roger said. "For that matter, neither is my brother. I bet it was Janine who did the beating of your friend, not Edward. I won't beat you. I'll fuck the shit out of you, I'll use your body hard, but I won't give you anything but pleasure and exhaustion. But you will have to give me full control; you will have to put your full trust in me. I require total surrender. You must be bound—fully captive, vulnerable. Can you do that?"

Kyle whimpered and panted with shallow breaths as Roger bound him to the cube on his back, the cube raising Kyle's pelvis but dropping his head off one side. His wrists were bound to the lower side of the cube on either side and his legs were spread and bent and bound at the ankles at the lower corners of the cube.

Roger knelt between Kyle's spread legs and slowly sucked his cock and ate out his ass until Kyle's hole was yawning open and he was begging for the cock. He didn't get it right away. Roger came around to Kyle's head, slid his cock into Kyle's mouth, and, as he slowly face fucked Kyle's throat, he toyed with the young man's nipples. Only when he was fully engorged, dripping, and sensed Kyle's full relaxation to the shaft moving in his throat did Roger come around to the bottom of the cube, insert his hips between Kyle's spread legs, and fuck him. And fuck him and fuck him and fuck him.

Roger commanded Kyle to remain relaxed and open to him, and panting shallowly and willing his passage to open to the limit, he took the cock deep in his core, only flinching a bit when Roger flooded him deep with cum—again and again and again.

Both men exhausted, Roger lay on top of Kyle's still-bound body on the cube and kissed and fondled him.

"You gave it all to me," he whispered, his voice reflected awe.

"Yes, I wanted to give it all to you."

"If I wanted to whip you?"

"I'd let you do whatever you wanted," Kyle answered.

"Don't worry, I won't. But I'd like to be with you."

"Whatever you want. Wherever you want it."

"You know where I'd like to be?"

"Where?" Kyle asked.

"Back in the snow. It's almost Christmas. I want to be back in Jackson Hole for Christmas."

"Then you should go. I wanted to stay in the snow for Christmas too."

"I want you there with me. Would you—?"

"I said anywhere you want me, whenever you want me. You demanded total surrender. I surrender totally."

"Key West has a commercial airport."

"Then let's—"

"Eventually," Roger said, climbing off Kyle and releasing the restraints, but only to turn Kyle on his belly, rebind him, mount his ass, and fuck him again.

While Roger was making airplane arrangements, Kyle returned to the ship to tell Jerrod he was leaving. Jerrod wasn't in the cabin. But Kyle had the pass card for Roger's cabin and, on a hunch, he went there. As he suspected, he could hear evidence from the cabin next door that indicated that Jerrod was being double teamed by Janine and Edward Ange again. He left a note, pushed under the connecting door of the cabins, packed his bag, checked out with the purser, and rolled his bag off the ship.

On Christmas morning, the *Empress of the Seas* was at anchor off Cozumel, Mexico. In cabin 9122, Jerrod was earning $300 fucking Janine Ange on the bed while Edward Ange fucked Jerrod.

In Roger Ange's snowbound Jackson Hole log cabin, Roger was fucking Kyle on a bearskin rug laid out on the floor in front of a roaring fire in the fireplace. There was much to be said for tradition.

Merry Christmas to them all.

~

Addicted to Dick

The cot in the room behind the guard's room at Hollins Prison was narrow, but it fit young, below-average-height inmate Ricky and not as young, taller, and more muscular guard Tate. The proof of that was that Tate was managing to lie on top of Ricky without either of them being dumped to the floor. Ricky was panting, tongue flicking out of his mouth and grimacing slightly with each deep thrust of Tate's dick inside him.

They were doing a missionary, Ricky on his back, naked from the waist down, thrusting his pelvis up a bit by the leverage of his feet dug into the rim of the cot surface on each side and his legs spread and bent. Tate, fully dressed in his guard's gray uniform except for his fly unzipped and flared and shirt unbuttoned to expose his muscular torso, lay, weight taken on his knees, between Ricky's spread legs. His muscular arms were laced under Ricky's armpits and grasping the top rail of the brass headboard behind Ricky's head.

Both men were concentrating on the throb and slide of the cock inside Ricky's channel. Tate moaned and came in for a hurried kiss but then dug his knees in and thrust harder and deeper. Ricky's groan was punctuated with sliding his hands under the waistband of the back of Tate's uniform trousers and digging his fingers into the guard's meaty butt cheeks.

"I think I'm gonna—" Tate muttered, starting to withdraw from Ricky's channel.

"No, don't pull it out. Inside me. Cream me deep," Ricky begged, and he clutched Tate's buttocks hard to him, not letting the guard withdraw.

Both men jerked and exclaimed a "Shit. Fuck," almost in unison as Tate shot a load, shuddered, and shot another one.

Tate made to pull out again, but again Ricky clutched at his buttocks and muttered, "No, don't. Last time. I want to feel you go soft inside me. Keep your dick inside me."

"I don't think I'll go soft," Tate said, with a low growl. "You're too sexy. I got cum left for you."

And, indeed, he didn't really go soft. He quickly recharged, and, young, virile, and in great shape, he fucked Ricky again without having pulled out. That obviously was quite all right with Ricky.

Afterward Tate sprawled out in a wooden swivel desk chair, legs spread, and his hand on his meaty cock and his other hand holding a lighted joint, while he watched Ricky on his back on the cot, slowly jerking himself off.

"Gonna miss you, Bud. And I'm sorry," Tate said after he'd watched Ricky ejaculate. "You're a good kid and a great lay."

"I didn't do it, you know. I took the rap for a friend. He said he'd die in prison if he had to be locked up here. I didn't do drugs, let alone sell them."

"Yeah, I believe you," Tate answered in a "that's what they all say" voice and taking another drag on the joint they were passing back and forth. "Don't matter now, anyway, does it? You served the time and you're getting out tomorrow." He could just as well have added, "and if you didn't do drugs before, you sure as hell do them now." To accentuate that, he handed the joint to Ricky again, who took a drag on it and handed it back.

"So, you're sorry we can't do it anymore," Ricky said. "That's why you said you're sorry?"

"Yeah, that's it," Tate answered, but it wasn't why he said it—or why he felt it.

"So, you going back to this boyfriend you took the rap for?" Tate asked.

"I can't leave the state. And he skipped down to the Caribbean at the first sign of trouble."

Tate gave Ricky another drag on the joint. "You know you don't have to be lonely when you get out. We can see each other on the outside if you want it—need it." He'd added the last because Ricky always left the feeling that he needed the cock, that he needed a dick inside him. Like just now, when he had said he didn't

46

want Tate to take it out of him. Tate didn't think Ricky was just shitting him about that.

"I'll be across state, up near Winchester. Probation officer's got a job lined up for me there, and my brother's there. I can live with him until I get back on my feet."

"On your feet is better than on your back, Ricky." Tate didn't know why he cared about this guy—so young and vulnerable—and so good looking. True jail bait. But there was something about him that made Tate feel protective, and he was always willing to be dicked when Tate could arrange it. It had been a chore keeping him out of the hands of seasoned inmates like Butch. He'd had to extend his protection over him. Fat lot of good that would do now, though.

"Yeah, I hear you. It's just that I like—"

"Addicted to dick. That's what I think you are. And it's not going to do you any good. As soon as you get out of here you need to find a sugar daddy young enough to keep it up, keep it in you, and keep you from reaching for the drugs."

"You're one to say that. You're addicted to male pussy." Ricky laughed, turned on his stomach, gave Tate a provocative look, and raised his bare buttocks a bit off the cot. "And I see that you're hard again now. Come and get it, guard."

Tate *was* hard again, and he *did* go and get it again, lying stretched out on top of the smaller, younger man and taking him from the rear. Showing his prowess in exercise regimes. Once he was mounted on Ricky's ass, with his dick buried, Tate showed his strength by taking a pushups stance and doing a hundred on a groaning and moaning Ricky. When Tate at last lowered his body on the young man's back, Ricky reached back and clutched at the guard's butt cheeks, holding the dick inside him for as long as possible after Tate had given him another double load.

Eventually, both of them fully dressed again, Tate stood and said, "Gotta take you back to your cell now. So, I guess this is it. You could find me in the Nottoway phone book if you wanted to link up after you get out, but it would be dangerous. We can't exchange anything on paper now. It would be my job—and probably a breach of your probation for us to connect on the outside. Something for both of us to think about. But I'll remember you. You're a great lay, you just should be using this release as an opportunity to turn your life around."

"Thanks. You've been good to me Tate."

Not that good, no, Tate was thinking. He'd extended the protection to this point because he wanted to fuck Ricky. There was no other honest way of looking at that. And, God, was he sorry about what came next for Ricky. But it couldn't be helped. He had no control over it. He'd said he was sorry to Ricky, which was the best he could do, even though Ricky had no idea why he was sorry.

* * * *

When Tate walked him back through the minimum security section, Ricky looked around in the cell that had been his for nearly a year. His suitcase was packed, and everything else he'd accumulated—what they'd let him accumulate—was in two small boxes. He could manage to walk out the next day with those, carrying them himself. They'd probably make him carry them himself, he thought, a small smile forming on his lips.

In many ways he'd miss it here. He'd been kicking around in life in Richmond with little motivation and few plans when he'd been arrested for dealing. He hadn't lied to Tate. It had been Lyle's stuff, not his. He'd done some underage drinking, but he hadn't done drugs, let alone dealt them. He had to laugh as Tate had done earlier when he'd handed Ricky the joint. Ricky had learned to do drugs here in the prison to which he'd been sent before for doing drugs before he'd actually done them. Of course liquor was a drug, as the judge had reminded him before he pounded his "I don't care" gavel on his desk, and Ricky had arrived in the judge's court drunk.

Ricky only did minor drugs here and not much of that— he'd found early, though, that he had to do some or he'd have been beaten on by the other inmates for thinking he was above them. As it was, he'd taken a few beatings until he'd hooked up with the guard, Tate, for protection. That hadn't been hard on him. Lyle had been fucking him, and Ricky did have a thing about having a man's dick inside him. Luckily, Tate had taken him up before the other inmates knew that, or Ricky would have been brutalized as well as fucked. Tate just gave him the cock; he didn't beat on him. And Ricky couldn't have gone this year without having a cock inside him regularly.

The others in the prison—the inmates and guards—just didn't know how regularly Ricky needed to have a cock inside him.

Lyle would have been a three-striker and Ricky believed him when he said he'd die in prison. They hadn't done so badly by Ricky. It was a minimum security prison and he'd had just a few routines he had to follow. He only rarely was locked in his cell, other than at night. He got to work outside in good weather, helping with the landscaping, and he had plenty of gym time, which had toned his rather small body up nicely. That had increased the cat calls he got from the other open-door cells as he walked the section, but knowledge that he was Tate's punch had kept the other guys in their cells—and Ricky outside of their cells. He'd let one black bruiser fuck him, early on, and he'd reveled in having a big black cock inside him, but Tate had put a stop to that. He'd let Ricky know in no uncertain terms how rough life would get for him if it became general knowledge that he'd put out casually—and for anyone but Tate—and, especially, for a black bull. There weren't many young guys in the prison who could take a black bull without damage.

Ricky had also done work at the Warden's house, painting his upstairs bedrooms. And the warden had done him in an upstairs bedroom too. He'd bent him right over a bed, knelt and eaten him out, and then given him the cock hard and deep. Instinctively, the warden knew exactly what Ricky wanted and needed most, although it surprised him that someone so evidently innocent would be so anxious to have a man's cock inside him. When he had first driven the cock home to where short and curlies were tickling Ricky's ass cheeks, he grabbed Ricky's hips and held hard, steady, and deep, while Ricky fucked himself in his own way on the hard staff, rhythmically pushing his buttocks back onto the cock. When Ricky had come, the warden then pumped himself to an ejaculation in the young man's well-open channel—and Ricky went with him.

Afterward, the warden told Ricky not to tell anyone about it. He hadn't told Tate about that. But it was the warden who had arranged for a probation officer who all said was the most lenient of the lot and it was the warden who had gotten Ricky set up with a job up in Winchester, near Ricky's brother. So bending over the bed for the warden once—well, three times to be honest—had worked out well for Ricky in the end.

Ricky was still thinking about what part of this experience he would miss, when the sound of a policeman's nightstick running along the bars of his cell caught his attention. One of the other guards—not Tate, but one who was meaner to the inmates—stopped at Ricky's open door and motioned for him.

"Come with me," he said. "You're spending your last night elsewhere. Leave your stuff. You can pick it up tomorrow when you're released."

* * * *

"Where are we going?" Ricky asked as he followed the hulking, unsmiling guard through the corridor of the minimum security section. The man let his nightstick run across the bars facing out in the corridor, causing a racket. It was late enough that some of the inmates might have turned in for the night. The guard obviously didn't care.

"You're being released tomorrow," the guard answered.

"Yes, so?"

"You've had it pretty cushy here. This is a state prison, so they have standards that coddle the inmates—if you ask me—and check frequently. You're in for drugs, aren't you? And it's your first conviction, isn't it?"

"Yes to both," Ricky answered.

"Well, our deputy warden here has a little program of his own. He likes to give guys who have lived a certain way here and are being released a little incentive not to be sent back. And next time you come—for a second conviction—it won't be to the pansy side of the house. You'll go to the medium-security wing. Understand?"

"Not really," Ricky responded.

"As I said, the deputy warden has a little incentive program of his own. We know Tate has been your protector here and what you've done for him to get that protection. We're going to medium security and you'll spend the night there. Warden wants to get in the minds of the minimum security guys what the difference is between that and being in medium security. You've been in for one offense. We want you to think twice before getting yourself sent up again. And here we are."

The cells here didn't have open doors. The guys hanging their arms through the bars as the guard guided Ricky down this corridor sang out cat calls and offered rough propositions and suggestions that were much more ominous than anything Ricky heard in minimum security.

Half way down the corridor, the guard turned, pulled out a ring of keys, and opened a cell door. The cell was dark, but Ricky could see a figure in the shadows—a hulking figure, more than a foot taller than Ricky and more than a foot wider too—a regular body builder with a thick, hairy body. The figure came closer. The face was battered, ogreish, and with a sneer planted on it. All the guy was wearing was gym shorts hanging low on his hips, under a beer belly.

"Here he is, Butch, as promised," the guard said. "He's yours for the night. Have fun. Just don't kill him or mark him up too noticeably."

The guard pushed Ricky into the cell. "Don't fight him, kid, if you want to be able to walk out of here on your own tomorrow. Like I said, you come back to this prison, it will be to this section, and every day for you will be like the next six hours are going to be for you."

Ricky turned his head and watched the guard leave the cell and lock the door, but he remained there, hands on the bars, looking in, with a smirk on his face. When Ricky looked back into the cell, he saw stars and dropped to his knees as a fist smashed into his cheek. On his way down, a knee caught him in the stomach. He retched in pain and shock, as he was pulled up by his hair, punched in the face—but with a last-second holding back that, nonetheless, conveyed what a full-force punch would be like—and lowered to his knees again. A monstrous, hard cock was

51

pressing at his cheek and then at his lips and then at his inner cheek. Ricky opened his mouth to the cock, and gagged as bulb went into the back of his throat.

"Well, OK, Butch, have it your way," the guard said and laughed before he walked away from the cell.

"I kinda would like you to try to struggle against it," a deep, threatening voice said. Fingers from a hand gripped the hair on the back of Ricky's head and guided his face to a deep-throated intake of an erect cock. "Suck it good or it won't go well for you," the voice said.

The guard hadn't gone far. He returned and put his hands through the bars and held Ricky's shoulders in place. One of his hands released the shoulder but only to take hold of his nightstick, run it down Ricky's back inside the waistband at his back, and into his cracker. The guard ran the club over the rim of Ricky's hole.

Ricky sucked the cock good—probably better than either the guard or Butch expected. That didn't keep him from being beaten down again after the cock was hard as a rock, bent over the bed in the room, and his ass eaten out while Butch worried Ricky's cock and squeezed his balls until Ricky's eyes watered.

Ricky instinctively struggled against the assault but only until Butch covered his body from behind as he was bent over the bed and forced himself inside Ricky's ass. Ricky had been opened but not well enough, and the invasion of the monster cock took some time, effort, and screaming. But once Butch was in, Ricky settled down for the plowing. Now he was in his element. He was addicted to dick, and there was a big club inside him. He didn't have to look at the guy fucking him. All he had to do was concentrate on the cock inside him.

To Butch's surprise Ricky settled right down, begged for the deep fuck he was given, grabbed at the frame of the other side of the bed to hold himself steady, and moved his pelvis with the fuck. He was beaten badly enough, though, to moan more from Butch continuing to prod and punch his body as from the size of the staff inside him. The staff inside him was just fine. To some extent Butch felt cheated. He and others had watched Ricky in lust, being frustrated that he was protected by Tate and assuming that Ricky only took Tate's cock for the protection. But now he was discovering that once a guy got his dick in Ricky, the little piece became a firecracker of want for the buried dick.

When Butch had come the first time, he stepped away from Ricky and the guard entered the cell, saddled up behind Ricky's bent-over body, and pushed the end of his nightstick inside Ricky's hole a couple of inches and fucked the young man with it. Getting bored with that, the guard mounted Ricky's ass himself and took his turn for a fuck, muttering in Ricky's ear, "This is in case you think the guards will come to your rescue if you wind up in prison again." Once skewered, Ricky enjoyed the guard's cocking too—the nightstick prodding, not so much.

Butch was ready again when the guard was finished and lifted and slammed Ricky down on his back on the bed and took him again in a missionary fuck, while he choked Ricky into submission with his fists around the young man's neck.

The ogre slept on top of Ricky, keeping him pinned to the bed, although he rolled over onto his side after an hour or so and a third fuck.

The fourth fuck, to Butch's surprise, was on Ricky. Butch woke up, on his back, with Ricky straddling his pelvis, impaling his ass on Butch's erection. Ricky leaned over and whispered, "Just stay hard for me," which, in amazement, Butch did, and Ricky rode him hard and in frenzied gyrations to another mutual load dump such as Butch had never experienced before.

When Ricky was pulled out of the cell the next morning, it was with a promise from Butch to be his protector if another conviction sent Ricky back to this prison.

When Ricky walked out of the prison gates to be greeted by his brother, Allen, and Allen's wife, Katie, his eye was blackened, his cheek was puffy, he was hobbling, and his arms, legs, and torso were bruised, but he was smiling, and an impressed medium-security prison guard was carrying his boxes and his suitcase.

* * * *

"That must be him now. He's wearing a clerical collar."

"That must be who?" Ricky asked his brother. They were at the barbecue in the Baileys' backyard. It had been nearly two weeks since Ricky's brother and his wife had brought Ricky home from the prison in Nottoway. Ricky had started his job with the landscaping company in Winchester, but he didn't see his probation officer until the next week. He was jittery, but it had nothing to do with drugs. He hadn't gotten into them enough in prison to be missing not having them now. He wouldn't have any trouble with that part of his probation at all. No, that wasn't what he was missing from his prison experience.

"It's Father Thomas—I think that's what his name is," Allen answered. "You have been referred to him for any adjustment counseling you might need. It's OK, Ricky, I told him that you—that we—aren't religious. He said that was OK. That he'd just be there to listen to any concern you have, knowing that, as a priest, he wouldn't be passing anything you had to say to anyone."

By then Father Thomas had reached them and Katie had brought the two small children out of the house and was setting the table for a picnic.

Father Thomas was a big man—big across the shoulders but thinner at the waist. He was a handsome devil with red hair and a ready smile. He could be a hockey player as much as a priest and he didn't talk preachy to them over the picnic lunch. He took a beer readily, something Ricky couldn't have, since he was on probation, but none of them made a big deal over that. Ricky wasn't quite old enough to be drinking beer anyway, and it was another thing he had no trouble giving up in his probation. There were other, stronger urges, that he was having trouble giving up— and looking at the robust priest, so comfortable in the situation and putting everyone to ease, didn't help Ricky fight his urges.

"Sure, I'm fine," Ricky said at the end of the meal. "Just nervous about the new job I've started."

"Are you getting along with the boss of the outfit?" Father Thomas asked. "Ned James is a friend of mine. If there's any developing trouble there—"

"No, everything's fine there. Mr. James is nice to me and patient with me learning the business. And he's fair to all the guys. No, everything there is fine." Nice was a comparative word for what Ned James was, though, Ricky thought. Ned James was sexy as hell. Muscular and handsome—and deeply tanned from working outdoors. Ricky had developed a crush on him from the beginning, and James was, indeed, respectful and nice to Ricky. That had been fine until Ricky had seen Ned spiking one of the male Hispanic seasonal workers over a wheel barrow behind a shed. Having seen that, and knowing now that Ned James was a power top, nice, in terms of fair and polite and patient in the workplace wasn't the brand of nice Ricky was looking for.

Tate had fucked Ricky regularly over the last year and Ricky had become addicted to his dick. He'd needed regularly. Ricky hadn't had a dick for two weeks. He was skittish as hell.

"Well, you are tense about something, Ricky," Allen said. "We're trying not to crowd you and watch you too much, but you seem to be having trouble adjusting to life. I know that you've just been under lock and key for a year and this is all hard on you, but we worry . . . Kate and I worry—"

"Which is where I come in, Ricky," Father Thomas said in a soothing voice. "Your brother didn't call me. I don't want you to think that. Warden Avery called me. He's concerned about those who have been in his system who he thinks need special attention when they get out because they are basically good people and he doesn't want to see them being sucked into the system again. You need someone to talk to. I'd be happy to be that person for you."

They sat there in silence for a few minutes before Katie spoke up. "We can have dessert later. Maybe the reverend and Ricky would like to take a walk in the park before that—to talk, or not, as they please. I can't keep the kids from being rowdy here, and we have a very nice park on the lake, with an entrance just down the street from here."

The two men walked, side by side, but conscious that the other one was silent, down a woodland trail, paralleling a lake bank. The trail kept coming close to the lake and then was hidden from view from the lake. Deep in the woods, Father Thomas put a hand on Ricky's arm to interrupt the walk and said, "Is there someplace more private from the trail that we can go, Ricky? Bill Avery really is worried about you—but not quite for the reasons I mentioned back at your brother's house. He told me you likely weren't getting everything you need, and asked me to come check on you . . . and to provide what you needed if I found you weren't being taken care of."

"I don't think I understand—"

"I think you do, Ricky. Is there someplace more private—where we can't be seen or heard from the trail?"

"Off toward the lake here, there are benches facing the lake. But I don't think—"

Ricky struck off into the woods, off the trail, toward the lake. They found a bench that was a good distance from the trail and also was hidden a bit from being seen from the lake, although those sitting on the bench could see the lake.

When they were seated, Ricky said, "Really, Reverend, everything is just—"

"I don't think so, Ricky. Your brother is concerned about you. He says you've been jittery, and I can see it myself. It isn't from drug withdrawal, is it?"

"No, certainly not. I don't do drugs—and I didn't do drugs before. I was in because I was covering for a friend."

"You didn't do drugs in prison? I find that hard to believe. And you're so jittery now. I think you need these, just to help you adjust down. Here, take these. Go ahead. It's hard to just cut them off altogether." He was holding two pills in his hand. Ricky looked at them for a minute but then shrugged, took them, and popped them in. Almost immediately he didn't feel so jittery.

"You say you were covering for a friend," the priest said then. "It was a boyfriend, wasn't it?"

"A friend, who was a man, yes," Ricky said.

"You don't have to pretend with me, Ricky. It's OK, I'm not going to judge. I'm gay myself."

Ricky turned and looked directly at the man sitting beside me.

"In fact, I find you very attractive. Can you say that you don't find me attractive?" And then, when Ricky didn't—or couldn't—answer, Father Thomas said, "No I didn't think so. I can tell when a man is interested in me." He put an arm around Ricky's shoulders and Ricky didn't move away.

"I'm going to say why I think you were jittery and needed a little help, Ricky, and you only need to interrupt me if I'm wrong."

His face was close to Ricky's and he was giving Ricky a close look. He moved his face to the side of Ricky's head and inhaled the scent of him. "You smell nice, Ricky. You're a beautiful young man," he said in a low voice. Ricky shuddered but didn't move away. He felt himself going hard. He almost moaned. He needed it so bad.

"Warden Avery has told me everything, Ricky. He told me he laid you. He told me he found that one of his guards Topped you regularly the whole time you were there. He told me you needed a cock inside you regularly. Tell me if you disagree with any of this. You needn't be ashamed. It's a natural condition. Something to be celebrated more than hidden."

Ricky said nothing. He was trembling. He needed it so bad. Father Thomas was fiddling with Ricky's belt buckle and his zipper—and then with his own.

"I think you were jittery because you aren't getting it. I've talked with Ned James—he's a friend of the warden's and mine too—and he said he isn't fucking you yet."

The "yet" got through to Ricky and he moaned. Father Thomas took advantage of this to fish Ricky's cock out of his fly with a hand. Ricky was hard and throbbing. He moaned again as Father Thomas began to slowly stroke him.

"You aren't getting it from anyone now, are you? You haven't gotten it since you got out of prison, have you? But you want it. You want it bad. Disagree with me if you can."

Ricky couldn't disagree and so he didn't. He offered no resistance as Father Thomas moved one of Rick's hands to Father Thomas's crotch. The priest as thick and hard.

"Warden Avery is coming to Winchester in a couple of weeks and he wants to see you. Until then and after he's gone, you have me. Tell me that you don't want me—that you don't want my cock."

Ricky couldn't tell him he didn't want his cock and he didn't tell him he didn't want it. The priest pulled the young man's face around for a deep kiss as they both continued stroking each other's cocks. Father Thomas began pushing Ricky's shorts and briefs off his hips.

Ricky rode the priest's hard cock by sitting in Father Thomas's lap, facing him, with the priest's hands holding his waist and Ricky leaning back, leveraging off his feet on the bench on either side of the priest's hips and locking his fists behind Thomas's neck. Thomas, fully clothed except for being unzipped and his trousers flared, just provided the hard, eternally hard, cock, while Ricky bounced up and down on it and brought himself to a much-needed ejaculation.

The priest's shoot off came behind the bench, with Ricky on all fours in a carpet of fir tree needles, and Father Thomas mounted on his ass and bringing them to a mutual ejaculation.

Afterward they were back on the bench, watching the sun dip down over the lake, kissing and fondling in a cool down. Ricky was sighing from a much needed release.

"I believe a twice-weekly counseling session at my rectory is in order," the priest said.

"Yes," Ricky answered.

"You'll tell your brother that we had a very nice little chat and you are working through some concerns with me, but that there's nothing for him to worry about. I'll tell him the same if he asks me."

"Yes," Ricky answered.

"And he won't see any signs of nervousness or jitters now if you make your sessions with me."

"Yes," Ricky answered.

"Any other questions for now?"

"Can you make it hard for me again . . . now? You don't have to do anything. I'll do the riding. All you have to do is keep it hard."

"Yes," Father Thomas answered, "I think we have enough time."

* * * *

"Strip and sit back in the chair with your legs over the chair arms, please. Scoot your butt to the front edge of the chair."

Now Ricky knew why his probation officer had set his first appointment in Harrisonburg for 6:00 p.m., when the office really was closed. The man had had his dick out and had been stroking it all the time he was telling Ricky what was what and what Ricky had to do for his probation officer to be giving him good reports.

Ricky also knew now why the warden had set him up with this probation officer. They must have some sort of club going, Ricky thought. And then he was sure when, after the guy had knelt in front of him and sucked his cock and balls and eaten his ass out, while Ricky leaned back in the wooden chair and grasped the ankles of his spread feet, the guy crouched over him, hands grasping the top of the chair back on either side of Ricky's head, and buried his cock inside Ricky's hole.

He did what the rest of the club did, with his own variation. He gave Ricky all of the cock to the hilt and held there, deep, while Ricky squirmed in the seat, jacked himself off, and panted to an ejaculation. The probation officer's variation was that, although holding deep inside Ricky for Ricky to come first, he moved his cock in shallow, but deep, strokes, kissing Ricky's walls deep with his cock bulb and making Ricky's channel wall muscles ripple on the hard shaft.

After Ricky got what he wanted—even though it wasn't fully expected—and what he undoubtedly needed, the probation officer got what he wanted. He had Ricky turn, with his knees in the chair seat, his chest hanging on the chair back, and his arms dangling down to the side, as the man covered him from behind, mounted him, skewered him, and pounded his ass to the man's own ejaculation.

He then told Ricky that all of their appointments would be late, if here in Harrisonburg, but that on occasion, he'd come to Winchester and they could meet in the rectory at Father Thomas's church.

So, yep, Ricky knew, it was a club. But as long as they all knew how he wanted and needed it and satisfied him, he didn't give a shit that they got pleasure from it too.

Still, he wondered about when his probation was over. It was only for six months.

* * * *

Over the next three weeks Ricky went from satisfied to frustrated to panicked. He was being fucked by Father Thomas twice a week and by his probation officer every other week, which went a long way to satisfy him. Increasingly, though, he was attracted to his boss, Ned James, who didn't come after him, even though Ricky strongly suspected he was part of Warden Avery's group of tops. Instead, James fucked a couple of the Hispanic seasonal workers where Ricky could see him doing it. The last time he'd done it, he'd even kept his eye on Ricky, watching him from across the terrace of a house whose yard they were grooming while the family was on vacation. It was almost like he was taunting Ricky—and it made Ricky want him all the more. The man was big cocked and virile and made no bones about letting Ricky see that he was.

This was the nonrelationship that frustrated Ricky. And it increasingly did so as Ricky's other servicing went by the wayside.

The first sign of trouble was Ricky's probation officer being arrested for just the sort of favoritism-for-sex behavior that he was going to be conducting with Ricky. Ricky was too new to it with him to become part of the case against the probation officer, but suddenly, without warning, Ricky had a sour old ugly woman as his probation officer.

The fallout from this was probably what made the other changes in Ricky's sexual life. Warden Bill Avery did come to Winchester, as Father Thomas said he would, and he did fuck Ricky at the church's rectory. Father Thomas fucked Ricky that day too, the warden taking him first and then the priest taking him. Between the two of them, they exhausted Ricky, who was sprawled out on the bed in the priest's bedroom, tongue hanging out in satisfaction, and lightly panting, as the two men who had fucked him sat in the next room, chatted, and drank beer together.

"I've taken a transfer out to California," Ricky heard the warden say. "I'm hoping I can get ahead of this and stay ahead of it."

"Good move," Father Thomas agreed. "There's a church up in New York State that is interested in having me. I'll be gone from here in another week myself."

And that's what came to pass. Going from having two dicks inside him in succession, Ricky went to having none.

And it frustrated him. It frustrated him to the point where, when the landscape company was grooming the grounds of another mansion near Middleburg with no residents present two weeks later and Ned James declared it was too hot to work and stripped and dove into the estate's swimming pool, Ricky did as well.

He swam over to Ned and begging him, "Please, Mr. James, I can't take it anymore. I know you fuck men, and I'm in a bad state. What's wrong with me that you won't fuck me too?"

"Nothing's wrong with you, Ricky," Ned answered. "I've been waiting for you to ask me for it. Warden Avery recommended you for this job because he knew you were what I liked to fuck. But I know that, with the rest of the men in the warden's circle, you were in the position to have to do what they wanted you to do. I want it to be a longer term relationship with me, if we do it at all. And I want it to be because you freely want it from me."

"I want it from you," Ricky sobbed. "I want it bad."

"Then you'll get it." Ned embraced Ricky and moved over to the side of the pool, where he could stand in a crouch. He maneuvered Ricky around to in front of him, facing him, palmed the young man's buttocks, and began to pull him into his lap.

"Don't you first need to—"

"I'm already hard for you, Ricky," Ned said. "I've been hard for you since I first saw you. Every time I made sure you saw me fucking someone else, it was you I was hard for."

"What I need—what I want—"

"I already know what you need and want, Ricky. I've known since Bill Avery called me about giving you a job."

And, indeed, Ned James did know what Ricky wanted and needed. He turned them both so that his back was to the side of the pool. And then, lapping Ricky, he pulled the young man onto his cock—all the way on it until his short hairs were mingling with Ricky's, and then he whispered, "I'll hold it hard inside you. You do what you want to do to get off and then I'll do what I want to do."

With Ned holding Ricky in his lap, one arm around the young man's waist and his other hand stroking Ricky's cock, and Ned keeping himself ramrod hard inside Ricky, Ricky used the leverage of his feet on the side of the pool to fuck himself on Ned's cock until he shot his load.

Then, moving them both down to the shallow end of the pool, Ned pulled Ricky up out of the water, laid him down on the terrace of the pool, with the small of his back on the pool lip, positioned Ricky's ankles on his shoulders, entered Ricky again, and fucked the shit out of him to a mutual ejaculation.

Ricky was crying when Ned was finished with him and Ned asked him why.

"It was so good. I'd like to have you inside me forever. But I'm scared. They're after the warden's group. They've all gone. I'm afraid you'll go too."

"Not a chance," Ned answered. "I own a business here I can't just walk away from. Besides, they all are in a position to lose big if their fucking of young men becomes public. I don't hide that I fuck men and I work for myself. I don't give a shit who knows that I do. I don't give a shit that everyone knows that I take care of your addiction for dick. And I'll do that if you let me."

"You'll do that? You'll always do that?"

"Continually. Like now. You're so sexy and sweet that I've got it up for you again already. These folks have a nice pool house, with nice beds in it. Unless you tell me you don't want to do it, I'm carrying you in there now, lying on my back on one of the beds, and I want you to climb on top of me and do a cowboy ride on my cock."

Ricky didn't tell Ned he didn't want to do that.

~

The Jacket

It was the first time I'd worn the jacket and I'd lost it. I had other jackets, but when I'd gone out the day before, I'd decided this one would be best to wear, and I was right. The temperature in Paris was changing, and there was a great variation between late morning and mid afternoon. It was too nice out to want to go to indoor cafés. The Parisian way was to settle in outdoor cafés, drink coffee, leisurely read the paper, and ogle women—or, in my case, men—as city life drifted by you.

I'd been transferred directly and unexpectedly from the Mediterranean, so most of the jackets I had with me before my goods arrived in Paris were lightweight. They weren't up to the slight chill in the Paris morning, and yet I didn't want to be the only one sitting inside a café for my morning break from my international export company job. I had sought out the Paris assignment because I also worked as a male model and Paris was the Eden of high fashion. I'd acquired a bit of a reputation for walking the runway, and Paris was a big opportunity for me.

The jacket had been just right for this weather. I'd had it for years and had only kept it for sentimental reasons, because most of those years I had been living in the tropics. The jacket was much too heavy for where I'd lived before now. It was a soft grayish-green wool, woven in an intricate pattern and with leather inserts of nearly identical color as side panels, elbow guards, and wrist bands. But it had come from my father, who had had it made in Oslo during his stint there as the military attaché at the U.S. embassy in Norway. It was much too nice to give to a charity organization in its nearly new condition. I knew my father must have carefully picked it out, as he was as style conscious as I was.

I always had assumed that someday I could put the jacket into service myself. I'd even bought an expensive cashmere neck scarf to go with it in a bazaar in New Delhi that was of a color I thought would match the coat and that, victoriously, had done so perfectly. I'm sure I could be considered overconcerned about style and clothing, but fashion was a major aspect of my life. I took great care with the grooming of my wardrobe and my body, and I'd always found it easy to fall in with men who appreciated the care I took with myself as well. I expected the same of them.

And now, after only one day of wearing the jacket around Paris to various offices and cafés in a flurry of activity in setting up my new life in the French capital, I somehow had lost the jacket. The day had warmed as it had progressed. There were any number of places I could have entered, wearing the jacket, and left, not feeling the need for a jacket. The worst part was that the jacket had had so little part of my life, other than sentimentality and being a timeless style, that I couldn't be sure I'd even recognize the jacket if I saw it somewhere other than in my closet or on the back of my chair.

Thus it was that, when I was walking past an outdoor café on a Paris street near my apartment late the next morning, I did a double take when I looked into the café and saw a jacket that very easily could be mine draped over the back of a chair. The young man seated in the chair caught my eye as I stood there, wondering and speculating, and gave me a smile. He was a beautiful young man—dark and sultry, with a day's stubble of beard that added to the sensuality of an athletic-frame European male, and with an infectious and teasing smile that went beyond his full-lipped mouth with dazzling white teeth and into his dark eyes. He was impeccably—and casually—dressed and could well have been a model himself.

I stood there, gawking at him—or, rather, at the jacket, although he obviously didn't understand that it was the jacket, not him, I was staring at—for a moment longer than needed for him to get the impression that I was interested in him. In hindsight, I could see that he was justified in thinking that I had been coming on to him from the beginning. In response, he turned in three-quarters profile to me in the chair, leaned back, and smiled again in a "what you see is what you get" fashion. And what I could see was very presentable indeed.

If I'd given him my full attention, I, of course, would have been interested in him. But my focus was on the jacket. Had I been in this café yesterday? Yes, I think I might have been. Had I sat at that table? Yes, possibly. Could I just have left the jacket on the back of the chair when I left and no one had taken it away? Unlikely—at least that no one would have noticed it as abandoned and taken it away—but not impossible, if the café, one that was open twenty-four-hours a day, remained as busy as it often did.

The smile on his face broadened and he gestured to me, inviting me to sit at the table. The gesture refocused my attention on him more fully, and a couple of parts of me took note—my heart gave an extra bleep, and another part of me noticeably hardened. He was a beautiful young man, fully masculine, but totally sensual. His clothes fit him like a glove, including across the bulge at his crotch. There was a type of man I melted to lay under. This was such a man. I mostly went with older men, but occasionally I preferred a younger one—when I was in the mood for vigor.

I accepted his invitation and sat at the table. In the blink of an eye, a waiter was at my elbow and I had ordered coffee. I would be there, with this dark and sultry hunk, at least as long as it took for me to finish my coffee. The young man's cup was refilled when my coffee arrived. He was willingly staying around too.

We couldn't communicate with each other in other than hand signals and the occasionally mutually understood word. He was French and I was American and had unexpectedly and on short notice been transferred to Paris. It would be months—possibly never—before I'd be able to converse in the language, although I did have a facility for learning languages and knew several. I'm pretty good at figuring the essential meaning of a word out when given in context of the situation.

We managed to maintain interest in each other and keep the interaction animated despite the language barrier, with some misunderstandings and, increasingly, at least one quite clear shared understanding—he wanted to fuck me and I was quite willing for him to do so.

He was a university student, making that evident by pointing to a pile of books on the table, and saying the words "Sorbonne" and "*architecture*," the latter word pronounced differently in French and English, but perfectly understandable to me when he said it in French. I got across that I very much liked the jacket hanging on the back of his chair, but not that I wondered if it was *my* jacket. In turn, he admired my Gucci polo shirt, saying "Gucci?" with a question mark, and I nodded and smiled and said "*Oui,*" which was about the extent of my French vocabulary at that point. I wasn't sure—at least then—when he motioned, with a twinkle of his eye, the act of pulling the shirt over my head, that he was propositioning me. Not completely understanding, I smiled back at him and said "*Oui.*"

That served as some sort of ice breaker and deal maker that I didn't immediately understand, but had no objection to when I did understand it. The conversation, such as it was, became more intimate, with touching, and lingering gazes, and him pointing to himself and saying "Jacques" and then pointing to me and waiting for me to say "Ryan."

This was followed with him smiling that million-dollar smile again, pointing up—which I only understood in reliving the moment as meaning he wanted us to go up to someplace private—and popping his tongue in the side of his mouth. I didn't fully understand that, but I was getting the message. His hand went to my thigh, above the knee, and he looked dreamily at me. I didn't try to remove his hand, which told him all he wanted to know.

What I *did* fully understand was when he folded over the fingers of one of his hands to form a sheath and pointed at me with a quizzical look and a "*Oui?*" and then showed me the middle finger of his other hand, declaring "*Oui,*" inserted that finger in the sheath formed with the other hand, moved it vigorously in and out, and popped his tongue inside his cheek again. He wanted to ensure that I was a bottom and was declaring himself as a top. I now understood what the popping of a tongue in the cheek meant. I was to think about how I found out and smile, every time I saw a Frenchman do that when a sexy woman passed him on the street.

What could I do but answer with the only French word I'd mastered. I said "*Oui,*" made a folded-fingers sheath with one of my hands, and pointed to myself and smiled. Just to be sure, he gave me the universal, underhanded, pumping of his fist that was understood anywhere as a jacking off sign, and I smiled again and said "*Oui.*"

There was some confusion as we stood and each dropped coins on the top of the table and he reached back for the jacket, showing that he knew it was there and thought it was his, no matter how recently acquired. I knew then that he would fuck me and I wouldn't make a fuss about the jacket, but I realized that we hadn't established where this coupling would take place. I took my wallet out and extracted one of my personal calling cards, pointing to an address. He smiled and pointed in the direction where my apartment was, not more than two blocks from here, and I nodded in agreement.

I also extracted some euro notes half way from the wallet and gave him a questioning look. But he smiled at me, moved his hand back and forth in a "not needed" gesture and then diagrammed an hour-glass figure with both hands—denoting a woman's curvy figure, but getting across that he found me attractive enough to fuck me for free. I never had had to pay for it before, but he was beyond irresistible. I would have paid him for sex. His eagerness was enhanced by a thrust of his pelvis back and forward, a licentious smile, and another pop of his tongue in his cheek.

I don't know if any of the others at tables around us at the café observed and correctly interpreted his mime, but I didn't care. I laughed. At this point I was also hard as a rock and fairly panting for him.

He was a highly competent lover, his body beautifully proportioned, muscular, and slightly hirsute, with curly dark hair swirling on his chest and down into his trimmed pubes. His cock was thick and long in erection, his balls plump, and his technique straightforward, powerful, and vigorous. He was everything I could want in a fuck with a stranger, especially one that was unexpected and impromptu.

We needed no language. We kissed inside the door as we undressed each other and showed in gestures and groans that we both approved of the goods we'd gotten in the deal. Naked, but still standing inside the closed door to the apartment, we rocked against each other. Jacques frotted our cocks while we kissed. I too reached down and found him to be uncut. I was cut. I pushed the foreskin back off the bulb of his cock and fluttered my fingers over his sensitive cockhead, which made him groan. I worked his cock for a few moments, reveling in the feel of his loose skin gliding on the hard steel of his erection as I worked him.

In breathy French, he murmured something to me. All I recognized from what he said was his interjection in English of "fuck you" and "bed."

I took him into my bedroom and sank to my knees between his legs as he sat on the bed and sucked his cock, again pushing his foreskin back with my lips, where it stayed because of how hard he now was, as he guided my deep throating with moans and his hands on the back of my head. He knelt behind me, in turn, as I was bent over the bed, my arms outstretched in submissive supplication, as he ate out my ass and alternated pulling my dick through my legs and giving it suck. I writhed under him, moaning and groaning, as he covered me close from behind, entering me slowly and deeply. I struggled against him half-heartedly and ineffectually, until he was fully saddled, and then gave into him completely, letting him have his way with me as he wished. When I relaxed, I opened more to him, and we both realized and appreciated that I could take him deeper then. He took his victory in long, deep thrusts, and pumped me to his ejaculation. I had already come for him while he was working on opening me up with his tongue.

There had been a moment of awkwardness before I realized he hadn't come with protection and managed to gesture to him that there were condoms and lube in the drawer of my nightstand. He hesitated but did take out a disk and crowned himself.

He wasn't in a hurry to leave, and we spent time in each other's arms stretched out on the bed, kissing and fondling each other, and engaging in a mutual language lesson. He palmed my chest, flicking my nubs and said, "*es nichons*" and "*les nibards*," and, taking one of his nipples between my thumb and finger, I twisted and pinched it and said, "pectorals and nipple." He pointed to my

68

cock and said "*le pénis, la verge, La bite,*" and "*la pine.*" I said "cock, dick, and shaft." He laughed, leaned over, and took my cock in his mouth. I moved around to where I could take his in my throat too and we sixty-nined. He moved a finger to my hole, penetrated me, and whispered, "*l'anus,*" which I readily understood, but, with a low laugh, he added, "*une coquille.*" I knew from his gesture that he was referring to a vagina, having used my ass as one would a woman's cunt. Panting and breathless, I murmured, "Male cunt. Hole. Yes, oh god yes," as he penetrated to the prostate with his index finger and rubbed.

He freed his hands and moved them to in front of my face, repeating the gesture from the café of folding the fingers of one hand into a sheath and thrusting the middle finger of the other hand into it. He growled, "*coucher avec quelqu'un*" and "*copuler, s'accoupler*" and then, in broken but clearly understandable English, smiled and said, "I fuck you again now." "*Forniquer*" and "*niquer,*" he murmured, and added, in broken English, "You understand?" and, strangely enough, I did understand he was going to fuck me again. He also gave me a questioning, pleading look and murmured in English, "No rubber? OK now. Raw fuck? Is better, how you say, feel."

"Copulate, fuck. Yes, raw fuck. Fuck me now!" I cried out, lost to him to the point of risking it. He rolled over on top of me, stuffing a pillow under the small of my back, as I spread and bent my legs, placing my feet flat on the mattress, and rolling my pelvis up to receive the strong, deep thrust of his cock and prepared to thrust with him. I clutched, alternately, at his shoulder blades and his buttocks, as he plowed me deep and hard, vigorously and with abandon. Young, strong, virile, he took me harder, rougher, more insistently now, and I cried out in passion and ecstasy at the intensity of the fuck.

We needed no language to be lost to each other, to become one, smoothly undulating fucking machine. Him giving me all, taking it all from me. Me luxuriating in a thick, uncut cock, raw barebacking, velvety smooth and loose skin sliding along steel erection, caressing and rippling along my channel walls. Until, with explosive ejaculations and his cry of "*Tirer un/son coup!*" and my answer in a cry of unbridled passion, "Yes, shit. Fuck. Blast me with your cum!" we both came, together.

I had meant to take him in a civilized, pleasant fuck, the celebration of two beautiful bodies working on consort, but the feel of him moving inside me, unsheathed, raw, hard as steel, as thick as a club, and the intensity of his attack and ravishing of me drove me to distraction and completely undid me. Older men were more experienced, nuanced, but there was no beating the occasional raw vigor and virility of a younger man.

After resting, we fucked again, with abandon, like two rutting animals in heat, and I melted under him, orgasming again and again and again at the sensation of him exploding inside me, flooding me deep in my core. I thought he was going to stay here forever, fucking me forever. And I wanted him to.

He held me, both of us panting heavily, in a close embrace, as he went flaccid inside me, me clutching his buttocks to hold him inside me as long as possible. Young, virile, vital, he recovered yet again to be able to reengorge and fuck me in long, languid strokes, his cock sliding easily through the cum of his previous deposit, bringing me to another ejaculation as well, before we both collapsed in exhaustion. He whispered words and short phrases in my ear, obviously in French. I hoped they were dirty. I took them as such. We dozed off in each other's arms.

When he left me as twilight was stealing into the windows of the bedroom in my third-floor flat, I watched him put on the jacket—possibly my jacket—give me a smile and a salute, and then turn and leave without a word.

I didn't begrudge him the jacket. It was well worth the night of fucking. Even the barebacking—the glorious barebacking with a young, uncut man. I'd have myself checked, of course, but it was worth the risk.

As it turned out, I didn't have to begrudge him the jacket. The next day as I passed the door of the barbershop I'd gone to two days previously, one of the barbers came to the door and hailed me. He held my lost jacket, complete with cashmere scarf, in his hand.

Elated and feeling like celebrating, I planted a kiss on his lips that had him staggering and wide eyed and went directly from there to the café where I'd met Jacques the previous day, hoping that I might find him there and ready for another fuck. He wasn't there, but sitting at a table—our table—and reading a book with a jacket I recognized—Thomas Mann's *Der Tod in Venedig*, *Death in Venice*, which I knew dealt with the subject of homosexuality—was a young blond man who was to die for. He was a muscular Nordic god with an impeccable sense of casual dress style. Draped on the back of his chair was a jacket almost identical to the one I had thought I'd lost but now was wearing. He looked up and smiled. He pointed to my jacket and then to his in recognition of the amusing coincidence that such a distinctive jacket could appear twice at any given time in a Paris street café.

I smiled back, gestured at the empty seat beside him, and gave him a quizzical look. He smiled and motioned for me to sit. The waiter appeared immediately, as if by magic, and soon we both had a fresh cup of coffee before us.

I gestured to the book and said, "Thomas Mann?"

"*Ja*," he answered. "*Sprechen Sie Deutsch?*"

"Sorry, I'm American. I speak only English," I answered, not bothering to add that I spoke Arabic, Greek, and Farsi also, but knowing that had no application here. But, as he smiled and put a hand on my thigh, I figured that differing languages need not be a barrier between us.

We drank coffee and spent time trying to bridge the language gap with small talk, but it was clear that he didn't want to leave and that I didn't want to leave—both of us not wanting to leave because he wanted to fuck me and I wanted him to fuck me. He gave me a sexy look and said, "*Ich bin Dieter. Du bist sehr sexy*," he added, going right to the familiar form, and I didn't have the least problem understanding what "sexy" meant.

"I'm Ryan, and you are very sexy too, Dieter," I answered, putting my hand on the one he had on my thigh, moving them both slightly up my thigh. He closed the distance between there and my crotch on his own.

"*Ich will dich ficken*," he said, his voice almost pleading. "*Sex mit mir? Ich will dich ficken.*"

Yes, you damn well can "ficken" me, I thought. And then, what the hell, I said it too.

I took him back to my apartment and he "fickened" me all afternoon . . . and he was damn good at it.

* * * *

Jacket Found

I was walking down the street from my apartment in Paris to the café where I'd been twice lucky in getting laid. I was having a horny day, having taken the morning off from the international export firm where I'd recently been reassigned to Paris from the Mediterranean to attend a meeting of the models in a coming runway production. I'd come to Paris because I also was trying to make it as a male model and this was a center for that industry. I had a show coming up of swimwear, and we'd been shown and had tried on what we'd wear. What we'd wear was close to nothing, and all of us were horny from looking at each other before we left. Unfortunately, most of the male models were submissives, like I was, so I had to go shopping for relief, if I was going to get any.

I was hoping to pick up another young hunk at the café for a dalliance this afternoon.

Instead, as I passed a barber shop, a strong hand reached out, clamped on my wrist, and pulled me inside the shop. Before I had any idea what was happening, I was in the embrace of a big bear of a man, who planted a kiss on my lips—and not just a friendly peck. He gave me tongue.

I pulled away from him, feeling bewildered and looking bewildered too, I was sure. "Rene. What was that for?" I asked.

It wasn't like I didn't know the man. I'd come to him to cut my hair twice since I'd been in Paris. He did a great job and I was quite careful about my appearance and what I wore. He also gave great shoulder and neck massages in the barber's chair that made me purr.

I'll have to say he gave a great kiss too, and he was a handsome brute of a man—tall; hirsute, with dark hair, graying at the temple; and thick bodied without being fat really. I'd gone hard in the chair when he gave me the shoulder and neck massages—and the temples too.

"You kissed me earlier this week . . . when I gave you back the jacket you had left in the shop," he said. "You didn't do that just because I found your jacket and returned it, did you?" His accent when speaking English was pretty heavy, but he must have a lot of English-speaking clients, because his English was quite good—certainly better than any French I could manage, having found on short notice that I was coming to France.

In fact, that's exactly why I thought I did it—why I had kissed him. Because I was so happy to see my expensive jacket again that I was afraid was lost forever. The kiss was impromptu, not that I hadn't been thinking about doing it. He had very sensitive hands and an intoxicating male scent, and he was very close to me when he was cutting my hair. I was highly sexed. I looked at every man I encountered with a "would I?" or "wouldn't I?" comparison going on in my mind. Rene, although older than me by at least fifteen years and a big bear of a man, was one I'd already categorized as "I would."

"It was an expensive jacket. I'd looked everywhere for it. I was just delighted that it had been found."

"And you're grateful that I saved it for you and gave it back to you?" Rene said, turning and looking at me expectantly. He'd been busy flipping the shop sign to "closed" and lowering the blinds.

"Yes, of course I was grateful—am grateful—to you, Rene."

"And you only kissed me because I found your jacket and returned it to you?"

"Yes . . . well . . ." I had to pause. Was that the only reason I'd kissed him? Hadn't I thought about kissing him before? Hadn't I thought about doing more than that with him? I'd been so randy since I'd arrived in Paris. I'd just earlier this week taken French and German studs home and let them fuck me on back-to-back days. That's where I was going today—back to the café where I'd picked them up, with the hope of picking up another hung stud. I'd been looking at all of the men as possible sex partners. I hadn't been put off when I'd thought of Rene as a sex partner. When he'd been cutting my hair, I'd taken glances at his basket, wondering if he was as big there as his feet looked and as I knew his hands to be.

Rene took the pause to mean more than I had meant it to mean at that point. "You kissed me because you like me, I think. You go hard in my chair when I'm touching you. I've seen you checking my crotch out. You're—what is the word?—your penis— same as French, I think, your *pénis*—likes my massages. It gets big for me. You like me, yes, I think. I like you too."

"Well, yes, I like you fine, Rene," I admitted. I saw no reason to deny that. And then my mind started to whirl. Wasn't I on the street today to find a stud to cover me? Did I really have to go all the way to the café to get that going? I took another hard look at Rene. He was older, but he was a big brute—who knew just how big? And he might be big where it counted most. And he seemed to be panting for me.

"Then maybe you would like to go with me, lay under me." Rene said. "You tell me you have a modeling job."

"Not my main job, Rene. Just something I'm doing on the side. But I don't see—"

"All French models are whores. Everyone knows that. Women models lay down for men and men models lay down for men. I mean no disrespect. Whores are fine in Paris," Rene said, and the way he said it made it sound like it must be true. I'll have to admit that I'd often thought the same myself. "The men on the street say you are a whore—that you go to the café to find men to take back to your apartment. The men in the street who like men all say they want to fuck you. Jacques, the student, says he's fucked you and that you fuck good, like a whore. He told his German friend about you, and the German said you were a good fuck too. He said you were a good whore. The Italian bicycle boy says he is in heat for you too. He described the sexy young foreigner in the fancy wool and leather jacket, and I knew in an instant he was talking about you."

"The Italian bicycle boy?" I murmured, my eyes glazing over. Hmm, the Italian bicycle boy—who could that . . . ? Well, yes, I'd let him fuck me. Well, shit, I thought. I'd heard that Paris was just a small town covering a lot of territory. So everyone in Paris does know everyone else's business?

"I'm not a whore, Rene. I just do the modeling on the side. I'm a respectable businessman." That sounded a bit hollow even to me. Could I be a whore? I'd been fucked by two different strangers already this week and here I was, out looking for more of it. But I wasn't being paid for it. Maybe that made me just a slut.

"A respectable businessman who likes men and whose *pénis* gets big when I give him a shoulder massage," Rene said, and then gushed on before I could decide what to say to that. "That is fine in France. Respectable businessmen are expected to have a piece on the side. Some have women. Some have men. It makes no difference—well, little difference. It is still best to be the one who gives cock. But there have to be women and men who take it too. I like men too. I give cock. I like you. I've heard that you take cock. When you are in my chair, I think it's clear that you like me too—that you would take my cock. I have a very nice cock. When I returned your jacket and you kissed me, I had no question that you liked me a lot. I think very much that you would like to be under me—that you would like to have some of this cock." He took my hand and plastered it to his basket. He was hard and huge . . . and, yes, I'd like something like that very much. It was what I'd come looking for this afternoon. I was looking for it from a younger man, but . . .

"You like men this big inside you? Yes?" he asked.

"Yes," I answered, involuntarily, but it was the truth. And although he'd taken his hand away from holding mine to his crotch, I didn't take my hand away.

He cupped the back of my neck and pulled me in for a kiss. I didn't try to draw away from that either. And the kiss was quite sensual. When he pulled back, our eyes locked and I couldn't hide that I was melting to him.

"I have a lot of experience with men. I will cover you good. You told me when you were last in my chair that you had a model job coming up. In less than a week I think. Swimsuits, you said. You said you'd have to shave your body for it."

Had I said that? Had I been so open to Rene about my life while he was cutting my hair? I must have been for him to know this. And, yes, I was a bit worried about having to shave myself all over. I'd done it before, but it was a chore and had its dangers when I couldn't afford to have any nicks.

"Yes, but—" I responded, but not with a lot of conviction.

"I have a deal for you," he said. Even as he spoke, though, he was unbuckling my trousers and pulling my zipper down. He was that sure of himself. And that was the key to me—a man who would take command. "I will shave you—all over—and give you a good massage. I have a table in the room behind the shop. I'll do a good job. In exchange, you will let me fuck you. I will do a good job of that too." He already was encasing my cock in his hand and stroking it.

He fucked me in the barber's chair, the chair reclined back, me slouched down in the chair with my legs spread and hooked on the arms of the chair. He was standing on the foot rest, crouched over me, his hands gripping the arm rest under my knees, and fucking me with a very nice, thick, long cock.

It's what I'd come out to find this afternoon, if not where I had thought I'd find it. And I was going to get a nice body massage and a free all-over shave, as well, a task that had been facing me and I was antsy about doing myself.

What a deal. What a cock. What a fuck! He was a power fucker, hard, deep thrusts. Just what I was after.

* * * *

Rene hadn't lied to me. He did have a back room with a massage table in it. I nearly melted when I saw that the table had wrist and ankle restraints on it and I turned to him as he was taking out the lotions and razors he was going to use and gave him a pleading look.

"You want to have these used? You want the full body massage before the body shave? And you want me to tie you down and have my way with you in the process?"

He'd already fucked me in his barber's chair—sucked my cock as I sucked his, eaten me out, held me close, taken me hard and deep, licked his cum off my ass. There wasn't much in the way sexual intimacy we hadn't experienced already. And he was looking like he might shoot off in excitement at the prospect of controlling me to that degree.

"Yes, please."

"You *are* a whore," he muttered, with a laugh. "On your back on the table." It was an authoritative command now. He'd gotten the message that I liked to be dominated. "I see you are hard for me again—as I am hard for you. Get up on the table. Now."

Giving me a sensual, deep-tissue massage after he had restrained my ankles and wrists at the four corners of the table, being careful to give me enough in the leads to writhe under his attentions, which I did in no uncertain terms, he concluded the "on my back" portion of the massage by stroking me off, and, eventually, blowing me to an explosion while he penetrated me with his fingers and worked my prostate. The "on my stomach" portion ended with him straddling my hips and riding my ass to his own second ejaculation.

We rested and I, still on my back and bound to the table, moaned as he explained what would happen in the body shave.

"Not my head, please," I whimpered.

"No, not your fine head of hair. Everything else, though. Off with the hair."

The foam used was edible, and he'd be cleaning the cream off with his tongue as he went along. As I lost body hair, he'd be sucked, I'd be sucked, and I'd be fucked again. At the end, he promised, I'd have a hairless body other than on the head, and I'd be sexually exhausted.

That all sounded quite nice to me.

Whereas before, during the full body massage, I had strained against the bonds and, at his direction, tried, ineffectually, to struggle against him, I knew that now, when he shaved me, I wanted to be as docile and relaxed as possible. That wasn't easy when, from the start, he hovered over me from the top of the table, with my head arched over the end, my mouth open to take the whole of his cock deep into my throat while he creamed my chest, shaved it, licked the cream off, and slowly face fucked me. It was only I who was being shaved clean. Rene was hirsute. His curly pubes tickled my nose as I took him deep in my throat.

He took extra time cleaning up the cream in my armpits after he'd shaved them and had me groaning as he hovered over me in reverse, shaved my pubes and my thighs while I sucked his

77

cock, and then sucked mine in a sixty-nine after tonguing off the cream from my crotch and thighs.

"You may have noticed I hadn't finished around your nipples nor had I done your face," he whispered, as he climbed off of me. "I saved those for last."

"Stubble on the face should be fine for the catwalk," I answered. But I admit I hadn't noticed that he hadn't finished my chest.

"I like to do a complete job."

"I've noticed," I responded. He'd done a complete job on me twice already.

"And you are mine to do with as I wish," he growled. "I have you tied up. I could do anything to you I wanted to." To make his point, he cupped my scrotum and rolled the testis in them around while I writhed within the bindings and emitted yips and precum. Then, humming, he very delicately shaved my balls while I held very, very still.

I moaned for him on that assertion of control.

He came back up onto the table below me, on his knees; lifted, bent, and spread my legs; and scooted into me, running his knees under my buttocks, lifting my pelvis. He slapped his cock on my belly and thighs for a few seconds, making it go rock hard.

"Are you—?" I started to ask.

"Yes, I am," he answered. And then he did. His cock invaded my channel for the third time and he slow stroked me while I lay as quiet as I could and he wielded the razor on my face and the rest of my chest. He licked the remaining cream off, threw the razor to the side, grabbed my hips with his hands, and fucked me vigorously and with a fury that had me bouncing around under him, straining at the restraints again, and crying out in passion and ecstasy, while he fucked me to a mutual explosion.

Afterward, as he, off the table, glided his hands over my body while we both cooled down, he said, "Such a beautiful body. As long as you maintain your beauty, you will be desirable to men. You can make good money with this body."

"Become a prostitute? A whore?" I asked.

"As I told you, to be a prostitute in France is not a disgrace. To have a body like this and not let others worship it—that would

78

be a tragedy in France. And as far as being a whore"—here he gave me an exaggerated shrug—"you can buy many nice things—like that fancy jacket you thought you'd lost—if you are going to be giving it away anyway, and the deal you made with me was a full body shave for fucking. You have already whored yourself. Do you feel any worse for having done so?"

I couldn't disagree with him. The deal had been very satisfying. Just the other day I'd considered paying for sex that had been far less exotic and satisfying—well, no, the sex the other day had been very satisfying—than this.

"Ah, so I think it's not too bad you feel about being a whore," Rene said and laughed. "I will make another deal. I will cut your hair and give you massages and body shaves whenever you wish it in exchange for letting me use your body when I am in heat for you. You will be a whore if you agree to that. Deal?"

"Deal," I said. And, no, I didn't feel any different in thinking of myself as a whore.

I almost forgot my fancy jacket again at the door, and Rene had to tell me to remain there and went back for it. I rewarded him with a kiss for finding and returning it to me just as I had the first time. This time he copped a feel, though. Our relationship certainly had progressed—and for the better, I thought.

In the downstairs vestibule of my apartment building, I had to stop momentarily as another resident moved his bicycle out of the way. It was the young Italian hunk who lived in the apartment at the back on the ground floor. He was wearing tight bicycle shorts and a pullover shirt, pads on his elbows and knees, leather riding gloves that left the fingers exposed, and a bicycle helmet.

The Italian bicycle boy. It was, I was sure, the one Rene said was in heat for me.

He was a hunk and the look he gave me there in the vestibule more than hinted that he was, indeed, in heat for me. I smiled, reached a hand forward, and traced the line of his dick in the tight Spandex shorts. He smiled back, making no move to disengage my hand—rather, he thrust his pelvis forward, into my hand—and going noticeably—and quite satisfactorily—hard.

I didn't have to know how to speak Italian and he didn't have to know how to speak English.

I turned and moved up the steps to my apartment, two flights up. The Italian boy followed me, close behind me. On the landing, he cupped one of my butt cheeks with a hand. I wiggled my butt for him as I climbed the remaining steps. His hand slipped deeper between my thighs, and he was palming my basket from the rear.

Inside my apartment door, he reached out, gently took my fancy jacket off me, pulled me to him, and roughly took my mouth into a kiss while pulling down the zipper of my trousers.

There would be no money exchanged. I didn't have to be a whore all of the time. Some of the time I could be just a young man with a toned body and fine face who needed and wanted another young, handsome man's cock inside him.

One thing I thought of, though, when I was on my back on my bed and Sergio was on top of me, his fists trapping my wrists over my head, showing every glorious sign of wanting to take me hard and rough and his thick cock already pushing up inside me, thick and demanding. I must remember to wear my fancy, attention-getting jacket on the street more. And maybe, just maybe, if I was careful and clever enough, I could manage, on occasion, to lose the jacket where I knew it would be found and returned to me by a hung stud. I was already scheming to hang it on Sergio's bicycle, which he kept in the apartment house vestibule as a signal that I wanted him again. And, god, as he pounded me hard, I was sure I would want him again . . . and again and again.

~

Snow Crash

I picked the extra wine glass up from the coffee table, took it into the kitchen, and put it back in the cupboard. I wasn't surprised. In fact I'd really known for a couple of hours that Emmet wasn't going to make it up to Wintergreen for the weekend. It had been snowing all day in the mountains, and my vacation house was nearly the last one on Pine Trail, winding around the mountain a third of the way down from the ski lifts at the top of the Blue Ridge Mountains resort.

The house further in from mine, the Albrechts' A-frame, had a few lights on, but I'd seen them down in Waynesboro Thursday evening, at the Kroger grocery store, and they said they'd be up in D.C. for the weekend. They must have loaned the house out. I hoped their guests wouldn't be disappointed about being snowed in. Of course, if they'd come to ski, they could wade their way up to the lifts and ski back down a short way to the house. I wonder if they knew that. I might go over and make sure they did—if I could get the gumption to go out in this snow myself. It was beginning to drift.

The house on the other side of me, the more substantial log house the Logans owned had had lights on earlier too—I got more of a glow from that direction over the treetops than being able to see the actual house. It was a good bit lower than my house in elevation and on a nasty twisting and rising curve that would be hard to navigate in this weather.

I went back to the living room and settled in to watch the DVD I'd put on, a gay male sex one that was making an attempt, not too successfully, of padding out the sex scenes with a background story. I'd picked it because I thought the actors were hot—not necessarily as actors, but certainly as sex partners—and there was a black guy who looked a lot like Emmet and a bit older blond who I could see as me. I had been warming myself up for Emmet's appearance, but now he wasn't coming. He'd called me and said he didn't think he could chance it unless he hopped on a snowplow. I'd told him not to bother, hoping that he would bother, but he'd said he wouldn't.

So, there went the weekend. I didn't even know whether the electricity would hold up here on the mountain in snow like this. At least I had a lot of firewood in and had had this house built with fireplaces and double insulation that could provide for heat, as necessary.

I was deciding whether to go take a shower and dress more warmly after the DVD was finished when I heard the door chimes sound. In anticipation of Emmet, I wasn't wearing anything under the Henley shirt and faded low-rise blue jeans I had on. I'd really planned on a sexually satisfying weekend.

And maybe, I thought, as I clicked off the DVD and went out to the foyer to answer the door, Emmet had hopped a snowplow after all and the weekend would be saved.

But that wasn't the case. When I turned on the front porch light, I saw that a stranger, bundled up in a parka and a floppy-eared hat, was standing out there, shivering in the cold, and blowing on his hands to warm them.

I opened the door.

"Excuse me," he said. "I'm looking for someplace I can make a call. My cell phone is dead and I've just gone off the road on a curve. Banged my car up pretty bad. I need to call AAA."

"On the curve?" I asked. "That would be in front of the Logans' house. They should be home."

"I didn't see any lights in any house but yours. Sorry. I can go back and—"

"No, no," I said. "Sorry, I wasn't thinking straight. You certainly can come in and make a call—assuming I still have phone service. The electricity is still on, so maybe the phone . . ." Just then the lights flickered, though, so I reached out and tugged on the arm of his parka to let him know he could come in. "You'd best hurry in and try to make the call," I said, "And you may be out of luck on AAA for a while in these conditions. There's a landline phone over there on the kitchen wall, but you can use my cell phone, if you

82

want. I have AAA dialed in. The cell phone is on the kitchen island over there."

"Thanks," he said, as he entered. He shook my hand as he slipped off the parka and was going by me. I was surprised to find that his hand was warm. I was also surprised to see that he was wearing a muscle T-shirt over tight jeans under the parka and was built solid and had a dark, sultry look about him. He looked like one of the porn stars I'd just been watching in the DVD. "My name's Brad," he said as he moved beyond me.

"I'm Justin," I said. "Can I get you something to drink while you're making your call?"

"If you have it, a beer would be nice, thanks," he said, as he picked up the cell phone and moved back into the corridor to the bedrooms to make his call. Before I went into the kitchen, I watched him slouch against the corridor wall, the small of his back against the wall and his legs stretched out before him into the corridor and spread a bit. I thought of it as a Marlon Brando stance. He reminded me a lot of Brando in his *Streetcar* days rather than his bloated afterlife. The man had that sensuous, pouty aura about him that Brando exuded in the sexy phase of his life.

I felt tingly inside. It obviously was from having been watching sex DVDs while waiting for Emmet and anticipating what Emmet and I would be doing tonight. But not doing now, I remembered, as I went into the kitchen and broke out a beer. I took the wine bottle back into the living room along with the beer and replenished my wine glass while putting his beer—Brad, he had said—on the coffee table. The big leather couch faced the TV. There were leather recliners set across from the couch and beside the TV credenza and, on second thought, I moved my wine glass to a side table beside one of these.

As I passed the opening to the bedroom corridor, I could hear him on the phone. He wasn't sounding too hopeful. I wasn't surprised by that, and my mind was already working on what could be done other than offering him a place to stay. But I couldn't think of any reason I shouldn't ask him to stay other than that he was a complete stranger and, despite that, I could feel I'd gone hard in comparing him to Marlon Brando. But was I set up for a house guest? Emmet, of course, would have slept in my bed with me. The bed wasn't made in the guest room. I'd have to do that, and I couldn't remember if there were towels in the guest bath. But I was getting ahead of myself. Maybe AAA was on its way and he wanted to be on his way as well. I found myself looking at myself in the hall mirror and wondering if I was good enough for him. That made me laugh and chastise myself. Talk about getting ahead of yourself.

"It's no go on AAA for a while—not until tomorrow they said," Brad said when he came back and put the cell phone on the kitchen island. "Guess I'll have to try to hoof it out to the main road. Is it better for me to go up or down? I didn't see much that might be open at the foot of the mountain. Is there a lodge up at the top?"

"Yes, there's a lodge up there, but it would be tough going on foot in this snow. And you have an open beer here. Come on in and take a load off."

I don't know if I was planning even then for him to stay and fuck me, but all the signs pointed to that. I was keyed up for an Emmet visitation—had even gotten a start on viewing the DVD— and this guy was a hunk in a tough guy Marlon Brando sort of way. His T-shirt was showing off a great set of pectorals with hard nipples standing out under the tight material, he had a mighty fine six pack, and his jeans were tight enough that I could see an impressive bulge and follow the line of a long cock. I was close to hyperventilating from the buildup of need.

I wondered if he was straight. I had to say he didn't act one way or the other yet. Most of my friends were gay, though, so I didn't often have to wonder about someone I met who I was interested in sexually.

But was I interested in Brad sexually? I'm afraid that ship had sailed. I had been so keyed up for Emmet and had just watched a gay fuck video. Why wouldn't I be interested in a hunk like Brad sexually?

We chatted for a while. I told him of the restaurants I owned in Waynesboro and Charlottesville and that I was up here for the weekend to take in the skiing with a friend of mine, a professor at the University of Virginia, but that the friend couldn't make it up here tonight.

"Your friend a man or a woman?" he asked.

"A man," I said without thinking of what inference he could get from that. But it was meaningful that he asked and was prepared to hear the friend was male. I tried finding out something about him, in turn, that would help me categorize him, but other than saying he worked in construction, he didn't reveal much. He even deflected the conversation the couple of times I asked how his car came to be in a snow bank this far into a dead-end mountain road. I probably should have pursued that more closely, but I found him disconcerting, sitting—more slouching—on the leather couch, with his legs spread and being all sultry and pouty, across from where I was sitting in the recliner.

The conversation had come to an awkward halt a couple of times, with him saying he should get out in the snow, but accepting a second beer, and then him saying he should start trudging up to the lodge but not moving, so I got the message that he wasn't that anxious to get out in the snow.

God help me, but I wasn't anxious for him to leave either. And it wasn't hard to figure he was playing me—taking me to the brink of begging him to stay. He must have known by now that I wanted him to fuck me. I wasn't too subtle when I was heat, and I moved deeper in heat the longer he sat here in my living room. I didn't care if he was playing me. It was part of what aroused me. At this point, if I had to beg him to stay, I would. My ass was twitching. I wanted it; I wanted him.

"It's still snowing," I said, looking out the wall to ceiling window that looked up the hill at the Albrechts' house, where the lights were all off now. "You won't get anywhere on foot tonight, and you'll need to be here for whenever AAA can get to your car. You'll have to spend the night here. I've got a guest room. Just let me go in and get sheets on the bed and make sure there are towels in the bath. I'll get you another beer while I'm up."

He didn't object to spending the night. He didn't object to having another beer either.

As I was leaving to go back to prepare a bedroom for him, he said, almost casually, "You know, now that you mention it, I know about you and your restaurants. John Knowles told me about you. Do you know John Knowles?" That stopped me in my tracks.

"No, I can't say that I do," I answered. But a chill had gone up my spine. I knew John Knowles quite well. He moved in my social circle in Charlottesville. He was a bottom, as I was. What did Brad know about me, I wondered. Was he playing me. I stopped at the kitchen counter and picked up my cell phone and checked the last call made on it. It was one of my calls, not a call to AAA. My mind was spinning as I went back to the bedrooms. What the fuck was going on here?

When I came back out, he'd rid himself of the T-shirt, had his legs spread and his feet on the coffee table. His fly was unzipped and a fat ole cock was standing straight up from the flared jeans. He'd turned the DVD on and was watching a sex scene and stroking his cock.

"You know, you don't have to set up a guest room just for me," he said. "I could sleep in your bed with you."

"Uh, I didn't mean for that to be on," I said, my voice slightly shaking and not having something to come back with on his direct proposition. "Maybe you should turn it off, and . . ."

"And stop beating off?" he asked, turning a sneery look at me.

"Yeah, I guess so. I didn't—"

"You didn't actually say you wanted me to stay and fuck you, but you do, don't you?" he said. "You don't want me to put my cock away, do you? You don't want me to use the guest room." He made to do so—to fold his cock back into his fly—and I groaned and involuntarily reached a hand out. He laughed. He slouched down more on the couch, pushed his pelvis up, and fingered his cock.

"Pretty nice, isn't it?" he said. He didn't seem really to want me to say anything—just notice his cock—so I remained silent. But I couldn't take my eyes off it. He gave a little laugh at that. He ran a finger up one side of it from root to tip and then down the other side. It bobbed against his finger, hard as a rock.

I couldn't think of anything to say to that either. Is that what I really wanted? And, if so, had it been so obvious?

"One of these guys, the blond there, looks just like you," he said, pointing at the TV screen. "Is that why you're watching this vid? You're fantasizing being fucked like the blond in this vid is being fucked, aren't you?"

"This is getting a little out of hand," I said, putting a bit of bite into my voice. It was one thing for me to fantasize this guy fucking me; it was quite another for him to be so forward. "Maybe we should back up a bit."

"We could do that, but we'd be wasting pleasure time," he answered, with a knowing smile. "John Knowles claims he does know you. He told me you took cock. He told me you took it real good. You do, don't you?"

"Yes," I said meekly, defeated. I wanted someone to fuck me so bad—and now, not some later date.

"And one of the other guys in this vid looks like this guy who was supposed to come up here tonight, doesn't he?"

"Yes," I said in a small voice.

"Which one?"

"The black one."

"Nice. He does you real well in the vid. Does your guy— did you say his name was Emmet?—do you that well—as well as the hung black bull in the vid performs?"

"Yes."

"I can do you that well. Come over here. Come over to the couch."

"I don't know. I don't think—"

"Come here. Kneel to me. Suck me off. Do it."

I was a submissive. John Knowles had probably told him that too—that I folded immediately to domination. I responded to commands. He lifted a leg off the coffee table to allow me to slip in between his legs and kneel in front of the couch. He put the leg back down, bracketing my body, and I took his cock in my mouth. He broke contact long enough to pull the Henley over my head and I resumed sucking him even harder than he'd been before. The DVD continued to run, with the only sounds from the couch being the slurping sounds I was making, my occasional gag as he forced me to take him deep, and his mutterings of what he was going to do to me after I'd sucked him hard as hard could be.

At length he brought his legs down off the coffee table and raised me up, turned me and laid me down on my belly on the coffee table. "Up on your knees," he commanded. "Give me your ass," and I meekly did what he demanded of me. He laughed when he unbuttoned and unzipped my jeans and pulled them down to my ankles, finding I was wearing no briefs.

He kissed and bit me on both butt cheeks.

"You were ready for your boyfriend, weren't you?" he growled.

"Yes," I answered.

"He was going to come up here and fuck you good, wasn't he?"

"Yes."

"So, I'll be your boyfriend for the night."

"Yes," I answered. Then I was panting and moaning and rocking my pelvis back into his face as he pulled my cock through my legs and gave that, my balls, and my ass attention with his tongue. I opened quickly to him. I had been anticipating this all day. Just not from a stranger. That didn't keep me from opening for Brad, though. He fiddled around in the pockets of his jeans, now bunched on the floor in front of the couch under mine, came up with a condom disk, and crowned himself. Then he came up onto the coffee table—and I worried that it would hold us both, but it did—mounted me, crouched over my body, and forced himself inside, as I groaned and grunted and felt my channel walls give—actually pull him inside me. My channel muscles rippled over the hard cock. There was no question that I welcomed this—that I wanted it, that I needed it.

"You do it. If you want it, you do it. Show me you want it," he said, and he stopped pumping and held there, while I took over, rhythmically rocking back on the cock, fucking myself on it—embarrassed and cowed, but, yes, wanting it; wanting it badly enough to fuck myself on the cock. I stretched my arms straight out from my body in both directions, gripping opposite edges of the coffee table to hold myself steady while I rocked back on the cock. After a few minutes, he laughed, and took over the thrusting again.

He fucked me for several minutes, with the DVD still running. It was a two-hour show. It had nearly an hour left to run and, I couldn't help it, I hoped the fuck would continue for that whole time.

Before either of us were done, though, he pulled out of and off me and said. "Over in the chair. I want you to do it. You have to show that you want it."

He was off the coffee table and went over to the recliner I had been in, slouched into it, made it recline, and grabbed his cock and held it upright. "Come here. Sit on it. Ride it," he commanded.

I mounted him on the chair, facing him; descended on the cock; and rose and fell on it with him holding my waist and helping me to slam up and down on the cock. Just as we both came, the lights flickered and then went out. I collapsed on top of him and we lay there in the chair for a few minutes, him embracing him, both of us feeling him go flaccid inside me—but not all the way. He remained half hard. Only then, with the lights out, did I realize that the DVD had run its course. We'd been fucking for an hour or more.

I felt the beating of his heart as he cooled down. I wasn't cooling down as quickly. I was still excited. This unexpected fuck by a stranger kept me keyed up.

"Where is your bedroom?" I heard him ask.

"Down the hall and to the left," I answered.

"Is that where this boyfriend of yours—Emmet, was it?—was going to fuck you tonight? In your bedroom?"

"Yes."

He hauled us both out of the chair, slung me over his shoulder, and lunging this way and that way and barely keeping from banging into the furniture on either side, headed back to the bedroom corridor. At the opening into the corridor, he banged my head against the wall. But I didn't care. All I could think of was that I was going to be fucked again—on my bed—in the dark, by a young Marlon Brando.

"Where do you keep them," he asked after he'd tossed me on the bed. "No reason to use any more of mine if you have them." I rolled over and opened the top drawer of my nightstand and retrieved a condom packet.

While I was doing that, he went to the fireplace and lit it. I'd already laid the firewood in anticipation that the electricity—and thus the heat—would go off at some point in the storm. After he'd lit the fire, he came over to the bed and went down on his knees on the mattress beside me. "You do it. Crown me," he demanded. I rolled the condom on his erect cock.

Once again, saying it had to be because I wanted it, he made me do the work. He was controlling me with the tease and more than a hint of humiliation, making me beg for it and demonstrate my submissiveness to him. But he was reading me correctly. He had me under his control. I would do anything he told me to do as long as he gave me the cock.

He lay on his back on the bed and put me on top of him, in a reverse crab position, facing him, with my arms slung back, my fists buried in the mattress, and my legs bent, my feet planted on either side of his waist, with him fisting my ankles, and I was skewered on his cock. I rose and fell on the cock and he thrust up into me. I was trembling and nearly exhausted when we'd come.

He fucked me to exhaustion in various positions and we both dozed off, stretched against each other in the flickering light and heat coming from the fireplace at the foot of the bed. When I woke, he was gone. I turned and looked at the clock, aware that what had awakened me was the electricity coming back on. It was barely midnight. Still, the stranger had fucked me for over two hours. I wondered where he was.

I realized it wasn't just the restoration of the electricity that had awakened me. Someone was outside, ringing the doorbell and beating on the door. Had he—Brad, I think he said—somehow locked himself out of the house? I rolled out of bed, reached for the sleeping shorts I'd put in a chair near the bed earlier in the day in anticipation of sleeping in them, and padded out to the foyer.

Brad's parka and floppy hat were gone. It wasn't him at the door. It was Emmet.

"Emmet. You made it," I said, hoping that Brad indeed was gone and suddenly concerned about what had been left behind. Beer bottles in the living room. Emmet drank beer and that's why I had it on hand. I didn't drink beer. I drank wine, and Emmet knew I didn't drink beer. My clothes on the floor in front of the couch. The TV humming, with the DVD in the slot. And condoms. Where had the condoms gone?

"Yes. I did catch a snowplow. But I can only stay the night, I'm afraid. There's a crisis in my department and the chairman has called a meeting for tomorrow afternoon."

"Did you have to walk from the accident in front of the Logans' house? Did the snowplow have to leave you there?"

"What accident?"

"I think there was a car accident. A car went off the road on that curve we're always careful about."

"No car there, and no sign of one."

"OK, well, come on in and get that coat off." I was looking into the living room as he took his coat off, panicked at what I could see in there of the evidence of the debauchery earlier in the evening.

Mercifully, the power went out again right at that moment.

"Shit," I said, although only halfheartedly. Maybe this would be OK, I thought. Maybe after he went to sleep.

Right on cue Emmet said. "I'm bushed, and we don't have much time. Maybe—"

"Come on back to the bedroom," I said. "It's warmer there. I've had a fire going and I can lay another one."

I remade the fire as Emmet stripped and retrieved lube and a condom from the nightstand drawer. Even in the dark he easily found it. He'd done this before. When I came back to the bed, I stepped on something squishy. The condom from Brad's fuck, I realized, and I kicked it under the bed before I climbed in and laid down on my back.

"Umm, you smell nice," he whispered. "New cologne?"

"Yes," I said. I didn't have any cologne on. Brad had, though.

Emmet fucked me in the missionary position—satisfying but not the variety Brad had employed—his knees pressed under my buttocks, lifting my pelvis to him. He leaned over me, holding my arms up and out on the top of the bed, fisting my wrists in his big, brown hands. He was thick and long inside me. If he sensed that I already was open, he made no remark of it. He started slow, but we quickly found a more vigorous rhythm of moving together and he pounded me long and hard before tensing, jerking, and coming in the sheath inside me. He rolled off to the side and was snoring in short order.

Quietly, I rolled out of the bed on the opposite side of him and padded out to the living room. I was tidying that up when I realized that the lights were on in the Albrecht house at the end of the road. I went over to the window and looked at the house.

He was standing naked, in the full wall of glass of the A-frame cottage, backed by lights inside. He was smoking a cigarette and staring at my house. Brad's body was as beautiful backlit like this as it had been when he had been standing in my living room, under me in the chair, and fucking me in my bed.

I was sure he couldn't see him, but I realized there was a light on in my kitchen, so maybe he could. He certainly had been able to see me from there earlier in the evening, slouched in the sofa and jerking off to the sex tape.

He confirmed he could by waving at me and blowing me an air kiss. Instead of pulling away, out of his sight, I turned on the lights in my living room. Now we each could clearly see the other. He took his cock in his hand. I was as naked as he was. And now I was as erect as he was too. We stood there, facing each other from across the snowy divide, and masturbated. I watched him jerking off and he watched me jerking off.

As if there was a mental connection, we both were working to come simultaneously. We came close to managing it, with him, as could be expected, demanding that I come first. My spunk arced and splashed against the glass window. His did so soon thereafter. He saluted me and the power in both houses, as if on cue, went out again.

I had had a stab of disappointment when Emmet said he could only stay the night, not the weekend. But now, thinking of the possibilities with Brad if he was staying the weekend, I wasn't disappointed anymore.

~

92

Strangers Off the Street

"How is Brandon? I hope he is well."

That was the first thing Diego Medina said to Brett Williams upon meeting him in the arrivals area of the Barcelona-El Prat airport.

"Your guess is as good as mine," Brett answered. "I haven't seen him for six months or more. I've been in London. I haven't been in New York for more than a year. You two are business partners, so I probably would be asking you how my father was, if I were interested in knowing how he was."

Medina had found out what he wanted to know without directly asking if the young man standing before him—stylishly dressed, impeccably groomed, sexy, and a very attractive platinum blond of barely twenty years—was still estranged from his father, Brandon Williams, the American director of the electronics corporation for which Medina held down the Spanish holdings. Since Medina left the next day for a corporate meeting in New York himself, he wouldn't have to mention to the father now that Brett was in his Barcelona flat. It also gave Medina an idea of how far he could go with the young man without worrying about how his business partner would take it.

"It is good of you to occupy my flat for me for the two weeks I'll be gone," Medina said.

"It's my pleasure," Brett answered, taking a good look at the Spaniard, who was his father's age—almost fifty, if not a bit beyond, but who had taken better care of himself than Brett's father had. He was a good-looking man—heavy, but more to be described as solid. His body was in the right proportions if a little stocky. He dressed expensively, with casual elegance, with a silk shirt open enough down the front to show a gold medallion on a chain and brownish-gray curly chest hair. His head hair was wavy, and he had his sunglasses perched there and a cashmere sweater draped on his back, the arms tied at his chest, in a fashion that was out of style everywhere but, on him, looked very continental and classic. His hands were expressive and didn't stop long enough for Brett to count the number of gold rings he displayed.

If it might be thought that Brett was checking the Spaniard out as a possible sex partner, he was. Brett was highly sexed. He had very low standards, but he wouldn't have to lower them for Medina.

"I could use the vacation and I hate the dreariness of London in this season," Brett continued, as Medina's chauffeur took his bag from him and he and Medina followed the driver out to the hourly parking area. Medina placed a hand on the small of Brett's back and chatted as they walked.

Brett took the possessive gesture in the vein in which it was extended, and Medina clearly could feel Brett tense immediately but then relax under the pressure of the hand.

"I hope you aren't too tired. I want to show you my favorite restaurant tonight and then I wish to introduce you to some of my friends who can help show you Barcelona and keep you from being bored while I'm gone. You do play billiards, don't you?"

"I play pool," Brett answered.

"We'll be happy to help you transcend over to the more gentlemanly sport. I understand that you have moved significantly up into the gentlemen's world. The friends I will introduce you to are in that world in Barcelona."

Medina was saying more, but Brett was smitten with the Maserati sedan that awaited them in the parking lot. "The car will, of course, be at your disposal while I'm gone. I'll leave you Fausto's number and he will come for you on short notice any time you need him."

Brett and Fausto gave each other a quick body scan and Brett decided he might, in fact, be calling on the dark and handsome chauffer to come for him while he was here.

"You're so generous," Brett said. "We'll have to think of some way I can show my appreciation."

"I don't believe we need to think too hard upon that to settle on something, Brett." Again the easy Spanish smile.

The restaurant Diego took Brett to indeed was a fabulous one on the Barcelona waterfront, but Brett quickly decided it wouldn't be one he'd be going to at his own expense. His father's business partner certainly was being generous to him. He hadn't thought twice when given the opportunity to fly to Barcelona at Medina's expense and watch over the man's flat in a fashionable area of the city center, on Carrer dels Tallers, while the executive was gone. Medina flew out for New York the next morning. And that being the case, Brett was surprised that Medina said they'd be going to a bar and pool hall on Carrer de Villarroel named Manuel's Lounge after dinner. They didn't get out of the restaurant until after 10:00 p.m. Of course, this was early in Spain. The dinner hour was just getting going when they left.

"These are the friends I wanted you to meet," Medina said when they reached Manuel's Lounge. As they had approached it, Medina had pointed out that this street and one running parallel to it, Carrer de Casanova, were the center of Barcelona's gay district and might be an area he'd want to avoid when he was out by himself. "If that's a district you would want to avoid," he said, turning a searching eye on Brett; giving him an opportunity to turn this evening around, if he wished. Brett just smiled back and didn't say anything.

Manuel's Lounge certainly met the "gay district" criterion. It's was obviously an all-male watering hole, but it was one of diverse application. They walked through a bar area that was mainly catering to an age split of men—some were young and among these some were professionals and others were drifter types and then there were areas of the room dominated by older men, looking fairly well heeled and ogling the young men. They all ogled Brett as Medina guided him by them. At the back of the room, two other rooms were sectioned off. There was a pool hall, dominated by younger men and then the room where Medina led Brett—a room with billiard tables, in use primarily by the older, more wealthy clientele.

Medina introduced Brett around to the men who were playing at one of the tables. "Sebastian Acosta. He owns a winery in the countryside north of Barcelona." The youngest of the men Brett was introduced to, Acosta was also the most in shape and muscular, no doubt because he probably worked with the vines himself. He had something of a thuggish appearance, but in a sexy way the Spanish men were prone to be. He gave Brett an openly assessing look as Medina turned to the next, significantly older, and to Brett's experienced eye, more patrician British man. "Alastair Cowden, retired here from England. He was a senior partner of our firm. Now he explores the Mediterranean in his yacht, ported here in Barcelona." The man was tall and gaunt. He'd been handsome at one time, but the ravishes of time hadn't been polite to him.

"And this is Valentino Nardo, he's into movies." The short, somewhat pudgy and baldheaded man held out his hand to Brett. When they shook, the man folded his index finger into Brett's palm and rubbed. He smiled when it was evident that Brett knew what he was signaling. He was declaring himself a top and checking on whether Brett was a submissive. By not pulling his hand away, Brett was affirming that. Brett, in fact, knew the name Valentino Nardo and what kind of films the man produced. "He's Italian, comes here periodically to recruit talent," Medina added.

"Yes, I know of Mr. Nardo's work," Brett said. He returned Nardo's smile and the Italian took his time giving up Brett's hand.

"Would you like to join in on the billiards?" Cowden asked in a raspy voice. He handed Brett a billiard cue, and Brett accepted it.

"Perhaps I'll watch for a while to see how it's played," he said and positioned himself in the doorway into the main bar room. He watched the other men play—it didn't take them long to become engrossed in their play, and Brett understood that Medina hadn't been making it up when he said he and his friends met here regularly to play. They played fast, expertly, and nearly silently.

From his vantage point, Brett could both watch the play and at least pretend that he was trying to understand the game and also look out into the main bar and case out the men there. He was leaning into the frame of the door with one of his legs bent and his foot pressed against the door frame. In this pose, he was as much being ogled from the bar room—and surreptitiously from time to time by the old friends playing billiards as well—as he was ogling.

Seeing a young man, swarthy and sexy, sinewy and sultry, come into the bar off the street piqued Brett's attention. Sensing something worthwhile was looking at him, the young man scanned the room with his eyes and lit on Brett. The two eyed each other—the foxy, dark, dangerous-looking stud and the almost androgynously angelic platinum blond beauty—and both sparks and an understanding flowed between them from across the room.

The foxy man nodded at Brett and slowly moved toward the corridor to what lay behind the club rooms.

"I'm going out for a smoke for a few minutes," Brett told the men at the billiards table. A couple of them nodded tersely without looking up, but they clearly were focused on their game. Perhaps this had all moved too quickly and smoothly for Medina in the unfolding of his plan. He obviously thought he'd established Bret as the entertainment for he and his friends later in the evening. He didn't taken into account that Bret had his own ideas about the evening's entertainment.

Bret pulled himself away from the door frame and moved toward the corridor to what lay behind the club rooms.

The room, not much bigger than a closet—a one commode bathroom, it turned out—was dark when Brett entered behind the fox. The door was slammed shut behind him and the lock turned with him getting but a glance of what fixture was where. The light wasn't turned on, but he knew, as his knee hit the bowl of the toilet that he was being leaned over the commode. Strong hands grasped his wrists and raised and spread his arms. The palm of his hands were pressed against the cool tiles of the wall behind the toilet. He heard the man mutter something in Spanish, and decided he'd guessed right when he left his hands pressed against the wall when the man's hands were taken away.

Brett didn't cry out. He was excited by this. It was a shock, though, when the man grabbed his hair and hit his head against the tiled wall. It didn't do damage, but it dazed him. Arms came around his waist and his belt buckle was being undone, his trousers unzipped, and this trousers and briefs pulled down to his ankles.

Brett laughed and then muttered, "Yes, yes . . . *si*. Oh, fuck, *si*, *si*," and then moaned as the man went down on his knees behind him, separated his butt cheeks with his hands, and buried his face in Brett's crack. Then, when he was eating Brett's ass out, with Brett muttering, "*si, si,*" over and over again, he reached between Brett's thighs, grasped his cock, and milked it.

When Brett came, crying out, "Fuck, yes!" which was quickly, as he had been keyed up and wondering how he was going to get this evening exactly what he was getting, the young fox man stood up, grasped Brett's hips with his hands, positioned the bulb of his cock, and thrust up, hard, inside Brett's channel.

Brett jerked, gave a little cry, and moaned. The man grabbed his hair again, bounced his head against the tiles again, and then, pulling Brett's head back cruelly into his shoulder, pumped him in earnest to his own ejaculation. Early in the pumping, Brett relaxed and concentrated on the cock working inside him. He was getting what he wanted. When the stranger had come, he pushed Brett, belly down, onto the commode, bounced Brett's head against the toilet tank—lightly, not hard enough to raise a bruise—adjusted his own clothes, and left the water closet.

The phantom man muttered the words "*Inglés putá*"— English slut—as he walked away,

Brett turned on the light, assessed the damage, of which not much was apparent, leaned over the sink as he washed himself, and stared into the mirror. He gave a little smile. This is what he'd wanted. This was what turned him on the most—an anonymous stranger from off the street. He pulled his briefs and trousers up, adjusted his clothing, looked at himself from this angle and that in the mirror to ensure that he was still beautiful, and went back to the billiard's room. He leaned into the frame of the door again, where he could see and be seen from both directions. The foxy stud wasn't to be seen in the bar room, though. He'd already gotten what he came for.

The older men taken up with their billiards game didn't seem to have missed him. He almost wished they had, so that they wouldn't be so smugly assured about him.

* * * *

Diego Medina's flat, on the third floor of an architecturally interesting old building overlooking the narrow Carrer dels Tallers, made narrower by the open-air street cafés below, was as impressive as everything else Medina exhibited. The rooms were large and ornate, the ceilings were high, and the windows were mostly French doors leading out onto small balconies. The layout was formal, with separate living room, dining room, kitchen—with an unoccupied maid's room behind it—library, and two bedrooms, each with an en suite bath of generous proportions and expensive fittings.

The two men sat, drinking brandy, on a leather sofa facing a fireplace, with a fire set, and chatted briefly. Medina moved closer to Brett, who was sitting in the corner of the couch, and pulled the young man to him. Brett didn't resist, and when Medina came in for a kiss, Brett opened to him. He ran his hand down into Median's open shirt front, opening other buttons as his hand glided down the muscular, hairy chest. They were still locked in a kiss when he pulled Medina's shirt tail out and then unzipped him, and took possession of the man's hard cock.

Coming out of the kiss, Medina unbuttoned Brett's shirt, pulled it off the young man's back, tossed it to the side, and, turning Brett's back to the arm of the sofa and hovering over him, let his mouth explore the luscious blond's chest and nipples. Brett had lost hand contact with the older man's cock, and Medina, in turn, unzipped Brett's trousers, fished out his cock, and slow stroked it.

As he was stroking Brett, he lay his cheek on Brett's chest, and murmured what the "deal" was. "There are two thousand euros on the table over there, Brett." The young man had, in fact, seen Medina put the roll of bills on the table as he'd returned with brandy glasses. "Your service in London told me that the going rate for you was five hundred euros for a night. What I've put over there will cover Sebastian, Alastair, and Valentino. They all wanted in. I have left cell phone numbers for them there too. You will call them to arrange your meetings. If you decide not to meet one of them, don't take their five hundred euros. If other meetings are desired by you both while you are here, they will pay more, of course. The other five hundred is for me. You will lay under me, yes?"

"Yes, of course," Brett answered, he arms going around Medina's torso and palming his shoulder blades.

"Now, here."

"Yes."

"And for the rest of the night, in my bed?"

"Yes."

Medina went up on his knees long enough to pull Brett's trousers and briefs off his legs and then to do so for himself as well. Brett turned more onto his back against the sofa arm, raised and spread his legs as Medina moved in on his knees, and rolled his pelvis up to Medina's hard cock. He gave a groan and a low moan as the older man entered him. They locked eyes. Brett had mastered the art of showing a mixture of pain and pleasure and awe in his eyes as a client drove his cock up inside him. The look wasn't lost on Medina, who gave a low moan himself, and began to pump. Brett dug his fingernails into the man's shoulder blades, and murmured, "Yes, fuck me. *Si, si.* You're so big. Give it to me. Just like that."

The golden words that every man wants to hear from a lovely sex partner.

"Oh, god, yes! Drive it in me!" Brett cried out. Whether or not the added passion was a prostitute's trained pretense, it had the desired effect of increasing Medina's arousal and thrust response.

And, having paid big bucks to get the London male whore in this position as a present for his three friends, Medina did just that.

* * * *

Sunlight was flooding Diego Medina's bedroom through two open French doors out onto mere inches of balcony depth when Brett opened his eyes. He groaned. He was on his back and his legs were spread and bent—the most comfortable position he could take at the moment. Who knew that he could take so much cock in the night? Who knew that a man as old as Diego Medina could get it up that often and keep it hard that long? He had really gotten his money's worth. Brett's jaw was sore. He gave a little smile of pleasure for managing to have been touched and well worked deep inside him. That didn't happen often in his profession.

It gave him an added thrill to have been screwed by his father's business partner.

He stirred, preparing to roll out of the bed, but a beefy arm flopped down across him and he heard a grunt from next to him in the bed. He tried to lift the arm off him, but that brought the man awake and Fausto, the chauffeur growled, "No you don't. I'm gonna do you again." He rolled over on top of Brett. He was a heavy man—young and muscular. A man of the street, which is why he was in bed, although Brett couldn't remember having asked him to be in bed with him. He couldn't remember when Medina and Fausto exchanged places—or whether they double fucked him before they did.

"Enough," Brett muttered, and made to roll out from underneath the hunk of a man. Fausto slapped him across the face.

"I'm not done yet, *puta*"—whore. "Take it," Fausto muttered, pressing his body down on Brett and grabbing for Brett's wrists. The bulb of his cock found Brett's hole and he slid in.

Aroused by the domination and rough treatment, Brett fell back onto the pillows. He wrapped his legs around Fausto's thighs, underneath the man's buttocks, and Fausto started plowing him in vigorous, deep strokes. That's why his jaw was sore, Brett now remembered. He'd struggled last night too, and Fausto had subdued him with two slaps to the face, calling him a whore then too. Whether or not the chauffeur was canny enough to realize it, it's what worked best with Brett. He had to play the high-class male hooker so much that, for himself, for his own pleasure, he wanted something rougher, something taken from him, with a little force. He wanted a stranger off the street. Fausto hadn't beaten him badly. It was as if he knew where the limits were. He'd just dominated Brett and Brett had dutifully fallen into the role of submissive.

That's what he did now too. He lay back, put his hips into motion to take Fausto rhythmically, and held the man's buttocks close against him with his legs wrapped around Fausto's thighs. They rocked against each other for a good fifteen minutes, Fausto grunting and whispering dirty words in Spanish in Brett's ear as

Brett moaned low and whispered "*sí, sí*" in Spanish and other words of encouragement and pleasure in French, which Fausto seemed to have some grip on and was the only language other than English that Brett knew. They came almost simultaneously, which was a point in the chauffeur's favor over Medina who, despite his age, had gotten it up four times but couldn't deliver on Brett's schedule any of those times.

After they had fucked the last time, with Medina on his back and Brett riding his cock cowboy style, Diego had whispered a few warnings about his friends. "You'll have to be patient with Cowden. He needs pills and even then doesn't always get hard enough or get off from penetration. You'll probably have to suck him off after he's tried getting inside your ass and failed. He's good for conversation if he can't perform, though, and would be content with that if you don't make him feel guilty.

And watch out for Acosta. He can be nasty. He's a real thug. Came from the streets. Nardo is OK, but he'll want to film you. He'll tell you it's for private viewing, but if he brings another couple of guys with cameras, make him pay more up front—that film is going to show in the art houses and then on the Internet." Then the older man had turned on his side and was snoring within minutes.

Five hours later, he was up walking around, finishing his packing, and Fausto, the chauffeur, was standing in the doorway, waiting to take the luggage to the car, but his eyes on Brett, stretched out, naked, on the bed. Brett had the sensation that Fausto had already fucked him at that point.

Fausto would certainly declare, if challenged, that Brett invited him back, and into bed again, after he'd delivered Medina to the airport. Brett couldn't remember having done so, but the man was a hunk and was from the street—and he slapped Brett around a bit that first time when he returned and got forceful with him and called him dirty names. And he'd proved to have been a real stud— young, vigorous, virile, forceful, and hung. After it had been done, Brett didn't have anything to complain about.

After this fuck, Fausto let Brett get out of the bed and pad off to the bathroom. Brett came back after soaking in the tub to answer a ringing phone. Fausto was gone.

"Alastair here," Brett heard when he picked up the phone. The previous night Diego had told Brett that he should call the clients to make arrangements for their encounters, but obviously the Britisher, Cowden, was too anxious to wait for Brett's call.

"I'm taking the yacht up the French Riviera this afternoon. Coming back tomorrow. I wanted to be sure I wasn't out of range when you called. I thought you might want to go with me. We'd be back by dinnertime tomorrow."

A day and a half on a boat with a man who looked like a skeleton and needed pills to get it up—and sometimes couldn't get it up even then? Brett thought. He wasn't ready for that. "I'm sorry, but I'm exhausted today. Jet lag. How about later in the week, or maybe early next week?"

The man was disappointed, but Brett made a date for the weekend on the yacht and that satisfied Cowden enough to get him off the line.

The phone rang again as soon as Brett put it down. It was the winery owner, Sebastian Acosta, who was quite direct. "I have tickets to a prize fight tonight. I want to take you to that and then take you to a hotel and fuck the shit out of you."

Brett asked the man what time he'd pick him up.

He was in the kitchen, eating his breakfast at 1:00 p.m., when Valentino Nardo called. "We will be filming at an old palace by the sea the day after tomorrow. The palace is fabulous as are the art works in it. You should see the gold gilt on the bed in the master bedroom. I thought you might like to—"

"Are you planning for me to be in that film—and on that bed?" Brett interrupted to ask.

It took a moment for Nardo to catch up to him. "It's a very nice bed, and I believe I have paid for—"

"You paid for private sex, Mr. Nardo. I know about the movies you make. I don't mind if you fuck me on film for distribution, but it would cost you another thousand euros—up front. Are you interested?"

He was interested, and the date was made.

His breakfast finished, Brett went into the bathroom of the guest room, where his suitcase was but he hadn't spent any time in there yet, and showered again, making sure to clean himself out

103

very well. He picked a form-fitting T-shirt and low rise, worn jeans from his suitcase and ferreted around in there until he came up with rope sandals. That was all he needed to take the walk he felt like taking. Fausto hadn't finished him; he'd just whetted his appetite.

* * * *

Diego had warned Brett about coming into the heart of the Barcelona gay district alone. The gay community in Barcelona was large—and bold, he'd said. Brett had listened to Diego say this, making his eyes go big, and clucking in apprehension—trying not to think at the same time of the sexy fox man who had fucked him in the dark water closet at Manuel's Lounge the previous night— who had taken him hard and banged his head against the wall and the toilet tank to subdue him and correctly called him a *puta*—and how he had loved the fuck.

Diego had warned him, in particular, about the men loitering on the Carrer de Casanova, the street parallel to the Carrer de Villarroel, where Manuel's Lounge had been located.

"When these men see a man they want to fuck, they just follow him until they can get him alone, and then they fuck the stuffing out of him," Diego had said.

"Really? How cruel. Just strangers off the street like that?" he asked, turning his face away so that Medina couldn't see his slight smile.

"Yes, just like that. Grabbing and fucking men who are on the Carrer de Casanova just to find some hookup with a suitable person, like you or me—and they grab them and have their way with them by force."

"Thank you for warning me," Brett had said in a breathless voice, not telling Medina, of course, why he was breathless.

Brett left the flat on foot and walked the short distance to the Carrer de Casanova. He started at one end and walked to the other. Then he turned and walked back. On his first circuit, he attracted the attention of several men who were leaning against walls of the buildings on the street and smoking and chatting with each other. As he passed them, many ogled him from when he first came into sight until he had passed out of sight. More than one man gave him a wolf whistle. Several even called out to him, some telling him what they could do with him, some telling him what he could do for them. They'd start with Spanish and then when he didn't react, they tried other languages. If they happened on English or French, he'd given them appreciative glances. By his second circuit, they knew to try English or French. When he passed a couple of bruisers, leaning against a wall, smoking and smirking, and one of them called out in English or French what they would like to do with him—to him—he stopped abruptly, turned and smiled at them, and then continued on his way.

With a little thrill, Brett learned from this walk that, on the whole, the strangers loitering and ogling walkers on the Carrer de Casanova were sexier and more brutish looking than he'd found on the streets of London.

On his second circuit, he stopped, one of the men built in more graphic terms on what he'd said before that he'd like to do to Brett, and Brett nodded slightly in their direction. One of them tossed out the *"puta"* challenge at him, flipping Bret and underhanded bird, and he just smiled seductively at the man and walked on. This time when Brett walked on, back toward the flat, the two pushed off of the wall and followed him. They followed him via several streets back to the Carrer dels Tallers. They followed him into the building where Diego Medina's flat was located. They followed him up two flights and to where he paused at the flat door.

Brett didn't let them into the flat, though. Carlos and Milo didn't let him. Carlos, tall, muscular, and swarthy, backed Brett up against the wall next to the flat door with his body and leaned in for a deep, possessive kiss, becoming busy with his hands in exposing Brett's naked body. Carlos fucked Brett right there, standing against the wall, beside the door, Brett trapped between him and the wall while Milo, also tall, muscular, and swarthy, went through the pockets of Brett's discarded jeans, found the flat key, and let himself in. Brett hooked his knees on Carlo's hips and took the Spanish stud's huge cock hard and deep to a mutual ejaculation.

Also nicely cocked, Milo fucked him doggie style over the arm of the same leather sofa Diego had fucked him on the previous night. Milo was similar enough to Carlos in every way, including the upward curve of his dark-brown cock, that Brett never did tell them apart and was never sure when one left off fucking him and turned him over to the other. Milo, crouched over Brett's back, was sunk into the sofa cushion with his knees, while Carlos stood on the other side of the sofa arm and fed his cock deep down Brett's throat. At some point Brett thought the two might have changed places, but they were too much alike to tell apart in the short time they used and abused Brett's body.

Before they left, they had Brett together, both of them astonished on how much into the fuck he himself was. The two thugs lay on the sofa, their heads on opposite sofa arms, their legs overlapping each other's so that their cocks were bundled together. Brett was mounted on both cocks—taking them together in his passage, and crouched at the center of the sofa, facing the front of the sofa, and stretching his arms over the back of the sofa in either direction to maintain his balance. He rose and fell on the cocks, taking them deeper with each movement, until all three of them were huffing and puffing and excitedly crying out in the passion of a shared explosion.

Each of the thugs, Carlos and Milo, fucked Brett again individually, while the other did his share of emptying the refrigerator of beer. They knocked Brett about a bit too, all of which he took like a trooper.

When they left the flat, leaving Brett in a fetal ball on the floor in front of the sofa, panting and moaning contentedly, they took a souvenir—but just one—with them. It took Brett a week to find a replacement of the bronze table statue that appeared to be one of Goliath fucking David, and the replacement was expensive. But it had been worth it to Brett. Two strangers from off the street. When they had left, he stretched out on the floor and masturbated to a reliving of what they had done with him and to him.

* * * *

A developing bruise check in front of the guest room bathroom mirror when Brett was able to scrape himself off the living room floor revealed that he really should call Sebastian

Acosta and beg off that evening, but the thought of watching fit men beating on each other in the ring with a thug like Acosta sitting next to him, both of them thinking about what they'd be doing afterward convinced him to carry through with the date.

The evening was everything he had dreamed it would be. Spanish prize fighting was as brutal as their bull fighting was. In fact the thought of bulls went all the way through watching three matches of one human bull beating another one to a pulp and to having Acosta move Brett's hand to his package during one of the fights and Brett discovering that Acosta too was a hung bull.

And Acosta was ready for Brett long before the prize fights were over. He couldn't keep his hands off Brett as the two watched the blood lusting and letting in the ring. And Brett was so much into the mood too that he shot a load in his trousers while their eyes were glued to the ring and Acosta was pawing his crotch. Brett was embarrassed, but Acosta just laughed.

"I hope you saved some for later," he quipped.

Brett had saved some for later and more for later than that. They didn't make it to the hotel before they had sex. They did make it to the hotel for a night of vigorous sex, but, for the initial bout, they only made it as far as Acosta's Alfa Romeo in the shadows of a parking garage. When Brett came up for air from kneeling in the well of the car and sucking Acosta ready for action, the big thug raised Brett up, pulled him down into his lap, skewering him on a gigantic cock, and slammed him up and down on his throbbing shaft, while he controlled Brett's breathing by choking his throat with both hands and Brett flopped around like a rag doll.

Acosta was no less brutal with Brett in the hotel room later, fucking him in every demanding position he could come up with, again using a choke hold to control Brett's breathing and to keep the young prostitute totally docile to everything Acosta did with him.

Brett loved it, but Acosta had to take him back to Medina's flat, carry him up the stairs, and deposit him inside the door of the flat, where Brett lay, moaning for nearly an hour before he was able to drag himself into the guest bathroom, soak in the tub, and assess the damage.

One thing was for sure. He wasn't going to be able to do a porn movie with Valentino Nardo the next day. He called Nardo, who was of another opinion. He wanted to film a scene with the bruises—but then he'd be happy to film another scene when they were gone. And he was quite willing to pay extra for it. Brett clicked off the phone with the feeling that he wasn't charging enough for this film work.

He dragged into the kitchen and made another 1:00 p.m. breakfast. When he was done, he went into the guest room and picked out a fresh form-fitting T-shirt. The low-rise jeans from yesterday would be fine again, as would be the rope sandals.

He left the flat on foot and walked toward the Carrer de Casanova and the lineup of the strangers from the street. He was on vacation. He'd manage with Cowden and Nardo. He'd already managed with Medina and Acosta. But when Diego Medina had invited him to house sit in Barcelona, he'd presented it as a chance for Brett to have a vacation. Vacation for Brett was strangers off the street, not the wealthier and more refined types of gentlemen he serviced in London—not that Sebastian Acosta, Brett thought, with a smile, had in any way been a gentleman. If he had to beg off of sex here in Barcelona, it would be from Cowden and Nardo, not the strangers off the street.

~

Avoiding the Inevitable

What was most maddening was the waiting. Not knowing what would happen and yet, in his gut, knowing exactly what was going to happen. If thirty-year-old hunky West Point grad six-foot-three Captain Joel Campbell was going to report them, he would already have done so. Nineteen-year-old Mike Gutierrez of Cuban ancestry and built low to the ground but of solid physique could hardly believe that the captain meant what he'd said when he'd caught Frank and him—making out in the jungle just beyond the camp periphery in Guatemala. In 1967, if you were a Green Beret, and you were caught with a man, you were drummed right out of the service. It didn't matter how frustrating and stressful this tracking down of guerillas in the Guatemala jungle was. You mess around with another man, Green Beret or otherwise, and you were out.

But when Captain Campbell had found them, what had he said? He'd taken Mike aside—he apparently had no interest in Frank—and he said, you give me what Frank got, Sergeant, and it will be just between the two of us.

When the captain had called him into the operations tent that evening, he just said one word—"Tonight." But Mike understood what that meant—if the captain wasn't toying with him. If this wasn't all just a tease before the captain reported both Frank and him and had them sent home. Mike didn't mind going home. Guatemala was hell. And he wouldn't have gotten it on with Frank at all, he didn't think, if Guatemala hadn't been a guerilla-fighting hell and the local women hadn't been strictly off limits to them.

Part of him wanted the captain to be sniffing around for it like Frank had. The captain was one handsome, squared-away dude. He had a body to die for, and that's how Frank had gotten going on Mike. They'd been showering together under the outdoor spigot and Mike had been hard. Frank had wheedled out of him that Mike had just seen the captain in the shower and the captain had one hell of a body and was horse hung. Somehow Frank had gotten to where Mike let him jack him off to discussions of the various bodies of the Green Berets in camp. It was an elite unit, so they were all cut and muscles—including Frank, who had gotten around to fucking Mike. And Mike had let him.

And the captain had caught them. And this evening the captain had growled "Tonight" at Mike.

Mike had been in his tent, wrapped in his sleeping bag—naked, because that's how he wanted to think about something like this with the captain going down, even if it wasn't going to happen. If it was all fantasy.

But it wasn't fantasy. The tent was in darkness, but the overhead lights were on in the compound. They never let it be totally dark in the compound in case the guerillas used the cover of darkness to steal in and kill them all in their sleeping bags. So, when the captain crept into the tent, leaving a slit open in the flap, he was backlit as, crouching in the tent, he stripped down to just dog tags.

Mike was breathing heavily, realizing it was going to happen, seeing the captain with a raging hard on. Horse hung. Certainly longer and thicker than Frank was. Mike was trembling inside the sleeping bag. He'd gone hard just from the thought of what the "Tonight" meant, and now he was even harder, having watched the captain, backlit by the light outside the tent, strip down.

Campbell pulled the sleeping bag cover back and Mike heard him take his breath in. "Shit, Sergeant, you've got a bod to die for." He touched Mike on the hip and could feel that he was trembling. "Don't be afraid, Mike," he murmured. "You went all the way with Frank. It will be fine with me."

"You're so big," Mike mumbled.

The captain gave a low laugh. He was stroking Mike's flank with his fingers, and it was hardening Mike up. "Yes, yes, I am. You'll love it. Roll over, onto your back," he whispered. He nudged Mike's shoulder and the sergeant went onto his back. "We're gonna sixty-nine now," the captain said, and he went into a pushup position in reverse over Mike's body. He opened his mouth over Mike's cock, causing Mike to moan and then to open his mouth as the bulb of Campbell's cock pressed at his lips.

"Relax. Take it. You'll take it better if you relax," Campbell murmured when they'd both come in each other's mouths and he'd turned Mike on his stomach and moved down to open up his hole with his tongue while he was waiting to recharge. Mike was tense and groaned and gasped while the captain prepared him. And then Campbell was urging him to relax and he was doing it. He had Mike on his side and was behind him. Campbell's hand glided over from Mike's hip, toward his lower belly.

"Frank told me about—"

"Oh shit, oh fuck. Fuck me," Mike suddenly cried out, writhing under the captain's touch now. Campbell clasped his free hand over Mike's mouth to muffle his exclamation, but his other hand continued stroking the spot on Mike's lower left belly that Frank had told him about. Mike clutched at him, trying to pull Campbell inside him, trying to be one with him. The captain decided that the sergeant was more than ready for him.

He was holding Mike's left leg up to give him access to his ass, and Mike was moaning and close to hyperventilating as Campbell was forcing his thick cock inside—moving deeper and cajoling Mike in soft tones, telling him it would be all right, that the captain would be gentle with him.

Fully saddled then, though, he rolled Mike over on his stomach, rolling with him, ending up on top of him. He nudged Mike up onto his knees, covered his mouth with one hand to stifle his cries of pain that eventually melted into gasps of passion and muttered, "Yes, yes. Fuck me. Fuck me hard," as the fit soldier with the fat cock did just that. He set a rhythm of thrusts that built on themselves as lust and passion took over, and before he ejaculated, which was after he'd stroked Mike off with his free hand, he was pounding Mike's ass like there was no tomorrow.

After blasting Mike's channel deep inside, Campbell rolled off him to the side. "Whooie, you've got one sweet ass," he growled. "Passage as tight as a virgin maiden. And believe me, I've had my share of virgin maidens."

Mike was breathing hard, grimacing at the intensity of the fuck, overwhelmed by what they'd just done.

In the silence, as he cooled down, Campbell got control of himself and the lustiness began to drain out of him, although not totally. He reached over, tentatively and touched Mike on the cheek. "I hope I didn't hurt you," he whispered. "Sorry if I did. You've got a beautiful body and a sweet channel. If you could have relaxed, we could have worked together well and you'd enjoy it more. Don't worry, I won't turn you in. Not now, of course. Now I'm in it with you. And I got pleasure from you. And I could have gotten more . . . and you could have gotten more if—"

"Captain," Mike whispered.

"What, Mike? Again, I'm sorry. I won't—"

"I can relax now, I think."

"What do you mean?"

"I mean I want it again. I want to try to please you more. Do me again, Captain. I can relax. I want to work with you. I want to get and give pleasure—with you."

"You want to take me willingly? This isn't just to keep me from reporting you?"

"Shit, no, captain. I've wanted you since I arrived here. I didn't know you would . . . that you were . . . that way. That we could. I want you to do me. You can do me hard again. I don't care."

"But Frank."

"When Frank fucked me, I was thinking about you. I want to do it with you, not Frank."

To prove what he was saying, Mike turned onto his back and spread and bent his legs, placing his feet on the ground and elevating his pelvis. "Fuck me again, Captain. Let's work at doing it right."

With a sigh, the captain rose up, moved between Mike's spread legs, pushed his knees under the sergeant's buttocks, slowly entered him again, leaned over to take Mike's lips with his, as Mike palmed his shoulder blades, digging in with his fingernails and Campbell moved deep inside him, deeper than Campbell had managed to sink when Mike was tense, and the two began moving together as one.

Weeks later, when they were redeployed, Captain Campbell to the Pentagon and Mike to Fort Bragg, in North Carolina, they had become seasoned lovers, meeting almost nightly; moving together in one long, synchronized, mutually explosive, passionate fuck; and striving for and often achieving a mutual ejaculation in raw, flesh in flesh stroking.

* * * *

For three years the two men exchanged guarded letters where their affection for each other that had gone beyond that of sex in the Guatemalan jungle was expressed between the lines. They often mentioned getting together again, but the Army was cracking down on homosexuality and it was as if they were purposely avoiding meeting because their coupling had been so explosive that they weren't sure they could keep their hands off each other if anyone from the Army was around them.

Joel, now a major, wrote Mike of an inspection tour he'd be on to Fort Bragg and, although the letter spoke of the possibility they could get together, Mike read more of a warning in it and he made sure he had those days off and went down to Fort Lauderdale, allowed himself to be picked up on the beach by a black bull who was using a PT course just off the boardwalk and admired Mike's workout while Mike returned the favor. He was thinking of Joel while the black bull was pounding his ass in a cheap motel room. Mike didn't give it out on base. It was too risky. But he went down to the Florida beaches whenever he could get time off and lived the life of a hungry bottom.

It was Mike who cracked first—or so he thought. He met a girl who worked in the Post Exchange at Fort Bragg. Rita was of Cuban ancestry just as Mike was, and she was one hot tamale. She was fascinated by his body and couldn't keep her hands off him, and he went along with that to provide camouflage on base concerning his real interests. She got knocked up, and it could have been him, so he married her on the quick in the fall of 1970. About the same time he was mustering out of the service and, because she wanted to stay close to the base, they bought a farmette east of Fayetteville and put in produce that went into the Fort Bragg dining halls. It was evident he was going to do well with that, and his life was taking a big U-turn. This was OK with him. He'd forget about his former preferences.

The problem was that he couldn't forget about Captain Joel Campbell.

To aid in the severing of all ties, Mike sent Joel a wedding announcement. That worked as he imagined it would, although it broke his heart. The letters stopped coming from Joel.

At Christmas in 1970, though, he and Rita got a Christmas card from Washington, D.C. It was from the Campbell family. It came as a hard blow to Mike. Joan Campbell, Joel's wife, must have added the Gutierrezes to her Christmas card list, having seen the wedding announcement and only figuring that Mike and Joel had served together in Guatemala and were service buddies. The card included a family photo. Joel, looking achingly sexy and masterful to Mike, his beautiful blonde wife, Joan, and their two children, a tall strapping, handsome boy, Andy, eleven, and a beautiful, all toothy-smile daughter, Candace, thirteen.

Joel had a wife and two children when he was fucking Mike in Guatemala. Mike had been twelve, nearly the same age as Andy in the photo was, when Joel became Andy's father. Joel hadn't said anything about being married and having children when he was fucking Mike—and beyond fucking him. Making love to him and saying how he wished and hoped they could be together forever.

Mike had been thinking of trying to resume the letter writing, but he gave up that thought now. And he had other serious matters come up to help push the Campbells out of his thoughts. Rita died in February, trying to give birth to a still-born son—one who was obviously black, so not Mike's baby at all. And the farmette became serious and demanding business. Whenever he could get away, he went down to Florida to get laid. He stopped thinking of Joel being inside him when some black bull or Hispanic was fucking him—well, most of the time he managed not to think of Joel being the one inside him.

He saw Joel again later that summer, the summer of 1971. They attended the same funeral. Frank had been caught fucking another Green Beret and was being booted out of the Army. The only life Frank had known was the Army. He accidentally shot himself in the head while cleaning a gun—at least that was the official story. All the men who knew him knew better, though. Joel, as a former unit commander of Frank's, gave a eulogy at the funeral. Mike sat near the back of the gathering. Their eyes met, but Mike left as soon as the ceremony was over.

Joel sent Mike a letter that was breezily worded as "I saw you at the funeral but didn't get to talk to you" but that obviously was really sent to let Mike know that Joel had split up with his wife. He also belatedly offered his condolences for Mike's loss of Rita. "We should get together again one of these days," the letter said, which was more explicit wording than Mike had gotten in a letter from Joel up to that point.

Mike, still upset at finding Joel had a family, even if he was separated now, didn't respond to the letter.

In 1974 Major Joel dropped a note to Mike that he'd be on an inspection tour at Fort Bragg again in May and maybe they could go to dinner together and have a few beers "for old time sake." Mike made sure he was in Florida for those days.

In 1978 Mike was heading up to New York to visit relatives in the city and, without really thinking about it, found himself getting off the Beltway around Washington, D.C., and checking out Joel Campbell's house in Falls Church—the address that the earlier letters and Christmas card had come from. An elderly couple lived there. If he'd seen Joel in the yard, Mike told himself, he wouldn't have stopped. But, since it was an elderly couple, he decided there was no harm in asking about Joel living there. They did remember the name Campbell as the people who had lived in the house before them, but they didn't know where the family had gone. They seemed to recall there was a messy divorce, that the husband was an Army officer, and that they had a son who had gotten a slot at West Point.

And that was that for the next nine years.

Then, from out of the blue in the spring of 1987, Mike got a birthday party announcement in the mail, address from a Captain Andrew Campbell, at the nearby Fort Bragg base.

Sergeant Gutierrez, it began, addressing Mike by the title he'd given up seventeen years earlier, *you don't know me, but you served with my father, Colonel Joel Campbell, in Guatemala. He told me quite a bit about you—the best friend he had in the Green Berets, he said. I'm a Green Beret now too, stationed at Bragg. Dad is finally retiring from the Army and turning fifty. We're planning to have a surprise birthday party here at our place outside Bragg on June 18th. As you two were best buddies and you live near here, I thought you might be interested and willing to come to the party for him. No gifts, please. Just a card. But if you could come over sometime before that, we'd like to pick your brain on surprises from Dad's past that we could spring on him at the party. Please let me know if you can come over. We have a little place in the woods outside Gate 3 at Bragg. Very casual. We have plenty of beer and wieners.* The note was signed Andy and Chris.

Mike propped the note up on a sugar jar on his kitchen table and stared at it during meals for the next three days. It caused an ache in his gut and dredged up a past that he'd tried to make the past, but now, even at thirty-nine, he realized it never really had been the past for him.

He wrote back to Andy and a date was set for him to visit Andy and Chris. It occurred to him that Andy would be the same age that Joel was when they were lovers. He wondered if there would be a strong resemblance. And he wondered if Chris was Andy's wife or a live-in—whether they were a cute couple. And then he thought again that Andy would now be the same age that Joel was when he and Mike were lovers.

* * * *

Andy and Chris indeed made a cute couple. The shocker, though, was that Chris was a man. He was another Green Beret officer. And the two were affectionate to each other. They obviously were a couple—and both were as sexy as hell. Chris was a black bull. The position on homosexuality in the Army had shifted—it still was taboo, but it was "don't ask, don't tell" taboo now, and whether or not Andy and Chris told, they certainly practiced it.

"You go on into town, babe, and pick up that lumber," Andy told Chris after Mike had driven up and introductions had been made. "I'll take care of Sergeant Gutierrez here." He patted Chris on the butt as the black hunk pulled on a T-shirt and drove out in a pickup truck. The two of them had been chopping wood, stripped down to athletic shorts. Andy, a six-foot-four strapping hunk, who was the spitting image of Joel Campbell when Mike had known the captain, didn't bother to top off his gym shorts. Turning to Mike, he said, "Go on up to the porch. We'll talk there. I'll go get some beers."

He came out onto the porch with a six-pack of cold beer. The two chatted about Guatemala and Joel, with Mike trying to avoid what he really could say about Joel, while they polished off the six beers. Both were mellow and sitting side by side on a wicker sofa on the porch.

They were mellow enough that Andy made a move—and that Mike did little to avoid it. He was still bowled over that Andy was gay and had another Green Beret for a partner and that he was the spitting image of his father at the age in which Joel was fucking Mike. The transference was easy—and probably inevitable, given Andy's intentions—and was aided by the beer.

Andy had left Mike briefly alone on the porch and had returned with another cold six-pack. Mike didn't really need more beer to warm to Andy, who had been working him since the second beers had been half drunk. When Andy sat back down on the sofa this time, he sat very close to Mike and put an arm around Mike's back, resting on the top of the sofa, but with his fingers touching Mike's bicep. Mike didn't move away.

"God, I can't believe what good shape you're in—that you've managed that with being out of the special forces for how long?"

"Seventeen years," Mike answered, his voice a little slurred from the beer. That didn't stop him from taking a deep drag on beer number four, though.

"Dad's in shape too," Andy said, "but he's just now getting out of the service, and he kept up with the personal training. You should see him now. Still a real hunk. But then you're a hunk too. I can see why it happened."

"Farming is hard work," Mike answered. "It's not hard to stay in shape when you're doing most of the farming work yourself." Then he stopped talking and went numb. "What do you mean that you can see why it happened?"

"I can see why Dad spoke of you in such glowing terms—on how sexy and sweet you were—what a good lay you were. How he couldn't keep his hands off you and you became his main lay during the Guatemala operation."

"Andy," Mike said in a weak voice. The young man was leaning into to him now, the arm around his back more clutching.

"I can see why he wanted you. You've kept yourself up great. I could easily want you too. I think I do want you. What was it he said about a spot you had? He said that if he touched you here"—and Andy inserted his free hand under the hem of Mike's T-shirt above the waistband of his cargo shorts and touched Mike on the lower belly on his left side—"that you just relaxed and opened your legs to him."

Mike moaned and collapsed under Andy, as Andy, nearly a foot taller than the slender Cuban and all muscle, moved his body over Mike and came in for a kiss. In the moments it took Andy to make Mike's lips yield to his and his tongue to get inside, Andy was rubbing the erogenous spot on Mike's belly. Sensing Mike was submitting to him, though, Andy moved his hand to Mike's belt buckle and zipper, and had Mike's fly open and his cock out and was stroking him as Andy brought Mike fully under his control with the kiss.

Still imagining the young hunk as his father twenty years earlier, Mike gave in with a long, low moan.

Andy was athletic and flexible. Trapping Mike in the corner of the sofa, backed into the arm, Andy moved over him in reverse, placing his knees on the arm of the sofa on either side of Mike's shoulder, with his body streaming down to Mike's pelvis. he took Mike's cock in his mouth and presented his own cock to Mike's lips, with dutifully opened to receive a long, thick, hard cock. Andy was hung, like his father was.

Mike was fucked there on the sofa, still backed up to the arm, his legs spread and waving in the air, as Andy crouched between Mike's thighs on his knees, and fed his long cock inside Mike's passage. He fucked him in long, deep strokes. He'd had a condom on when he'd pulled his gym shorts off. Mike didn't know if he'd crowned himself before Mike arrived or did so when he went to get the second six-pack, knowing only then that he planned to seduce the older man.

To Mike's shame, it wasn't much of an effort in seduction. He melted to the young man as soon as he saw his tall, muscular body at the wood chopping block, only wearing gym shorts and construction boots. Suddenly Joel Campbell was standing before Mike again, as he was in 1967, beautiful, muscular, and hung.

After fucking him missionary style for a while, Andy turned Mike over, with his belly on the arm of the sofa, and his torso and arms draping down to the floor of the porch. Andy crouched over him in a half-standing position, grabbed the older man's hips between his hands, mounted him, and growled, "Fuck yourself on it." Mike submissively pumped his buttocks back onto the hard, steadily held cock until, with a laugh, Andy took over the pumping.

With a low cry, Andy pulled out of Mike's ass, flipped him back over, jerked off and tossed away the condom, creamed Mike's face with his cum, and forced his dick inside Mike's mouth to be cleaned off. Mike submissively took him, but he jerked when he heard Andy exclaim, "There now, Daddy's favorite lay is *my* lay."

Giving a wounded, guttural groan, Mike struggled out from underneath Andy, stumbled to his truck, and started the engine, threw the truck into reverse, and laid gravel in backing out of the driveway. His last look at Andy was of a magnificently naked young man standing on his porch, laughing, and saluting Mike with a beer can.

Mike waited until mere hours before the birthday party for Joel Campbell was to start and then sent off an e-mail saying he was having trouble starting his truck and would have to beg off.

* * * *

Mike was at the horse shed near the house, spearing hay into a trough, when the spiffy Dodge Ram truck turned into the drive late the next morning. He wasn't expecting visitors and had been spending the hours since skipping the party running over in his mind why he'd skipped the party. If wasn't just because Joel's son had taken advantage of him. It wasn't the sex. It was that Andy had used him as some sort of "one-up-man-ship" chit in something he had going with his father. The fuck itself was something Mike needed and refused to be sorry for.

Was it that he still was avoiding Joel? Was it that he couldn't trust himself with the man and still was hurt that he'd been married and hadn't told Mike? Would he have let the captain lay him in Guatemala if he'd known the man was married? Yes, he had to admit to himself that he would have given Campbell whatever he wanted in Guatemala. If he could admit this to himself, than why need the family business be a barrier? Why did it seem to be important to Andy, the man's son?

He leaned on the pike he was slinging the hay with and watched the truck drive in and then swerve off into the field and drive toward him. He was just in gym shorts and heavy high-top boots he always wore while working in the fields.

The truck came to a stop in front of him and he and Joel Campbell remained in place, giving each other searching looks. Mike would have known Joel anywhere, despite the twenty years of separation. The man had good facial bone structure and he was still in great shape. Mike was the first to break the visual standoff. With a sigh, he dropped the pike, came around to the passenger door of the truck, opened the door, and climbed up into the cab, plopping down in the seat beside Joel. He tried to keep his eyes pointed to look out of the windshield, but he couldn't help taking furtive glances at Joel, whose face was turned to him and focused on him.

Joel moved a hand to grasp Mike's knee, flesh on flesh. That's all he needed to do to hold Mike there, captive and submissive to him. That's all he'd ever needed.

"You didn't come to my birthday party," Joel said in a low voice.

"I couldn't. My truck . . ."

"There's nothing wrong with your truck, is there?" Joel asked.

"No," Mike admitted.

"Andy told me what he'd done. Why it was that you probably weren't there. He was proud of it, happy about. Threw it in my face."

"Sorry," Mike said.

"Andy's my son."

120

"A son I didn't know you had when you were screwing me."

"Yeah, I'm sorry about that. There never was a good time to mention that. But I wanted you so bad. Would you have let me fuck you if you'd known I had a family?"

"Yes, probably," Mike admitted. "But it's important that I didn't know."

"You're right, of course. I should have risked it. I should have trusted my hold on you. And is that why you let Andy screw you? To get back at me?"

"No. I think getting back at someone is what your son is doing. I let him screw me because he was you—he was you back in the Guatemala jungle. He was the man I'd let do anything with me as long as he had his dick inside me. And the other day. I would have let your Andy do anything to me for the same reason."

"Because he was me? He did it because he's still mad at me for breaking up with his mother—for screwing his roommate from the Academy. For being gay, I guess."

"He's gay. He's got a male lover. And there was no holding back with me."

"Sometimes I wonder. Sometimes I think his whole thing with being gay is to rub it into my face. You know how he knew about you—knew that you'd take cock?"

"Knew that I had an erogenous button he could take advantage of?" Mike added.

"Shit, did he take advantage of that?"

"Yes."

"Fuck. Yes, that too. When he came to tell me that he was gay, I tried to help him with that by telling him I had sex with men too. I told him about you—about the best lay and the best lover I'd ever had. I was trying to make him feel better about himself. I think now, though, that it was all acting. That he was looking for vulnerability in his old man."

"I don't think it's all that," Mike said. "It wasn't all acting when he was fucking me. I could have told."

"Well, you *are* a great lay," Joel said, trying out a tentative smile. His fingers were playing with Mike's knee. "But I didn't come here because of Andy," he continued. "Andy's a problem that has to be tackled separately. I came here because of you and me. Unless you tell me to go away and not come back, we need to stop with this cat-and-mouse game of avoidance. We're grown men. We're both free now."

"So, you came here to fuck me?"

"Yes, repeatedly. I you'll have me. I'm tired of us taking turns of running away from it. Are you going to let me fuck you?"

"Yes, of course."

"You going to let me touch you here?" Joel moved his fingers up under the hem of Mike's T-shirt and touched him on the lower belly on the left side. Mike collapsed toward the passenger door and Joel leaned over him and pressed Mike's lips open with his and moved his tongue inside. Mike's hand went to the zipper in Joel's jeans, and he freed Joel's cock, which was quickly going hard.

"Where do you want to start? It's been a long time," Joel murmured.

"Too long," Mike answered. "I want to start by sucking you off." he pushed Joel back upright behind the wheel and, lowering his head, took Joel's cock in his mouth.

After several minutes, Joel said, in a husky voice, "Let's go into the house."

"Later," Mike said. "I want to do it here, so that anyone who drives by can see that I have a man. That I'm not keeping a secret about having a male lover anymore. Slide over into this seat."

Joel did so, and, stripping off his gym shorts but not his jock strap, Mike climbed into Joel's lap, his knees pressed into where the seat back on either side of Joel merged into the seat cushion. He held Joel's cock in position and started to descend on it. Joel grasped his waist, prepare to raise and lower his passage on the cock, but Mike whispered, "No, this time let me do it. Let me fuck you. After that I surrender to whatever you want, whenever and wherever you want it." Joel let loose of Mike's waist and let one hand go to touching Mike's erogenous spot, whereupon Mike went wild in riding the cock to Joel's ejaculation inside his passage and Mike's into the mesh cup of his jock strap.

In the master bedroom, on Mike's bed, Joel later proved that he still had the virility and vigor of youth as he hovered over

Joel, trapping the younger man's wrists above his head, and pounded away in his ass.

Afterward as they lay against each other, Joel on his back, and Mike on his side stretched out along the older man's body, Mike's fingers playing in Joel's curly pubic hair and with his cock, Mike murmured, "I understand you're retiring from the Army."

"Yep. Already did. My last day was last week."

"What do you plan to do now?"

"I was thinking of getting a little farmette someplace. Someplace close to an Army base so I can use my retirement privileges there. Someplace like near Fort Bragg, I think."

"I think I know of a nice farmette that meets that criteria," Mike whispered.

"Does it have privileges?"

"Privileges?"

"Fucking privileges."

"Absolutely, yes."

"Might be a good offer then."

"I'm glad you think so. Time to make up for lost time."

"You got that right, good buddy."

~

On a Snowy Afternoon

"Well, gentlemen, I'm for an after-meal hike on the mountain before this afternoon's short session. All this sitting around in meetings is making me sluggish." Professor Rab Rahmani stood up from the table in the dining room of the InterContinental Davos hotel, his eyes going to the rise of the Rhaetian Alps of Switzerland beyond the walls of the mountain resort hotel in the highest town in Europe. He took up the thick coat that had been draped on the back of his chair and had impeded the otherwise excellent waiter service during the lunch.

Across the restaurant, young and eager Erik Hinkel of the courtesy staff of the international nuclear physicists conference being held in the hotel popped up from his table and took up station at the exit. He had a heavy coat folded over his arm.

The men—and woman—who had been at the professor's luncheon table, fawning on the leading American nuclear physicist, had all taken in the coordinated movement of the handsome, young, Germanic blond Hinkel across the room. Rahmani was famous—or infamous, in some circles—for having solved the problem of being caught, as a defected Iranian scientist, working in the Iraqi nuclear program and being captured by the Americans in Operation Desert Storm in 1991, by defecting to the United States. Since then he had been one of the leading lights in the American nuclear program. Rahmani also had a certain reputation with young men, which the Americans seemed happy to overlook to have the power of his brain working *for* them rather than *against* them.

"Remember that the next session starts at 2:00," a German physicist said. "Although it only goes until 3:00. I would have preferred that they give us the whole afternoon off so we can get out and enjoy the snow."

124

"And don't stray far," the French professor Felix Dederaux added. "It looks like it is about to start snowing again." They all gazed out of the broad wall of glass overlooking the town of Davos, with the peaks of the Rhaetian Alps rising above the hotel on the right of the window. Light flurries had just started, but they promised to bring more snow to add to that already on the ground.

"I won't be long," Rahmani said. "And I will have a guide. Young Erik Hinkel has agreed to show me a path up into the mountains with a spectacular view of the town."

"Yes, we can see that Hinkel eagerly awaits," the somewhat sour Sun Park, of South Korea, a fan of Rahmani's work but not, in her verbal criticism, of Rahmani personally, quipped as she brought her coffee cup to her lips to hide the smirk on her face.

All eyes at the table watched Rahmani move gracefully toward the exit. Erik Hinkel's eyes also were glued on the elegantly turned-out man as he approached. Sun Park sighed at what she'd be interested in doing with the Iranian-America, but what she strongly suspected would never be possible. Rahmani was a striking figure—tall, dark, and handsome, highly presentable and charismatic even in his early fifties. The graying at the temples of his luxuriously waving hair made him even more distinguished looking than in his earlier years, which had shown the man off in newspaper photos as Bollywood movie handsome—tall and slim, with a dancer's body and movement and with a strut of well-earned self-assurance of receiving what he was due and that he was due quite a lot.

The snow flurries had picked up a pace as the two men climbed the mountain trail. The path was cut into the side of the mountain above the hotel, but still on hotel property, in such a way as to give hikers from the hotel a walk that would be as unchallenging as possible but still permitted access to a view above the hotel that took in not only the unusual sideway egg, golden dome shape of the InterContinental but also the ski slopes sweeping down into the center of Davos. The snow had been shoveled off the path that morning, but it was starting to drift in again as the flurries turned into something more blanketing.

By the time they reached the first lookout, the view—if the visibility hadn't already closed the view down—being of a ski slope, with the lights of Davos below, it was as if they were the only two men on earth. No one else was up here.

"I'm afraid there will be nothing at all to see in a few minutes," young Hinkel said, raising his voice to be heard by Rahmani, who was impatiently pacing back and forth ahead of him. "Soon, perhaps, we won't even be able to see the opening to the path back to the hotel. I suppose we'll have to go back down and try this again at another time." Erik turned back on the path, but Rab walked swiftly back to him, reached out, and pulled the younger, smaller man into his body.

"Let us linger for a moment more," he exclaimed into Erik's ear, having to raise his voice above the whooshing sound of the snow now falling heavily in the fir trees lining the upward side of the path. "We haven't had a time of privacy, and if I've read you correctly, you are interested in having privacy with me. True?"

The arrogance of the man was only superseded by his sterling assessment abilities. And he wasn't a subtle or shy man. He was comfortable in using his advantages, privilege, and charisma. And he was confident that he could just take what he wanted.

"Yes," Erik answered, understanding fully what Rahmani meant by the word "privacy" and tilting his face up to that of the taller man. They went into a kiss. Erik's soft-blue eyes opened wide in surprise at Rab's subsequent boldness, as, with the two men in a close embrace and Erik gathered into Rab's body with Rab's left arm wrapped around him, Rab fumbled around inside Erik's coat with his right hand. He found Erik's crotch, unzipped him, inserted his elegantly long fingers inside layers of material until he felt flesh on flesh, and grasped Erik's cock.

Coming out of the kiss, Rab gave Erik's eyes a searching, dominating look and asked in a throaty voice, "I am not wrong, am I? You will lay under me, yes? You will allow this as token of your willingness, yes?"

"No, you aren't wrong," Erik answered, opening his lips for a return to the kiss, closing his eyes, and nestling closer into Rab's overpowering figure. He lifted a leg, hooking it clumsily, considering the layering of the coats, on the taller man's hip, to give the Iranian-American professor greater access. He understood that Rahmani was going to masturbate him—the older man was already

126

masturbating him. He would return the favor if he somehow could manage in these conditions. And, yes, he understood that this was a preliminary commitment to let Rahmani fuck him when they got back to the hotel. That didn't bother Erik a bit. It was all part of his plan. He swayed slightly against Rab's body and sighed, as Rab slowly, efficiently masturbated his cock to an ejaculation that was as glorious as it was unusual and inventive.

It started slow, Rahmani squeezing the shaft as he stroked it. When Erik had produced precum, Rahmani drove him to distraction by rubbing it all over the bulb of the young man's cut cock. He put the tip of his pinkie finger on the bulb and pressed it to the piss slit, trying to invade it. Erik writhed a bit at that, disengaging from the kiss and throwing his head back and howling to the sky. Rab buried his mouth in the hollow of Erik's throat and pressed his teeth into Erik's flesh there, his tongue rubbing on Erik's throbbing jugular. The young man moaned, feeling both the pressure of the teeth, able at a moment's notice to slice into his throat if Rahmani so wished it, and the insistence of the man's pinkie finger to get inside his urethra channel. The finger tip somehow managed to push the urethra open, breach its rim, and was slow fucking it, his fingernail causing Erik to groan each time it flicked on the tender rim of the urethra opening. Erik panted heavily and begged Rahmani to fuck him there and then.

"Oh shit, oh Christ!" Erik screamed into the snowflakes assaulting his face. "Fuck me. Fuck me now!" He'd never had a man penetrate his piss slit and fuck it before. He'd never known that was possible. Rahmani had more than the tip in and the channel had opened to him. Erik's pants were matching the rhythm of the penetrations of the finger. Precum was surging up the channel, providing lubricant for deeper penetration. He was feeling as one unit with Rahmani in a way that he'd only felt from the penetration rhythm of a cock in his ass before. When Rahmani pressed in, Erik was thrusting up with his cock to meet it—to welcome the invasion.

Rahmani pulled his mouth away from Erik's throat, laughed, and, cupping the back of the young man's head, pulled his face back up for a deep kiss. Erik opened his mouth wide to the older man, and Rahmani pressed his lips inside Erik's, captured the young man's tongue, pulled it into his own mouth, and sucked on it. He also released the squeezing hold on Erik's cock, withdrew his pinkie, and loosed the sheath of his encircling fist.

Erik's pelvis had already been set into motion. He had been stroking his cock up to meet Rahmani's penetration of the cock bulb. The man's loosely cupped hand replaced his pinkie action and, slowly at first and then more rapidly, Erik stroked inside the sheath provided by Rahmani's hand. Rahmani was holding firm now, and Erik was fucking himself. Never before had a man made such a production out of masturbating Erik. The buildup was overwhelming, the release explosive.

"Yes, yes," The Iranian-American growled as he pulled out of the tongue-possessing kiss and put his mouth next to Erik's ear, running his tongue around in Erik's ear cavity before continuing. "Fuck yourself. Fuck yourself in my hand. Bring yourself to release. Fuck yourself and give me your cum." His mouth closed over Erik's ear lobe and he was sucking that when Erik exploded, dropping his load in Rahmani's hand. The older man rubbed the cum into Erik's cock, folded Erik's withering shaft back into his fly, and zipped him up.

When the younger man had come for him, Rab whispered in Erik's ear, in a thick voice, "My room, after the 2:00 seminar has concluded."

"Yes, oh yes," Erik answered, as he reached down and readjusted his coat and looked around, searching for the path back down to the hotel.

* * * *

The afternoon seminar session was nearly half over in the Seehorn meeting room. Rab Rahmani, whose drooping eyelids had indicated to anyone looking at him that it was past his naptime, had, in fact, been watchful. He caught the movement of the young staffer of the Japanese conference contingent rising from his seat along the wall and moving toward the exit. Rahmani waited until the slim young Japanese man had left the room and then he, too, slowly stood and worked his way around the periphery of the room. Several sets of eyes followed his movement, taking their attention away from the presenter at the front of the room, as Rahmani's fame and reputation outshone that of nearly everyone else in the room. Those who watched him leave included the conference courtesy service staffer, Erik Hinkel. After Rahmani exited the room, Erik stood and inched toward the door as well.

Rahmani bypassed the first men's room he came to, knowing that the young Japanese staffer was headed somewhere else. This was the only conference being held in the hotel and thus there was a corridor of meeting rooms beyond a swinging glass door that weren't currently in use. Rahmani went through this door and continued down the line of meeting rooms, entering the men's room at the end of the hall.

The young Japanese staffer was standing at a urinal in the dimly lit bathroom. Rahmani saddled up beside him, unzipped, pulled his cock out, and produced a strong stream of piss. The young man glanced down and sucked in his breath. The older Iranian-American scientist was hung. The Japanese staffer wasn't, but he was well enough endowed to have pride in it. Holding his cock in position, he produced a weaker stream of urine and was finished before Rahmani was. He didn't tuck his cock back into his fly, though, when he was finished. He just stood there, looking into the wall behind the bank or urinals.

He flinched but held steady when Rahmani reached over and under the young man's balls and pulled out the flash drive he had tucked up there. The Japanese man grimaced a bit when Rahmani was slow to extract his hand and the flash drive. When he did, the young man made to tuck himself in and zip up his fly, but the older scientist had quickly pocketed the flash drive and had brought his hand back, grasping the young man's cock.

The slight Japanese gasped and gave Rahmani a confused look. Rahmani whispered to him, "No, stay for a moment. Indulge me. You can hardly say no. What excuse would you give for being in here with me? Put your hands on the wall and lean slightly forward. I am going to give you pleasure and take mine as well."

Although exhibiting a worried, trapped look, the young man did as commanded, leaning forward and palming the hands of his spread arms on the wall behind the urinal. Fisting his own cock with his left hand, Rahmani kept his right arm crossed in front of the young Japanese man, his hand grasping the young man's cock.

The Japanese man moaned slightly and looked both perplexed and dreamy as Rahmani masturbated them both, both of them eventually arcing their cum—Rahmani's more prodigious than the young man's—conveniently into the urinal.

The young man, when he'd gotten past the shock, became increasingly lost to and aroused by the experience, and toward the end of the journey to climax, Rahmani was able to loosen the sheath provided by his hand, and the young man was stroking his cock in Rahmani's grip of his own volition and moaning deeply.

"Yes, yes," Rahmani murmured in a mesmerizing, sing-song voice. "Fuck yourself. Fuck yourself in my hand. Bring yourself to release. Fuck yourself and give me your cum."

The young man had leaned so far forward that his cheek also rested against the cool tiles of the wall, his hooded eyes were glued to Rahmani's face, giving and receiving evidence of mutual pleasure, and he was so lost to the sex act that he didn't realize that drool was running down his chin. If Rahmani had taken him into one of the stalls and fucked, him, the young Japanese staffer would have submitted to him. If the young man hadn't been so entranced, he would have begged Rahmani to take him into one of the stalls and fuck him.

They had all wondered why the American had specified what he had about the delivery of the flash drive. It had seemed bizarre at the time—at a men's room urinal, hidden in the young man's—a young man specified—crotch. Now the Japanese courier knew why. He also knew that it made sense. If anyone discovered them here, just the two of them in a remote bathroom, what they would see would be sordid, yes, but it would be believable and thus was a brilliant cover for the real reason they were meeting here.

When he was finished, Rahmani folded himself back inside his trousers; zipped up; and turned, without a word, and left the bathroom. He walked purposely, confidently, without a hint of guilt, to his seat in the Seehorn room, no doubt not having missed anything from the talk on nuclear physics that was anything he didn't know already. As he sat back down in his seat, he transferred the flash drive to the satchel, suspended from a shoulder strap, that he held close to his side. More than one set of eyes observed the transfer.

The young Japanese staffer remained in the position he'd been jerked off in, leaning forward over the urinal, hands and cheek against the wall, now-soft cock hanging out of his pants, trembling slightly. No one had told him this would happen in the exchange of the North Korean nuclear bomb status report. He'd had no question about his personal sexual identity to this point, but, shit, that milking by another man had been hot. He would have let the man fuck his ass. His ass channel actually twitched from the unrealized possibility of that.

Erik Hinkel, who had managed to slit open the men's room door enough to have seen the flash drive exchange as well as what happened later, was quick enough to be gone from the deserted corridor and back in the lecture hall himself before Rab Rahmani had returned. The young Japanese staffer was far slower in reappearing. When he had, he caught the eye of Sun Park and gave her a nod, indicating success. He wasn't about to relate to her all that had happened in the exchange—all that he would have done for the man.

The lecture concluded at 3:00 p.m., and all in the hall, including the lecturer, let out a sigh of satisfaction—more that the lecture had ended on time and that the rest of the snowy afternoon was free time than because of any new information they had picked up.

* * * *

Rahmani answered his hotel room door wearing just a loosely sashed hotel dressing gown. Entering the room, Erik Hinkel did a quick visual scan. There was a desk, with a briefcase on it and papers fanned out on its surface. Erik immediately wrote those off as camouflage. Rahmani's trousers and shirt were neatly hanging on the back of the desk chair. The satchel that had been hanging from his shoulder in the conference hall and where Erik had observed him hiding the flash drive was laying on the queen-sized bed that dominated the room.

The Iranian-American professor closed the door, came up close behind Erik, and wrapped his arms around Erik's torso. The young man leaned back into Rahmani and turned his head for the kiss that followed. While they were kissing, Rahmani undressed the smaller, slimmer, younger man, first unbuttoning his shirt and caressing his chest, bringing up sighs and moans from Erik. Next sounded the unbuckling of the young man's belt buckle, the lowering of his zipper, and the rustle of the trousers cascading down to the floor. Now only in red bikini briefs, Erik stepped out of the puddled trousers as the kiss came to an end and Rahmani released him from the embrace.

"Go into the bathroom, please," Rahmani murmured. He pulled Erik's shirt off his back and watched, with appreciation, the roll of the young man's buttocks as he walked into the bathroom.

In the bathroom, his dressing gown open, and his long, hard cock pressed up under Erik's ball sac between the young man's closed thighs from behind, Rahmani leaned a now-fully naked Erik over the toilet. Erik's arms were spread and thrust forward, his palms pressed against the wall behind the toilet in the same stance he'd very recently seen a young Japanese man in at the hotel's conference center. This obviously was a fetish of Rahmani's. His left arm embraced Erik's heaving chest, his lips were buried in the hollow of Erik's throat, his right hand grasped Erik's cock, and his own cock was dry humping Erik from behind between his pressed-in thighs.

When Rahmani's pinkie went to Erik's urethra opening this time, Erik relaxed, wanting it and welcoming it, and, as if his cock remembered that it was possible, the pinkie met little resistance as it sank in to the first knuckle. Erik came close to hyperventilating, as the pinkie fucked his cock head. After asserting that it could do so as the master wished, though, the pinkie was withdrawn and Rahmani provided a loose sheath with his hand and whispered for Erik to fuck himself in it, which he did until Rahmani took control again, fisting Erik's shaft hard and vigorously beating the writhing young man off, with Erik, pressing his cheek to the wall behind the toilet as the thrusts became stronger and giving a little yelp of release as he shot his load into the toilet bowl.

He had held his ejaculation for as long as possible—the man had whispered in his ear to do so—but Erik couldn't help releasing when he felt that Rahmani had done so, the feel the jerk of the man's cock at the base of Erik's ball sac and the sensation of the wetness, cum dribbling down Erik's inner thighs.

Rahmani had ejaculated, but he was half erect still and the cock still had steel hardness in it as the man continued sliding his cock inside his own cum between Erik's thighs.

"Run a bath for us, please," he said, as he, at last, released his hold on a trembling Erik. "I'll order up some champagne."

Erik stumbled over to the large marble tub that was backed by a large window overlooking the still-falling snow and the rocks of the alp rising behind the hotel, and started the water going.

In the bedroom, Rahmani first made a call on his cell phone. Then he extracted the flash drive and a small, handheld flash drive reader from his satchel and made a second copy on another flash drive. He careful returned the original back to the satchel and went over to the desk and fished a key from his trousers. He took the satchel over to his suitcase, which was sitting on a luggage rack on the other side of the bed. The case wasn't completely unpacked. There were shirts and pieces of underwear hanging over the side. He didn't lift the lid of the suitcase, though. Rather, he inserted the key at the side, near the base, and a secret compartment large enough to hold the satchel slipped out. Securing the satchel inside the compartment and closing it, he returned to the desk, returned the key to his trouser pocket, picked up the copy of the flash drive, and went to the door and opened it.

A man wearing the uniform of a hotel waiter and leaning over a cart with an ice bucket and two wine glasses on top was waiting outside the door. Rahmani handed the man the second copy of the flash drive, pulled the cart into the room, and shut the door.

When the scientist reentered the bathroom, Erik was sitting on the broad lip of the steaming tub, looking dreamy and stroking his cock. He was erect again. Rahmani was still erect—massively erect. Erik's eyes went big and he gasped when he saw what the Iranian-American was packing. He moaned at the knowledge of where that was going to be sheathed.

Rahmani placed the tray with the champagne and glasses on a broad corner of the tub, climbed into the tub, and reclined back. He opened his arms to Erik, who slipped into the tub, facing Rahmani, and placed his knees on either side of the scientist's thighs. He panted and huffed and gave little cries, as Rahmani grasped his waist and slowly pulled the young man's channel down on the long, thick, throbbing cock. Erik leaned back, away from Rahmani's chest, threw his arms back, grasped well-placed metal handles inside the rim of the tub behind him, and held on for dear life as, water churning around them, Rahmani slammed him up and down on the cock vigorously and cruelly until the Iranian-American blasted the young man deep inside his passage with three separate bursts of cum. He pulled Erik's chest into his, took him in another deep kiss, and continued stroking his cock up inside Erik's channel, sliding through the lubricant of the cum he had deposited there, as, slowly, he went flaccid and Erik's sighs and moans subsided into a soft purr.

Still sheathed on Rahmani's lap afterward, Erik did the honors of pouring the champagne, ensuring that Rahmani didn't see the packet he deftly opened and emptied into the scientist's glass. They toasted each other and tossed off the champagne. Erik refilled the glasses. They toasted each other again and sipped more slowly, cooing to each other, complimenting each other on their beautiful bodies and on how well they moved together in the fuck.

Erik felt Rahmani going hard again. Another glass of champagne, and Rahmani changed their positions, turning Erik over the rim on the tub, his belly on the wide lip, his fists pressed into the tiles of the floor next to the tub, his eyes focused on the pattern of the tile design on the side of the tub, and Rahmani on his knees in the tub, crouched over his buttocks. Grasping Erik's waist between his hands, Rahmani pounded Erik's channel to another coming, letting Erik know how much enjoyment he got out of Erik's cries of passion in the brutal taking.

Feeling drowsy after he'd seeded Erik a second time, Rahmani leaned back in the tub and closed his eyes. It hadn't been a sleeping drug—just something to make the man drowsy and lethargic for a short period. Erik had been told not to expect more than ten minutes of time in which Rahmani would be so far gone that he couldn't think straight. When the Iranian-American was well settled, Erik climbed out of the tub, dried himself off, and padded out into the bedroom. Time was limited but he knew what to do.

He made a call on his cell phone. After he'd closed out on the call, he went to the desk and fished around in Rahmani's trousers for the key to the secret compartment. Finding and retrieving it, he went to his own trousers and extracted the handheld flash driver copier he had brought with him. It only took him six minutes to retrieve and copy the flash drive and have everything back where they belonged.

He took the handheld device copy of the flash drive he made to the door and opened it. A man was standing there, in the corridor. He took the device from Erik. Erik watched him long enough to see the man safely back into the room next door. Then he closed the door, padded over to the bed, and laid down on the bed on his back. When he heard sloshing in the tub in the bathroom, he spread and bent his legs, placed his feet flat on the surface of the bed, and took up a pillow beside him and jammed it under the small of his back, elevating his pelvis. He turned his gaze to the bathroom door, put on a look of need and arousal, and fisted his cock.

Emerging naked and in full erection again from the bathroom, Rahmani took one look at the bed, grinned, and moved swiftly to climb up on the bed, knee himself in between Erik's thighs, mount the young man with a swift and deep thrust, and immediately begin to fuck him hard and deep. Stretching his arms straight out from his body and clutching at the bedspread with his fists, Erik arched his back, cried out, "Yes, yes, Fuck me hard, you daddy stud!" and thrust his pelvis upward with each cruel in-stroke to take Rahmani's cock as deep as possible.

* * * *

Erik closed the hotel room door quietly and looked up and down the corridor to ensure no one was there as he moved to the room next door, walking backward, with his eyes glued to Rahmani's door to make sure it didn't open and the man pop his

135

head out and demand another go at Erik. He'd had several goes at him already. Who knew that a man over fifty would have so many erections and so much cum in him? Erik wasn't leaving dissatisfied, that was certain. This was what made his job so worthwhile. He had not feigned his want for the cocking he got.

When he reached the door of the neighboring room, it opened without him having to knock, and he slipped inside. Two men, agents of Israel's Mossad intelligence agency, were sitting in front of a bank of computer monitors. The monitors showed everything in the room next door—wide sweeps of the bedroom and both the bathroom tub and toilet. One of the men watching the monitors—and now watching Rab Rahmani moving around the bedroom in his hotel robe—was the man who had taken the handheld flash drive recorder from Erik at Rahmani's door earlier.

"Quite a performance that was, Aaron," the man who had retrieved the flash drive said, without taking his eyes off the monitors. "Enjoyed yourself, didn't you?"

"Yes," Aaron—no longer Erik Hinkel—answered, with a bit of a blush. "The man is hung and he can fuck forever. Shit, what's that?"

The three men's eyes scanned the monitors closely. Rahmani had answered the door and had been pushed inside the room by three swarthy men in black, who overpowered him. Rahmani went limp and sank to the floor between them. Two of the men picked him up, supported him between them like he was dead drunk, and hustled him out of the room. The third man started a quick search of the room.

"You got out of there just in time," the first agent said, and Aaron wrapped his arms around his chest and shuddered.

"Who are they?" the second Mossad agent asked, reaching into his arm pit and unlatching the cover to his gun case. "Should we be doing something?"

The first agent put a restraining hand on his arm. "No, it's OK. I recognize them. They are MOIS—Iranian Ministry of Intelligence—agents. They are just retrieving one of their own. The Americans are well rid of Rahmani. That man, the waiter who delivered the champagne and who received a copy of the flash drive, he's SRV—Russian foreign intelligence. Rahmani was double-agenting the Americans. He was as much a whore as handsome Aaron here is. He'd laid on his back and screw with anyone who paid him well or saved his hide. He's served our purposes—passed on the fake North Korean nuclear plans. We can let this work its way out."

"So they *are* fake," the second agent said, "the documents in the flash drive."

"Yes, the South Koreans want as many players as possible to get their hands on the documents. They want us all thinking Pyongyang is further along than it is. They want us to stop it before it gets too dangerous. We've got what we want out of this. The Iranians are welcome to their defector and the Americans are well rid of him."

They watched as the Iranian agent circuited Rahmani's room and focused his attention on the papers fanned out on the desk—no doubt misleading documents Rahmani put there for someone to find if his room was searched. The search was far too limited and hurried to have found the secret compartment in Rahmani's suitcase. The Americans could find that later themselves and be duped like the rest of the world—other than the Mossad—on the actual progress of North Korean nuclear development.

Aaron had pulled away from the monitors and gone over to the window. The snow on this snowy afternoon had finally stopped. He could see all the way down into the town, which was lit up by the late afternoon sunlight, while the area surrounding the hotel was in near darkness, blocked from the rays of the sinking sun by the alp looming behind it. He saw that there was a black Mercedes, its trunk open, in a drive below that came up to a back entrance of the hotel. As he watched, he saw an inert figure in a hotel dressing gown being hustled out of the hotel and over to the Mercedes. The body went into the trunk of the car. By the time the two men had gotten into the Mercedes—which was being driven by another man—the third figure rushed out of the hotel, got into the car, and the car drove off.

Erik gave the car a weak wave. He was rather sad. Rahmani had had a cock to die for and was a great fucker. That little fetish of his was arousing as well.

"Wait, who is that?" the second agent asked, pointing to a monitor image from a camera trained on the corridor.

Erik came over and looked at the monitor. The young Japanese staffer he'd watched Rahmani jack off earlier in the afternoon was standing at Rahmani's hotel room door. He paused there and then knocked, tentatively. He waited for ten seconds or so and knocked again with a stronger rap. When there was no response, he looked disappointed and disappeared in the elevator.

"I wonder what he wanted," agent number two said.

Erik shrugged and went back to the window. He highly suspected that he knew what the young Japanese staffer wanted from Rahmani. The man had been a pied piper of sex. It was surprising how arousing that preliminary little jack-off fetish of his was—how easily it brought a young man under his control. Erik had been his from the moment Rahmani had masturbated him in the snow on the mountain trail.

"Joseph," the first Mossad agent was saying across the room. "I think the entertainment is over. Go on over there and pull the cameras. You can have your go at Aaron when you get back. You don't have to leave it with stroking yourself off while we watched the defector do him."

"You were jerking off then too," Joseph said in a sulky, "I've been caught," voice.

Agent number one turned and looked at Aaron. "I think our little whore is missing the turncoat already. I think he's a bit sad about losing the Iranian's big cock. But, that's OK, we have big cocks too. He told me earlier that this is his favorite part of the job—being royally fucked."

As the second agent we now know was named Joseph—or maybe not—left the room, the first agent turned and said, "Would you be so kind as to get on the bed and spread your legs, Aaron? This is your lucky day—a three-cock afternoon."

With a sigh, Aaron turned from the window. The display of the sunlight on downtown Davos had been short lived anyway, and the Mercedes was out of sight. Unbuttoning and pulling his shirt off his back and releasing and stripping down his trousers and red bikini briefs, he climbed up on the bed. Emitting another deep sigh, he lay on his back, spread and bent his legs, dug his heels into the surface of the bed, and stuffed a pillow under the small of his back to angle his pelvis to give the Mossad agent's cock, which Aaron well knew was big enough, a straight thrust angle. He had to admit that being fucked was his favorite pastime on a snowy afternoon. Three big cocks in an afternoon wasn't bad, snow or no snow—not bad at all.

~

Sugar-Coated Hot Pepper

He was young; cute; Hispanic; had a very nice smile; had a small, perfectly formed body; and moved like a dancer. Any three of those were good enough to make me hard. I immediately went hard for him. His name was Manuel. I guessed Brazil from his bronze skin color. But then we were only ninety miles from Cuba.

I was on a punishment assignment from the Agency. We had a listening post in Key West, at the very tip of the key, on the small naval base, and I'd been sent to head up the operation—and maybe to close it. The ice around U.S.-Cuban relations was thawing and Fidel was dead. The unit was on Key West to monitor every breath a Communist country just off our shore took and, historically, to cover Fidel's three-hour diatribes on the radio. Times were changing. We could squeeze more juice out of Cuba off the Internet than we could off the radio, and there was a shitload of Cuban refugees sitting in Miami who were more than happy to squeeze Cuba off the Net every day and to make sure the U.S. government knew what was happening there.

The Key West bureau was a dying office, and that's how my boss, Sam Winterberry, had pitched a hand-slap assignment for me to the guys and girls—increasingly girls these days—on the seventh floor. I'd been caught fucking the college-age son of the Agency's comptroller, Jerry Ortez, and he wanted me sent to Hades. What could I do? The lad—who was well of age, mind you—was young; cute; Hispanic; had a very nice smile; had a small, perfectly formed body; and moved like a dancer. Just looking at him made me go hard. He also was quite willing and made very nice compliments about the size of my cock and about what I could do with it. He had that "take me like a virgin" act that got to me every time—and I'd taken him like a virgin every time.

140

They couldn't spear me for spiking a man, even though that still was a separation offence in the Agency, because that was my job—I worked for Sam Winterberry's Candy Store unit, which put into play the truism that the world's two oldest professions—spying and prostitution—worked well together as an intelligence-gathering activity. So, I fucked women and men and, on occasion, got fucked, all in obtaining valuable intelligence for the Agency. Being a switch hitter, as I was—Sam Winterberry was fucking me—I was actually quite an asset for the Candy Store unit operations.

So, what officially was a crime in the Agency was, unofficially, premium good business, and the worst Ortez could subject me to was a dead-end assignment until my Candy Store services were vitally needed by Uncle Sam. So, Sam had emphasized the "business is dead, it's at the end of the world, and it probably is closing" aspects of the Key West bureau to the brass and the seventh floor and failed to mention that Key West is the gay male Mecca of the United States. And the seventh floor bought it. That there was male pussy romping from shore to shore down in Key West was a plus for Sam. He wanted to get my mind off Ortez's cute son. It took thinking of the honey pots down there to do it. As it was, I was still banging young Ortez, taking him like he was a virgin, on the night before I pointed the headlights of my Camaro toward Florida. And Sam banged me the morning I left. Both Sam and I well knew I wasn't a virgin.

So, I was sitting at a crowded outdoor café on DuVal Street two weeks after taking up residence in Key West, and he appeared before me on the other side of the café table I was at—one with two chairs at it and I only occupied one. He was holding a coffee mug and a croissant. I was folding up my *New York Times* and had an empty cup and a small plate with croissant crumbs in front of me. It was quite natural to get the idea that I was about ready to vacate the table.

"Excuse me. Were you about to leave? There don't appear to be any other open chairs."

I looked up at the young man. He was young, cute, Hispanic, and had a great smile and a small body to die for. His hair was black and curly, with a curl dipping down to an eyebrow. He was minimally dressed, with tight shorts, sandals—without socks, naturally—and a mesh shirt showing a nicely muscled, bronzed torso. There wasn't anything unusual about that; all men dressed gay in Key West, and most *were* gay. The interesting thing, though, which caught my attention immediately—other than that he wore the uniform very well—was that the tight mesh T-shirt revealed to me that he had a ring in his left nipple. The signal wasn't universal, by any means, but years ago a ring in the left nipple had replaced an earring in the right ear as a declaration of a seeking submissive bottom—my favorite brand of young gay men.

I did a fast look around the café. He hadn't been shitting me. The only available chair was the one at my table, the one he was standing behind while looking oh so fuckable.

"Sure, no problem," I answered breezily, "as long as you don't mind sharing the table long enough for me to have a second cup." I lifted my mug and looked for a waiter, there fortuitously being one almost at my elbow, and signaled that I wanted another hit of caffeine. It would be my third, not my second, cup of java, but who was counting?

With a smile and a, "Hi, my name is Manuel," he sat down across from me.

"Chaz here," I said. "It should be Charles, but this is Key West. We like to go very casual down here."

"Yes we do," he answered with a repeat glorious smile.

That led into a discussion of where we each came from, how old we were. I was relieved to hear him claim he was nineteen. He smiled when I said I was thirty-one and told me I looked a lot younger—and in great shape—but that he liked older men. I, of course, didn't mention that I didn't think thirty-one was an old man. We weren't yet at the point where I could indignantly say that I could keep it up for hours, reload fast, and achieve three ejaculations in an hour—with pretty impressive wads of cum too. He gave me an "I didn't mean to get into comparative ages" look and then we moved to what we were doing in Key West. I told him I worked for a news agency, which, in loose terms, was true. He told me he was a college student.

"Well, not what you would call a real college, I guess," Manuel said. "I go to the Key West Yoga College of India, over on

Southard Street. But I also do some part-time work with a caterer—serving at parties and such."

"An Indian yoga college?" I asked, making my voice sound like I was intrigued. And of course I was.

"Yes. It's a school of yoga. It helps with flexibility. I do some dancing, but I wanted to qualify as a yoga instructor, so—"

"Dancing?" I asked, fascinated.

"Yes. I dance a pole on weekend nights at the Bourbon Street Pub. Right up the street here, on . . ." He was blushing, as if he'd said too much. He hadn't said too much for me.

"Yes, on DuVal," I supplied.

"You know it?" he asked. It was a key question. It was one of the premier gay cruising and strip clubs on a premier gay island.

"Yes. I go there," I said. "I haven't been there on a weekend, though. Too crowded for an old man like me. But I'll have to make a point now of taking it in on the weekend."

"You're not an old man," he said. "You're in great shape. And you're a real hunk, if it's OK for me to say." He had a forearm resting on the table and I reached over and stroked it with the tips of my fingers while giving him "that" look with my eyes. He gave me a submissive's look back—a slight dipping of the head and looking up into my eyes under fluttering eyelashes. I could feel the tremble in his forearm as I took up a stronger grip of that with my hand.

"And, yes, Manuel, I'm gay. I'm a power top. And you. You're a submissive bottom, aren't you?" I didn't mention that, for the right man, I could be a submissive bottom too—and that, on occasion, I wore a ring in my left nipple too. That revelation wasn't needed in this transaction.

He managed a deeper shade of blush. "How do you know that?"

"The nipple ring. Unless, of course, you aren't following the convention, such as it is. Is it not true that you are a seeking submissive?"

"No, yes. Shit, I'm not good with sentences like that with the screwy negative words. Yes, I'm a bottom. But I didn't mean . . . I didn't sit here to . . ."

"Were you shitting me, Manuel, about not thinking I was too old? You said you liked older men. I heard that. Maybe you didn't think I'd heard you say that, but I did."

"Yes, I like older men. I had an older guy who took care of me, but . . ."

"But no one owns you at the moment? You don't have a master right now? Someone to control you and take care of you and use you right?"

I could see that my calculated use of the word "master" had not gone unnoticed—and, I think, unappreciated. "No . . . no I don't," he murmured.

"Someone to contain you and give you direction? Someone to use you hard—to take advantage of that flexibility that's important for you to maintain?"

"No. I don't have anyone like that at the moment." His eyes were downcast, his trembling had increased a bit. The café was still busy—busy enough that no one was paying attention to us. The world was swirling around us, but we were isolated in a bubble, an island in the ocean of people pursuing their own interests, not ours. I had his full attention. I already was seducing him, fucking his mind. It was something we learned to do in my business. I could talk to him as dirty as I wanted to here at the table, and he would be focused on it, seduced by it. If I wove a web of dirty talk and images around him here well enough, he'd let me do all of that to him when we were alone. I'd been taught how to do this.

There would be a barrier between us and everyone else at the café. I pulled my right foot out of my sandal and rubbed my toes against his lower calf. He widened the stance of his legs. He probably didn't even notice he was doing it. It happened involuntarily. He was opening to me. I could, if I wanted, fuck him right here at the table—on the table, under the table, in his chair. He'd take me here and now if I told him he would.

"This man of yours—your daddy, Manuel, was he a big man?"

"Yes."

"I mean where it counted."

"Yes."

144

"At least ten thick inches?"

"Almost that."

"So you like men who are big—hunky—you can take it thick and long."

"Yes, that's the way I like it."

"Good. That will be good then. You know what I'm saying?"

"Yes."

"Long, thick, vigorous. And you want your man to be a little cruel, don't you?"

I felt his shudder through my grip on his forearm. "Yes," he whispered.

"Here, Manuel. Here's a card with my home address on it. An apartment house over by the Truman Annex, near the gate into the naval station. In case you are free this afternoon . . . now, and in case you lose sight of me as I walk home from here. You're going to follow me back to my apartment. Now. Do you understand?"

"Yes," he said meekly.

"Good. I'm leaving money here, enough for both of us. I'm finished my coffee. I see you have a bit more to drink—and a few more bites of your croissant. That should take long enough that you can walk behind me but not lose sight of me, right? The master always walks ahead of the submissive, right?"

"Yes . . . sir," he said, still looking down at his unfinished croissant. I stood and dropped money on the table.

"If you follow me out of this café, I will be your master," I said and turned and slowly sauntered out of the café and toward the Truman Annex. I didn't look back as I strolled back to my apartment house. I was that sure that he was back there somewhere, following me.

I lived on the fourth floor. There was an elevator, but I was a fitness nut. I had to keep my body toned when I was in Sam Winterberry's unit. But I had time to make it upstairs and get packets of condoms and a bottle of lube out and placed on the nightstand in the bedroom before I heard the buzzer sound down at the street door. I buzzed him in without looking to see whether it was Manuel or not. I was sure it was. And I went out into the hallway and looked down into the well, following glimpses of him as he wound around and around stairs and landings, rising up to me.

I pushed him down to his knees in front of me inside the foyer after I'd closed the door, unzipped myself, and made him service me for a few minutes. This was the mark on whether he was going to be coy or not—or even back out—whether he'd deep-throat me, on his knees, just inside the apartment door. No preliminaries; right to business. After exclaiming how big it was— "Well, I did tell you," I said—and gagging at his initial efforts to deep throat it, he handled it like a pro.

When I knew that we were going to have smooth sailing this afternoon, I lifted him up on his feet. He was a good foot shorter than I was, and his body was small, but it was perfectly formed—just the way I liked it.

"I want you cleaned out, and I want to be clean," I said. "The bathroom is through the bedroom over there. You first in the shower. Then me."

When I came out of the shower into the bedroom, he was leaning in a provocative pose, naked, in the frame of the floor-to-ceiling window of my bedroom, with the golden light of the sun glistening on his beautiful, small bronze body. He hadn't bothered to dry himself off, and I was excited enough to take a fast shower, so beads of water were still taking their long, slow journey down the curves of his glorious body. The pose was studied, but I could tell that he was nervous and a bit scared at what was to come. That was the way I wanted him to be.

I fucked him there, at the window, from behind, as he leaned his chest into the frame of the window, rose on his toes and grabbed the brace for the curtain rod above his head, rested his cheek against the frame when we weren't kissing, and jutted his bulbous little buttock out to me to take the thrusts of my cock up into him.

And I fucked him a second time standing on the floor half way to the bed, with his little body plastered on my front, his legs hooked on my hips, his fists locked behind my neck, me clutching and spreading his buttocks with the palms of my hands, while he bucked vigorously against me, riding my cock hard, fucking himself. He was a firecracker, a regular hot pepper below the surface of his cute sugar coating.

And I fucked him a third time on the bed in inventive positions that emphasized his flexibility and aided my ability to ram him hard again and again and to mine his ass deep. He exhausted me, but after that afternoon, I had to rephrase my pitch of being able to shoot three times in an hour. I made it four with him before the first hour was up.

He was so sweet that, despite obviously being a professional at whoring, he also could take me in a way that made me feel I was taking a luscious young man for the first time. It was by no means the first position on the bed, but when we went into a missionary position, him on his back, legs spread and raised, back arched, and his hands clutching my shoulder blades, he cried out as I entered him and tightened up his channel to make me force my way in. He writhed and cried out a passionate, "Yes, yes, god, you're a monster. You're splitting me. Yes, take me hard, daddy!" And I did, giving it to him hard and deep, both of us crying out as he allowed his channel walls to open for me and his muscles to ripple over my cock and to draw me deep inside.

He was docile then for several minutes, lying still, his head turned to the side, sobbing quietly, the undone virgin. I gave it all to him, holding steady, ramrod straight stretched out over him, buried to the hilt, listening to him sighing and murmuring, "Yes, yes, yes," until slowly coming to life, he started moving under me, setting his pelvis in motion, moving to slow writhing and then, crying out, "Finish me. Give it to me! Cum me!" he bucked against me, with me deep inside him, where I tensed, jerked, and gave him my seed, with him moaning and clutching my buttocks in his hands to hold me inside until he'd gotten every drop out of me. God, he knew out to milk me dry. He had to be a seasoned pro.

I zonked off on my back on the bed, with Manuel doing a writhing cowboy on my still-hard dick. When I woke, he was gone. He hadn't left me a contact number, but I had a line on him. I should be able to catch him at the Bourbon Street Pub on the weekends, where I could watch him shake the cute little butt that I had split with my throbbing cock again and again.

I dozed off again, trying not to smile at the hardship tour to this backwater that Jerry Ortez had demanded and Sam Winterberry had slyly acceded to with a sigh of sympathy for me.

The sugar-coated hot pepper that was Manuel had gotten it good. And he knew he had. He was a mouthy little thing and boy did he know some dirty ways of telling me he had been fucked so hard his eyeballs were swimming in cum. He hadn't wanted to use the condoms and I hadn't been in the mood to insist. He'd declared his was checked weekly, and I knew I had a standing appointment to get checked after every fuck and, unbeknownst to the rest of the world, the Agency had its own miracle pills for such problems—both before anticipated sex and after unanticipated sex. One thing we didn't want to do to marks we were trying to compromise and blackmail was to give them something that would kill them before we'd squeezed all of the value out of them.

"When you got it, you got it," I murmured to myself as I drifted off into an exhausted sleep.

I fretted through the rest of the week, counting the hours before I could make a weekend appearance at the Bourbon Street Pub. I didn't want to admit it to myself, but I was smitten with the sweet sugar-coated hot pepper Manuel—enough that I was questioning who was master and who was slave. My mind kept going to that moment in the missionary fuck when he went docile, completely open and vulnerable, laying there, sobbing quietly, his passage walls pulsating over my cock as I held it ramrod hard, deep inside him, sinking in an inch deeper than I'd managed ever before, the master subduing the virgin, waiting for him to come alive on the cock, which he did. He knew how to do undone virgin magnificently.

When I finally arrived at the pub that Friday night—and then returned on Saturday—he didn't appear. For solace, I settled on another small, cute, young, Hispanic honey named Emilio, who perched on my lap as I sat on a stool at one of the bars, with my arms wrapped around his bare chest, while we watched the dancers on the poles and then the male strippers, and who gave no objection when, after stuffing a wad of compensating five-dollar bills in his waistband, I slit the tight nylon bikini briefs he was wearing along the line of his crack while he moved to the music on my lap and then unzipped and exposed my erection. After I rolled on a rubber handed to me by the bartender, who kept returning to watch us, Emilio slid down my pole and fucked himself on me as we sat on the stool and watched the world dance around us. No one seemed to mind that we were fucking. The bartender certainly didn't seem to mind. He watched us like a hawk and lifted up a trashcan to take the rubber when I was done.

God, I loved this hardship assignment in Key West.

* * * *

The next Tuesday I was back at the open-air café on DuVal at the same rush hour time I'd been there when I hooked up with Manuel. I hoped he'd show up. I didn't have any other way of contacting him than through the yoga place he said he attended, and, not wanting to leave tracks, I'd try that as a last resort. He didn't show at the café, but I ended up having a good time anyway.

The guy was older, perhaps late forties or early fifties, Hispanic, built like a tank, very capable and distinguished looking, and he had a nice smile. I was dressed in the casual office style of Key West—white shorts, white Polo shirt, and sandals, without socks—and thought that I might, if I didn't strike it lucky, actually check in with the office after my coffee and croissant. The office didn't need me. There were too many people and too little work already. Fidel wasn't ranting on the radio as much as he once did.

Even though he looked like a Fortune 500 executive, he was dressed in Key West casual: red gym shorts, sandals, and a black mesh athletic T that showed the musculature of a Zeus. Although he had been similarly dressed, Manuel exhibited as a David. This man's torso was that of a mature man—but a well-toned mature man, and looking closer, I took in my breath. He didn't have the nipple ring that Manuel had; he had a sleeve and pec tattoo—a colorful one that depicted a Japanese Samurai warrior looking down into the face of a vanquished foe. The tattoo flowed up the arm and around to where the warrior's war-like grimace of a face was staring through the captive mesh of the shirt on the man's bulging left pec. If the vanquished foe didn't look like

149

a submission about to be put to the sword I didn't know what would.

He was standing across the table from me. The café was crowded, and once again it appeared my table had the only open chair. He was holding a steaming coffee cup in one hand and a black leather bag in the other.

"Sorry, you look like you're about to leave," he said, looking apologetic. He also was looking Hispanically handsome. Argentina, I wondered. But then Cuba was only ninety miles away for Key West. "Do you mind if I take this chair?" he asked in a deep, rich voice.

"As long as you don't break my heart and take it to some other table," I said, giving him my version of a radiant smile. "Please, pull it up and sit with me. I was about to ask for a second cup of coffee." He smiled and sat, as I flagged down a waiter wading around the room with a coffee pot and received another hit.

"You don't have to be anywhere?" he asked, as he took a black case out of his black bag and placed it on the surface of the table. Once again I sucked air in as I looked at the case and recognized the logo of a gray G entwined with a lower-hanging yellow S embossed on a bronze medallion embedded in the case's top. I look up into the man's eyes and find him watching me closely. I knew what the logo represented—G. S. Instrument's Van Buren sounding wand set. From the way he looked at me, I knew he knew I recognized the emblem.

That was fine. That cut out a lot of preliminary fencing for both of us. "No, I'm on my own," I answered. "I have whatever time free that I want." Even though I was here as the chief of one of the Agency's listening posts, as the bureau chief, I pretty much was free to come and go as I wanted as long as I got the administrative work done. So I wasn't lying to him. I had planned to go into the office from here, yes, but that little black case of his just might change my plans.

"Hector here. Hector Lopez," he said, giving me an expectant look.

"I'm Chaz Findley," I answered.

"Are you a tourist here in Key West, Chaz?" he asked.

"Not really. I've recently arrived, but I'm working for a news agency down here." It was the same job story I'd given Manuel, and it still technically was true. "And you?"

"I'm a doctor," he said, with a smile, lifting the black bag that he'd taken the black case from. The black bag did look very much like a doctor's bag, I thought, now that he'd mentioned it. I gave a little shudder at the thought of what the doctor could have in that little black bag of his.

"That case isn't the normal medical equipment for a doctor," I said.

"Ah, so you recognize that it's for."

"Yes," I answered giving him a level stare.

He shrugged and said, in what could be taken as a nonsense answer, but I didn't take it that way, "I own various other businesses in the keys. Pity that you aren't a tourist."

"Why so?" I asked.

"Handsome, well-built men like you who come down here as tourists are usually looking for one of two things. I'll have to admit that I like to help these men get what they want, assuming they want something very, very special." One of his fingers went to the edge of the black leather case and he nudged it an inch toward me. He wanted me to look at the case, which I did. I don't know what more he wanted me to do, but I stole a march by moving my hand and extending a finger that touched both the case and his finger.

He smiled and said, "That's why I asked you if I could join you—in case you might be interested in joining me. I did mention that I was a doctor, didn't I. I have some special skills. I am quite careful with my work."

"Tourists are looking for two things, you say?" I asked, knowing what his answer would be.

"Tourists with the roving eye such as I saw you have, and magnificent bodies such as I see you have come to Key West to lay or be laid—and with added benefits they normally couldn't get where they came from. And most of them are looking for other men to take their pleasures with."

"And residents down here can't have the same interests as tourists have?" I asked.

"Of course they can," Hector said, with a smile. "Men who come to live in Key West can be connoisseurs in the art of personal pleasure and satisfaction fulfillment. Many men come to live in Key West precisely because of the special pleasures the key provides. I think perhaps that you have done so. You had that look of refined tastes about you when I looked over those at the café. Have I thought incorrectly?"

"No, not at all," I answered. It must have been the answer he desired, but he then slipped a foot out of its sandal and raised it, pressing it between my thighs from across the table. I spread my legs enough so that he could place the heel of his foot against my crotch. He pressed it into my crotch hard, and I grimaced for him, but I reached down with my right hand and held the foot in place.

He smiled again. "Which kind of tourist are you available to be, Chaz? Do you lay or get laid?"

"Yes," I answered and he laughed.

"Do you have any special tastes?" Again, he touched the case containing the sounding wands.

"Yes."

"Do you like to be used or abused?" he asked.

"Yes," I again answered. His eyebrows went up.

"You recognized the logo on this box, didn't you?" he asked. He opened the box to reveal graduated sounding rods— which were used to invade and stimulate men's urethra channels. There were eight of them, slim silver rods with curved tops, arrayed on a red velvet lining.

"Yes."

"You have observed these in use before?"

"Yes."

"These have been used with *you* before?" He closed the case almost as quickly as he had opened it, presumably not to attract too much attention.

"Yes." I was giving him a level stare, and he was returning the same, gauging me, looking for any sign of withdrawal. I gave him no such sign.

"All eight?"

"I believe only six."

"But you would have liked to have taken all eight?"

"Yes."

He gave me another small, cruel smile and then he dug the heel of his foot into my crotch, and I held him there with my hands under the table, taking the pressure and the pain on my genitals.

"I keep a motel room not far from here, over near Lands End beach. If you will go with me there now, I will pay you $200 if you let me fuck you--$200 more if you let me fuck your cock. I will use all of the wands. Again, I'm a doctor. I can be both careful and give maximum pleasure."

I rose from the table and dug into my pocket for money to pay for my coffee and croissant. The man retained a nearby motel room for these trysts. He obviously was a serious player—and rich. I felt myself trembling, my cock going hard.

"No, I will pay for us both," Hector said in a commanding voice as he too stood. "And let us be straight. You will be bound. I will use you cruelly."

"Yes, it's what I want," I murmured, lowering my eyes. For him. For men like him and Sam Winterberry, I would be submissive. The money was immaterial, but the feeling of being a fully used whore was, in itself, arousing.

"You will walk at least ten paces behind me to the motel," he said.

"Yes . . . master," I answered. I had tried, but never been successful, in explaining the psychology of a switch hitter in this business. All I can say is that I found it supremely arousing to dominate a younger man while at the same time found it equally arousing to be dominated myself by an older man.

I panted heavily as I lay, curled up into myself, on the small of my back at the foot of the bed in the motel room. We were both naked. His body was beautiful for a man his age, solid, muscular. My legs were painfully bent and angled to the side, one restraint gripping my legs below the knees and linking them with a strap running around the back of my neck and other restraints on either side binding my wrists to my ankles. I was drooling and biting into a rubber ball mouth gag. I jerked each time one of the balls in a string of balls surfaced from my ass as he gently pulled on it. I'd watched at least six graduated balls, the string having come out of that black bag of his, being pressed inside my channel, which struggled to open to take them—but which *had* opened and taken them.

The third larger sounding rod was buried in the piss slit of my cock. Hector was holding the cock steady and erect with one hand while tugging the balls out of my ass with the other. He was crouched over me, staring down into my face, savoring every subtle change in my reaction to his playing with me with his toys.

Two balls still in my channel, he left those with his right hand now free brought his fingers to the tip of the sounding rod still outside my cock bulb. I moaned deeply as he twirled the rod slowly in my urethra channel, and then I screamed through the gag as he withdrew the rod and my ejaculation came with it.

We held there for several minutes. He was waiting for something. He was cupping my cock, so I presumed he was waiting for me to recover from having ejaculated and my cock having lost its ram-rod hard state. I was still half hard, though. But he was waiting for me to harden again. He had the seventh rod out of the case and I knew he intended to use them all before he was done. I moaned as he started to slow stroke my cock and I felt myself going hard again. And then I was groaning and biting on the ball gag and he was twirling the next-to-largest wand inside my urethra, deep. As he had promised, I was going to get all eight of them. And when he did me with the eighth one, I ejaculated again.

The last of the balls came out of my ass, to be replaced with the slide of his hard cock up inside my channel. He grasped my hips and started a serious, building pumping of my ass. His eyes went large and he laughed when he realized that I was using every leverage I could get, despite being trussed up as I was, to move my pelvis with his—to be an active partner in the fuck and not just his prey.

* * * *

I was surprised when I went to the mail slot of my apartment house on Thursday to find an invitation to a swim party on Saturday afternoon from Hector Lopez. It gave an address on a street of exclusive houses above a beach on the water in the northwestern sector of the key. The invitation was written on stiff

154

vellum in fancy calligraphy. A less fancy note, in a scratchy hand, was enclosed in which Lopez asked me to come to the party to service a client he was trying to strike a deal with. I would be paid $500 for whatever the client wanted. A subscript to that said that Hector would pay more if it wasn't evident that I'd enjoy it so much.

Cheeky devil, I thought, but it made me laugh. It also made me want to go to the swim party.

That explained the invitation. What it didn't explain was how Lopez had gotten my address. I suppose, given my name, which I'd told him—at least the name I was publicly giving down here in Key West, would have allowed him to find me. But I hadn't really been in Key West long enough to establish connections. That he could have found me so quickly spoke to the power of the man here on the key. I put in a call to Sam Winterberry back in Langley.

The house was in one of those rare enclaves on Key West where private residences had beach access to the sea. The house itself was a rambling, two-story stucco and glass modern building with a huge swimming pool and an even more expansive terrace behind it, all sitting on a rock outcropping overlooking a beach. It was an all-male party, which didn't surprise me, but on the surface it appeared to be coed as many of those in attendance were transvestites, some very convincing in their skimpy bikinis.

Lopez took me almost immediately from the front door— with a stop in a guest bathroom, where I stripped down to a blue silky Speedo—to the pool area and, as he took drinks off a tray, he handed one to me and another to a large, bulky man, in the nude, as many of the party guests already were, and introduced the man to me.

"Chaz, this is Daniel Cruz, a business friend of mine I have told you about. And I've told you about Chaz, Dan. I'll have to mingle for a while, but I will speak to you both later. I'll want to know how you are enjoying the party—and each other."

With that, he was off, and I was standing there, talking to a naked Hispanic man who probably was in his mid fifties. He was about a zillion feet tall and broad and thick of body. He'd almost certainly been an athlete at one time but age had been getting to him. He had a beer belly—not a gross one, but a noticeable one—

and his pecs were beginning to be better described as breasts. He was covered in black and blue tattoos, most of which seemed to be crudely inked, and none of it telling a greater story. Still, he was a muscular man, with good bicep definition. and he had what was definitely a redeeming feature. He was hung like a bull. His balls hung low, the testicles plump and distinctive in the drooping ball sac, and his thick cock was making an effort to reach for his knees. At least it was until I was brought forward to meet him. The cock was already at half attention now, thickening, lengthening, and rising up the longer we stood there, looking at each other, neither fast on bringing up chit chat.

We both knew what I was there to provide for him. With each passing second of awkward silence his cock increasingly told the story of where we were headed. I didn't particularly mind. He was a huge bear, but he wasn't exactly gross. And boy was he hung. I appreciated a challenge in that department.

I'd only drunk half of the drink Lopez had handed me—I didn't even know what it was—when the man—Dan—was reaching out with a thick-fingered mitt, taking the glass out of my hand, setting it down on a table at my elbow, and saying, "Hector has such a nice swimming pool. I think we should try it out."

"Yes, it is a nice pool," I said. There weren't many in the pool. The party was already well under way. There was loud music and dancing, and I could already see that there was humping going on on the chaise lounges and even down on towels on the beach. Whatever Cruz and I did wouldn't surprise anyone or get much attention.

"I want to take you to the pool," he said, and then, before I could tell him that was just fine with me—that I was on board with the plan—he clarified. "I want to take you in the pool." In case I didn't understand, he reached out and cupped my balls and cock through the thin material of the Speedo. "Nice, very nice," he muttered.

"Yes, let's get into the pool," I said, making my voice sound breathy, like I couldn't wait to be riding that cock of his. And, indeed, I was looking forward to the challenge.

We dove in and swam around in our own patterns for a few minutes. He was a strong swimmer—strong swimming strokes which I assumed he could match with the thrusting power of his cock. He finally surfaced in front of me as I had my feet down in a section of the pool where the water came up to my nipples. His long, strong, beefy arms went around me and he took my mouth in a kiss. He was a good, possessive kisser.

"Take your swim suit off and give it to me," he commanded as we came out of the kiss.

"You want me to take it off?" I asked. "You don't want to take it off me?"

"It is your statement that you will let me fuck you," he said. "You take it off and give it to me and you are confirming I can fuck you."

I think the whole reason I've been invited here is for you to fuck me, I told myself, but It didn't' say that to him. As I pulled the Speedo down and off my legs and handed it to him under the surface of the water, what I said was, "You can have the suit. You can have anything you want from me."

He gave me a grin and then swam over to the side of the pool and deposited the Speedo on the lip of the pool. Turning then, he motioned to me. "Come here. Come to me."

I swam over to him and he wasted no time in taking me. He turned me belly to wall, my elbows on the lip of the pool, on either side of my Speedo, and pulled in close behind me. I could feel the insistence of his hard-on on my thigh and then his fingers at my hole. I cried out in surprise, my cry being covered by the loud music and largely unnoticed by those getting their own desires on, although a few turned their faces to me briefly and smiled in recognition of what I was getting. What I was getting was having my ass channel brutalized by thick, invading fingers, which were working on opening me up and not caring what I thought about it.

Cruz wrapped a beefy arm around my neck, pulling my head into the hollow of his neck and dug and dug with his fingers, as I writhed under his control and cried out—as much in passion as in pain—at the cruelty of his penetration. I cried out again when the fingers were replaced by the forced entry of the thick cock. He pumped me slowly for a few minutes, gaining a bit in depth with each push, until I was able to accommodate the size of him and quieted down to deep moans and groans.

157

Again, only occasionally did eyes focus on us, and the faces showed nothing more than admiration for the facial expressions and moaning that the big bear of a man could pull out of me. Lopez drifted by once, stopped, looked at us and smiled, and then walked on.

When he had completely cowed me, Cruz pulled out of my ass without coming and turned me so that his back was to the wall and I was facing him. "Feet on the wall, grab the lip of the pool with your hands, ass on cock, and fuck yourself," he commanded. I understood what he wanted, and it was quite OK with me. I grabbed the lip of the wall on either side of his shoulders, raised and spread my legs, placed my feet on the wall tiles on either side of his waist, and waited as he moved his cock into position at my hole. Then, at his muttered command, I thrust my pelvis forward, taking him deep inside me in one long slide. He worked my cock with one hand, palming one of my buttocks cheeks with the other, as I rode his cock.

He held there, rock hard, for a good ten minutes, urging me to take him deep and then deeper, while I huffed and puffed to do what he demanded. Eventually, though, he lost the patience of essentially just being a gigantic dildo, grasped my buttocks and started pounding hard, both pulling me to him and thrusting forward with his hips into me. I screamed for a while, with few noticing other than smiling and nodding their heads and agreeing with each other that I was having the hell fucked out of me. At length, I lost my hold on the lip of the pool, arced my back into the water behind me, and floated in semiconscious silence while he continued slamming me on and off his cock to what was an almost simultaneous ejaculation.

* * * *

I roamed the party on my own for a while, returning smiles and touches and gently pushing away grasping hands. Lopez had told me that my duties weren't over, that Cruz was resting, and not to leave the party yet. I didn't know what else they had in mind, but I didn't particularly care. Cruz might have had the biggest cock I'd ever taken. I didn't mind having another crack at it. Even with all that preliminary digging and opening up with his fingers, it had been a challenge to sheath the cock. But he'd made me take him to the hilt. It was an accomplishment to crow about. And it deserved an encore.

I was walking aimlessly about, reversing when it looked like I was entering the orbit of a big bruiser who was giving me the eye or when I saw a sweet young honey pot I wouldn't mind spiking myself when I saw him. Manuel was coming out of house, hefting a tray of drinks. He was in a skimpy Speedo, but it hit me that he was there as a waiter. He had told me he worked part time with a party caterer.

I caught his eye. He gave me a look of surprise and then a sensual little smile. We both paused, not knowing what to do next. He recovered before I did and nodded with his head toward the interior of the house. He put his tray of drinks down on a table just outside the glass doors into the house, turned, and was gone.

I followed him into the house. I saw him at the foot of stairs leading up to the second story. When he saw that I'd come into the house, he mounted the stairs to the second story and my eyes followed his cute, rolling buttocks. When I reached the top of the stairs, he was standing down a hallway, in front of a door. When he saw me reach the landing, he turned and went into the room.

The room he went into was a bedroom. He was lying on his back on the bed when I entered. He'd stripped his Speedo off and was lying with his legs spread and bent and his hand on his hard cock. I came down on top of him on the bed, slapped his legs even more open, thrust inside him, and fucked the shit out of him.

It was a while before we got to my favorite part—him playing the role of the undone virgin. He was flat on his stomach, angled on the bed, one arm drooping off the side of the bed, an expression on his face that managed both grimace and walking on the clouds. I was riding his ass, stretched on top of him in pushup position and doing pushups on his ass. His moans and groans egged me on to take him harder, deeper—to pop his man cherry. It was all very arousing.

We parted with his promise to come out to my car after he'd finished helping with party cleanup and to come back to my apartment with me. I didn't have long to think about what I'd do with—to—him that night in my own bed, because Lopez and Cruz found me and hustled me to yet another bedroom, one outfitted more in keeping with Lopez's kinky sexual interests.

I was bound to the bed, my arms stretched wide above me and restrained at the corners of the headboard, and my legs spread and raised, manacled by restraints at the ankles on straps suspended from the ceiling.

As if his cock wasn't big enough, Cruz fucked my ass with the biggest dildo I'd ever seen, while Lopez crouched over my chest and fed his cock into my mouth.

"Hold steady. You'll want to hold steady, Chaz," Lopez whispered to him as he crouched beside the bed, feeding a sounding rod into my cock. At the same time Cruz was feeding his monster cock into my ass channel. While, yes, holding as steady as I could, I let my mouth scream the pain-passion of their attention to my body.

The finale was a double, with Lopez under me, my spread-eagled and restrained body stretched on his, my chest pointed up and with Lopez's hands on my waist and his cock in my ass. Cruz knelt between my spread thighs, his knees on either side of Lopez's thighs, forced his cock inside me above Lopez's buried staff and pumped me to a three-way creaming.

"Attend us downstairs in the Library after you've cleaned up," Lopez said, as he unbound me. He'd already gone off and showered while Cruz was still fucking me. Cruz was gone as Lopez freed me, though. "The library is on the front of the house, down the stairs, to the right of the door into the front foyer," Lopez told me in a quite calm voice as he left. No "Good job" or "You were great." I'd done his work, and that was that.

When I entered the library, dressed in the clothes I'd come to the party in, sure now that the fucking was over and I'd earned the $500 Lopez had agreed to pay me, I'll have to say I wasn't surprised at what I found. The two men were sitting in chairs pulled up at two sides to a mahogany desk with miles of surface. A third chair was pulled up to a third side. All of the chairs were facing a laptop monitor. Lopez motioned me to sit in the third chair and focus on the laptop. I noticed that Cruz was now in some sort of khaki army uniform, his shoulders bursting with gold stars.

We watched the scenes being shown on the laptop for several minutes without anyone saying anything: Cruz fucking me in the pool; me fucking Manuel on a bed; Lopez and Cruz fucking me on another bed.

After the show had gotten into the third scene, I said, "So?"

"So, Chaz," Lopez said, "Daniel here isn't really Daniel. He's a general in the Cuban intelligence service. What do you think about that?"

"I'm flattered," I said. "I didn't think I'd rate more than a colonel."

"You seem awfully cool, Chaz—if that's your name," Lopez said, with some irritation in his voice. "Do you understand what sort of bind you're in now? We know you are CIA. The CIA doesn't exactly approve of their employees engaging in activities like these videos show. Look at that poor young man, Manuel. Why it looks like you're raping the young man. He may not even be a young man to someone watching the tape and being told he isn't. He may be just a boy."

"So, all of this is about blackmail?" I asked.

"It would seem so," Lopez answered. The general gave a snort. "What we would like for you to do is to work for us—for Cuba. That doesn't seem to be asking for much to not share these tapes with your employers."

"Is that it?" I asked, standing. "Tell me, how much does Manuel know about his part in this?"

"What do you think?" the general responded and gave another snort.

So, Lopez, who I thought might be an Argentine, was Cuban, and Manuel, who I thought might be Brazilian, might be Cuban. And the Cuban general I never gave a thought to in origin definitely was Cuban. Wonderful.

I got to the door to the foyer, and they both started to rise to, I don't know, follow me? Restrain me? Shoot me? Fuck me again? I didn't wait to hear. I stopped them momentarily by saying, "I suppose I'm not going to get the $500 you promised me either."

161

They looked at each other and laughed. "No, Chaz, you aren't getting the $500 I promised you," Lopez said, and then he turned his head to me, but I was already gone, making a dash for the door.

I had the front door open before they came out of the library. The general was unbuckling the gun holster under his arm.

"Before you think of doing that, general, you might take a look out front. It's just a guess, but I'll bet you didn't enter the country legally. That thing that looks like a derelict barge off the coast? Is that your yacht by any chance?"

Men in black were coming in as I was leaving. "I was a bit ahead of you, Hector," I said before I turned and left. "I called my guys on Thursday, and they hightailed it down here to join the party." I didn't bother to tell the Cubans that Langley wouldn't give a shit about any sex tapes they saw on me. That was my job at Langley—creating sex that looked good on tape. I'd let the two Cuban spies contemplate that one while they sat in a U.S. prison cell.

The next night, I heard the buzzer to my apartment go off down in the street and took a few minutes to prepare as I saw Manuel's mug in the street door camera shot.

I watched from the landing as he wound around on the stairs and landing up to the fourth floor. We'd done this before—in more happy circumstances. They certainly were more innocent circumstances on my part.

He was trembling when he entered the apartment and went directly on his knees in front of me. What could I do? I let him suck me hard and then I took him into my bedroom and fucked the stuffing out of him. It seemed to be what he wanted. It certainly felt good to me.

As we lay there afterward, he gave me an innocent little look with his eyes and said, "You'll have to help me. The Cubans will be after me. They'll say I informed you. They used me, and I didn't know what they were doing."

He'd just done the innocent, open and vulnerable virgin performance for me again that he was so good at. I enjoyed it immensely.

I called out that we were ready, and two agents dressed in black entered the bedroom. I'd ushered them in there when I'd seen that it was Manuel who had buzzed from the street.

"These men will give you protection," Manuel. "They'll take you somewhere. They'll ask you questions. You'll be safe with them one way or the other. What eventually happens with you is probably up to how good and convincing you are with your answers."

He was still bombarding me with innocent sheep eyes when the two agents were taking him downstairs. I sort of regretted seeing him go. You don't often come up against a sugar-coated hot pepper like him. I, in fact, liked him so much and wanted to believe him so much that I'd go check out the next day if he really was enrolled at the Key West College of Yoga in Indian. If so, I'd continue to check from there. If not, well . . .

That left Sam Winterberry who then entered the living room from the spare bedroom.

"I think you're safe enough here, Clint," he said—Clint being my name of the post-Cuban general caper operations. "But if you want, I could pull you back to Washington now."

"No, thank you," I said. "I rather like it here in Key West." I was already thinking about the café on DuVal Street and how I was going to snarf up a table for two the next time I was there when the café was otherwise jammed. "And you," I said. "You starting back to Washington now?"

"No, I think I'll stay here for at least the night. In your bed . . . with you." He gave me a pointed look.

"Yeah, I think I'd like that," I answered. And I certainly did.

~

Close-Up

He wasn't looking. He was talking to a woman sitting at a table across the pool from me, but he was looking sideways at her and giving me a full frontal view, so I snapped off a few photos. The whole effect of him, just out of the pool, body beautiful, with beads of water glistening off his body in the sun. Then a few close-ups. One of his male-model handsome face: reddish-blond hair, square jaw, clean-shaven dimpled chin, gorgeous smile. Another of his torso: muscular, but not muscle bound, beefy for a guy probably in his mid thirties, swirls of the reddish blond hair around his pecs, descending in a line down his sternum and flat belly. A hint, possibly, of a fringe of pubic hair in the same color, but what I could see of that was probably just wishful thinking. And then a close-up of his pelvis. His suit wasn't a Speedo, but it pulled nicely across his crotch. I think in a blow up I could get the curve of the cock and balls.

I didn't know his name. I called him Mr. Wonderful, and I had been fantasizing about him ever since we'd both been coming to the pool of the Beaufort Christian Academy in the mornings before the classes started.

The school had the best pool for swimming laps to be had in the Beaufort, South Carolina, area, and, through contact with the English department chairman here, Kate Hamilton, my publisher had arranged for me to be able to use the pool. Apparently others in town had the same arrangement, as there was a group of us out here swimming laps in the mornings before classes started.

I usually used lap time as a time to pull down inspirations for my writing—I wrote coming-of-age books; two kinds of them in genres I kept strictly separate by pen name. My Christian theme young adult books got me invited to book festivals and bookstore signings. My coming-out-gay books made more money. My publisher wanted more of each but said New York City had become too distracting for me—that I needed to get away.

Taking a long-term rental in the isolated town of Beaufort, South Carolina, off the beaten path of almost anywhere between Charleston and Hilton Head, seemed a good place to get away from the New York swirl.

"It's picturesque; a sleepy little southern harbor town. Movies are made there," Sara, my publishing house representative, said. "There should be inspiration aplenty."

She'd been right. My muse had latched onto Mr. Wonderful, here, mornings at the academy pool. It had blotted out any inspiration I might have for Christian-themed coming-of-age novels. I could feed my gay coming-of-age muse, though.

To be blunt, I ached to fuck Mr. Wonderful. I didn't even know anything about him other than he looked sexy in a bathing suit. I just knew that I fantasized about having him under me and being inside him.

I swam laps to clear my mind and let story ideas filter in. But he was usually in the pool swimming laps at the same time. All I could think of while I swam, with him one or two lanes over, was how many positions I could put him in. That certainly wasn't a Christian theme. And it wasn't a gay coming-of-age theme either. We both were way beyond the coming-of-age stage. Both of us were somewhere in our mid thirties.

Now that I had taken the photo shots of him, I was obsessed with getting them printed. I had already set up a darkroom in the old bungalow in Fiddler's Cove I was renting, because I wanted to indulge in my photography hobby as well as get two novels written to check off my contract with my publisher. Still I waited.

I waited until I saw Mr. Wonderful leave the pool area and then I followed him into the locker room. He was in the shower and I got in there too before he left. His body was even more beautiful naked than with the swim suit on. Our bodies were comparable. We'd both stayed in shape. His hair was that reddish-blond color all the way to the trimmed bush. I was dark haired. We probably had the same covering of body hair, which was slight and more a frame for our pecs and a trail down into our pubes, but mine was black and curly, so more noticeable.

We were both slim hipped, with pert buttocks and distinct hollows below the hips. And we were both hung. We could make beautiful love together, trading off who did what to whom. I was so turned on by possibilities that I had to turn away from him or he would have known it.

I deeply regretted that I couldn't somehow get a camera in to the showers and memorialize his naked body. I dreamed of taking a close-up of his cock and balls while just inches from them and before taking his cock in my mouth.

I drove straight home to the bungalow in Fiddler's Cove, which was south of the Beaufort waterfront and around the curve of highway 802 going on to the Marine training base at Parris Island. The house, a one-story Carolina-style bungalow clad in weather-beaten wood, was on a longish dirt and gravel drive off the road to Parris Island. The house was set off on its own just above the water and up against a bend in the Beaufort River, looking back at the Beaufort waterfront. It was the photogenic view of the town waterfront at various times of day from here that had sold me on the house.

The house itself was both too big and too derelict for what I was used to, but I'd been told that there was nothing I could do to it that would impact on a security deposit and I had immediately seen how a back bedroom would be turned into a darkroom and that a sun porch on the back, overlooking the river in three directions and cooled by the wonk-wonk of a ceiling fan would be perfect for writing, so I took it.

I almost exploded out of the car when I got there and went straight to the darkroom. Not too long after I had blowups of Mr. Wonderful that I could hang to dry and then I went to the kitchen to find a bottle of bourbon and a glass. I took a couple of swigs and then, carrying both glass and bottle, went back to my computer in the sunroom and sat there and pondered.

And pondered and pondered. I wasn't in the writing mood. I was in the fucking mood, to be honest. That was the mood my publisher had wanted to get me out of by sending me out of New York. It had bummed a ride with me, though.

I couldn't have Mr. Wonderful. At least tonight. Maybe sometime down the road, but not tonight. When the photos dried, I'd have some close-ups of him, I thought. I could pin them up somewhere and sit in front of them and masturbate—and no doubt I would—but not before they dried. I didn't want to take the chance I'd mar them with a smudged finger print.

In the meantime there was the computer. I'd already made use of my subscriptions to a few video sites and, desperate, and not having found anything in cruising on the one street of bars and restaurants in Beaufort, I'd even looked into the local hookup sites on the Internet. I'd paid for it occasionally in New York. I wasn't embarrassed to do that if I got value for the money. I'd been paid for it myself when I was younger. Indeed, my first coming-of-age gay books had been autobiographical, going from being a rent-boy on the streets of New York to an escort in my early twenties. There then had been the period of being paid in apartments and cars and travel rather than cash by sugar daddies. Now, at thirty-five, I got it by being interesting or recognized as an author. And sometimes I paid for it.

I would pay Mr. Wonderful for it if I had the opportunity. But I bet he'd be insulted. He'd either want it too or could get what he wanted elsewhere. And to have access to the pool he was swimming in, he probably had too much money already to need to fuck for money.

I'd found nothing in hookups on the Internet in the Beaufort area. There was Hilton Head and Savannah to the south and Charleston to the north. All three were lucrative sources for rent-boys and hookups. I had subscribed to the Savannah and Charleston sites.

I pushed everything aside and forced myself to put in a full day of writing. I denied myself more than one glass of bourbon, albeit it was a tall glass, perusing the hookup sites on the Internet or going into the dark room after the close-up photos of Mr. Wonderful until I'd written at least four thousand words to a Christian teen novel.

I won't say I'm not disciplined. I was able to carry out my daily contract with myself—indeed it was just such negotiating with myself that kept novels of mine in the pipeline well enough for the synergy of moving buyers of one novel right on to buying one coming out when they finished reading the previous one.

It was getting dark when I typed the last of the four thousand words, though, and, looking at the dirty dishes on the table by the computer, I couldn't even remember what I'd fixed myself for dinner.

I stood up and stretched. I was about to turn and go into the darkroom for the photos of Mr. Wonderful. But then I said, "What the hell," out loud to the river flowing just outside the windows in the twilight, poured myself a slug of bourbon and tossed it off, and sat back down at the computer.

I went to the Charleston hookup site. It would show me some photos, but not many and no specifics on the guys unless I joined and filled in portfolio information myself. What the hell, I thought, and opened the application. It wasn't so bad. I could answer truthfully, if generically, and be impressive enough, I thought. I'd tell the truth about the age off the top. No use spinning wheels, lying about that, and being closed down at the first face to face. Besides, bottoms didn't mind going with tops that old. The problem was the other way around usually.

E-mail: I gave it. Phone number (optional): I didn't give it. Height: six foot even. Weight: 185. Tell the truth about that as well. Build type: muscular. When you can say it, say it. Profession: novelist. That was true. That was an "advantage" answer too. Interests: writing, art, music, swimming, tennis, fucking. Race: Caucasian. Hair color: black. Smooth/Hirsute?: light pattern. Cut/uncut: cut. Cock length: seven and a half. Another area not to fudge too much with, and I was proud of mine. Finding by sight that you were off by a couple of inches meant a quick backout. Thick? yes. Preference: Versatile, but mostly top. Availability: Anytime. Location: Beaufort, SC. Range: From Charleston down to Savannah; have wheels and accommodations. Comments: Horny and ready to rock your world. Rates/Willing to Pay: either; I've been paid; I would pay.

Then the kicker. Download photos—bare body shot, head shoot, bare torso shot, cock shot.

God, they wanted it all. And they'd want it real. This wasn't about cyber sex; this was about face-to-face sex. And, it was OK with me. I didn't see any reason to be scared of this. I hadn't had any complaints—yet. I wouldn't give the head shot in New York, but this was out-of-the-way South Carolina.

OK, if I'm going to do this, I'm going to do this. I picked up my cell phone, went into the bathroom, where there was a full-length mirror on the back of the door. I stripped down. Holding the cell phone out of the frame of the picture on a stick, I snapped a full length. Then close-ups of my face and torso. They didn't ask, but I did two dick shots—flaccid and hard. I didn't have anything to hide there.

Application submitted and accepted and suddenly the world of gay male hookups in Charleston opened up to me. There were more than a dozen of them immediately. I'd just go through some of them tonight. I'd get more serious tomorrow. I was being distracted by going back and forth between guys in the search file and guys pinging on me. I got a dozen at once pinging interest in me and that was intruding in my own search of the files so much that I just sat back, sipping bourbon, and going over the expressions of interest.

I was leaning back on two legs of the chair, merrily watching the screen scroll through and rubbing my dick through the material of my shorts from the bluntness of some of the offers, with my cock going hard, when I whistled, set the chair back onto all fours, and muttered, "Holy Shit."

It was him—Mr. Wonderful—but it wasn't really him. It was what he surely looked like when he was in his early twenties. The smile was the same, though. The color of the hair was the same. He was slender, with a twink's body. He claimed to be twenty. Nice face, no body hair, very nice shy smile, nice cock. He looked fresh. From his join date, he'd only been there for a week. His stats showed a high number of interests, but no references. He liked my portfolio—a lot, he said. Both my photos and profile made him hard, he said. He charged $50 an hour during the act and $20 for side hours, plus travel and entertainment expenses, and would come to Beaufort, but I'd have to come get him in Charleston. He was a student—art and dance—at Charleston College. He'd travel but he didn't have wheels. He could meet me tonight. He'd love me to fuck him.

"Holy shit," I exclaimed. I bent over the computer and banged out a bid. "Interested. Rate is fine. I'd bring you to Beaufort and take you back. Soonest is tomorrow, May 10th."

A message came back almost immediately: "How about pickup and checkout at Dudley's, 42 Ann Street at 4:30 afternoon? They open at 4:00. I'd have to be back at college at 10:00."

I answered, "I'll be there. Can you shoot a shot of you naked jacking off to my cell phone now? I want confirmation you are your file photos and I want to get it off on you before tomorrow. $20 extra." I gave him my phone number. It was a crude request, but if I was going to do an hour drive to Charleston, I wanted to know he was serious.

"You first," came the reply, "and I won't charge for my live photo." He provided a cell phone number. I went into the bathroom, straddled the toilet seat, jacked myself hard, took a cell phone shot, and fired it off to him.

It took a few minutes, but he sent a photo back. He had a nice hard on. And he sent a short vid, not just a single shot. After hyperventilating for a few minutes, I took the phone, went into the dark room and retrieved the torso and crotch shots of Mr. Wonderful, which were dry; took the phone and photos into my bedroom; and stretched out on the bed. Bending my knees, I propped the phone and the photos up on my thigh so that I could see them in the background while watching myself jack myself off. Then I masturbated myself to a nice-load ejaculation and dozed off.

"Tomorrow I get laid," I whispered as I nodded off.

In New York, when I was selling myself, I got laid every night. Sometimes twice or three times a day. Here, in sleepy little Beaufort? Not yet.

* * * *

My first use of Ethan's ass—that was the name the rent-boy gave me, Ethan—didn't go real well. He kept clinching and telling me I was too big. I went for some time assuming he was being coy, the way rent-boys are prone to do. Rent-boys should be ready to take a big one. But I decided that maybe he was being

170

literal, because I only got it in a couple of inches and he was impossibly tight and closing his passage down. He'd been fine with the sucking, so I guess my observation that he seemed fresh was more relevant than I'd thought.

I didn't get irritated, though, because I'd been so horny and ready for it that the effort of spiking him and not having gotten any for a couple of weeks had me finished off with just that much. And, as I said, his sucking before that had been fine and had put me on the edge.

I had been so horny for the guy who looked like a younger Mr. Wonderful that I'd changed plans for the day.

When we met at the Dudley's "anything goes" bar and had both confirmed quickly that we were who we'd been in the photos we'd exchanged and that that was just fine, I said, "So, you'll go with me? I had the $50 out in two twenties and a ten and showed them to him."

"Sure, that's fine," he said.

"I've got a room at the Motel 6 on Ashley Phosphate Road," I said. "We'll do it there. Then I'll take you to dinner and drive you back to your college." I picked the Motel 6 because it was only one star and my experience with Motel 6s and my observation of the neighborhood it was in was that we wouldn't have trouble. I didn't know if the rent-boy was going to be a screamer. I wanted a place where nobody would care if he was.

"A motel here? I thought we were going to Beaufort."

"I couldn't wait that long for it with you in a car with me," I answered. That seemed to please him and it had the advantage of being the truth. Besides it was neutral ground. If this went sour, I'd just bail on him.

When we got out on the street and I took him to the car, a new Nissan 370Z sports coup, he whistled and said, "Nice ride, Chris." He said like he was surprised, and I knew why.

I'd given him my real first name, but not my last. "It's leased," I answered. And it was—not because I couldn't afford a flash sports car but because I normally lived in New York City and had no need for a car there. But so that he didn't get the wrong impression, I said. "I didn't book at the Motel 6 because I'm cheap, Ethan. I'll take you to a good restaurant for dinner. I booked there because we're using it to fuck, not lounge in, and we don't want to attract attention. Lots of people use Motel 6 to fuck anonymously in, and the Motel 6 people respect that."

That seemed to satisfy him. And no reason why it shouldn't, because it was the truth. I kept looking at him to see him as a younger Mr. Wonderful, and the similarities were there—the ready smile and the graceful walk.

So, inside the room we stood and swayed against each other, feeling each other up as we kissed. I backed up and sat on one of the beds—it was a double—two double beds—and there wasn't much room after what the beds took up—and he knelt between my thighs and went right for my zipper and my cock. He treated the cock right, although in retrospect I realized there wasn't any deep-throating. Worked up quicker than I normally was—because it had been an unusually long time since I'd had it—I lifted and bent him over the bed when I decided I needed to back up on the work on my cock, pulled his trousers and bikini briefs down, pulled around to kneel behind him, and sucked his cock and balls and got his anus wet and, I thought, open.

When I stood and crouched over him and put my crowned cock in position, he closed right down on me and started the "God, you're big. Too big," complaining routine. He was trembling and panting heavily too.

He obviously wasn't a seasoned rent-boy. Well that was OK. It was just as good to break one in. It just meant this was going to cost me more than the $50, though, because it was going to take more time. That was OK too. I just didn't mean to leave until he'd taken it all. That was the main point here. He wasn't trying to back out. He was making no effort to leave.

He clearly was upset after that. He knew he hadn't given professional service. Personally, I was a bit thrilled I had had a neophyte to work with. I took pains to assure him we were doing fine—and that we weren't finished. I coddled and cuddled him as we sat side by side on the bed. And I kissed and fondled him and exchanged small talk with him. He was calming down and relaxing. He stiffened a bit when I pulled him onto my lap and fondled and kissed him some more—and let him feel I was hard for him.

I didn't want to try anything fancy until he was mellowed out and was opening to me, so, assuring him we'd take it slow and easy, I took him in a bent-over-the-foot-of-the-bed doggie fuck again. I took it slow, taking my time getting in the first three inches and working his cock to take his mind off what was happening in his passage. He struggled against me and cried out when, feeling him relax, I quickly fed him nearly three more inches in a thrust. Then I held there, embracing him and calming him down and giving him time to adjust to me before I gave him the last couple of inches and pumped for a good fifteen minutes like that—beyond his shoot off—before I released into the bulb of the condom. By then, he was just lying in my arms, loose as a rag doll, and moaning.

I fucked him like this longer than I needed too—I kept edging off when I could have come—because I wanted him to be able to open to something this big and I wanted to work him until he was putty in my arms. I kept it hard by substituting Mr. Wonderful for him in my mind. My concept of Mr. Wonderful would be a fuck that went on forever.

We spoke only in monosyllables and surface comments as we showered separately and I took him out to the car and to Ruth's Charis Steak House and fed him a T-bone. I took him back to the motel and T-boned him again myself, doing him in a missionary and making him open up completely to me in short order and giving it all to him. He was fine that time, although he did a lot of belabored groaning and came across as a sacrificial lamb. I was having none of that; I fucked him good.

Afterward I whispered. "You can register that as a seven and a half."

"What do you mean?" he asked. I was still on top of him, still inside him, and we were both focused on me going flaccid—but still filling him.

"I was a rent-boy once too. When you talk among yourself about johns, you'll refer to a date like this in terms of how many inches you took. We mingled pubic hairs this time, so you can tell the guys this was a seven and a half inch date. You haven't done it for pay like this before, have you?"

"No. This was my first time with a stranger—for pay," he admitted in a small voice, turning his cheek to the sheet and not looking at me.

I pulled off him, stood up, and said, "You can use the shower first. Then I'll take you back to your college."

"Was it . . . did I . . .?"

"I'll send you a message when I get home," was all I said. I wouldn't have been surprised if I'd said more that he would have sworn off doing this ever again with anyone and pulled the plug on his hookup site listing.

At the college, we kissed before he got out of the car. "Did I . . . ?" he started to say again before getting out of the car, but I shushed him and told him I'd be in contact with him by e-mail. He gave me a worried look, and exited the car.

When I got back to Beaufort, I sent him an e-mail. "You're a sweet lay, Ethan. I wouldn't have sprung for a T-bone if you weren't. If you're willing, I'd like to see you again—maybe pick you up at Dudley's again next Tuesday at 4:30. I'd bring you to Beaufort this time and take you through enough paces that you'll become a top earner. I will teach you but I will take full pleasure from you. Your rates will continue to apply. Confirm if you're interested and if you want seven and a half each time."

I had waited to pose this offer until we were at a distance from each other and there would be no pressure for him to sign on for anything he didn't want to do. I wanted it to be clear that if we had another date, he would be worked hard.

He confirmed within the hour.

* * * *

I was standing, knees bent slightly to balance his body, as Ethan was arched off from me. His shoulder blades were pressed to the surface of the mattress at the foot of the bed, his arms stretched out straight from his body, his fingers digging at the edge of the mattress on either side, moaning deeply and looking into my eyes with an expression of pain, pleasure, and passion. His legs were hooked on my hips, and I was supporting his body with one hand palming the small of his back. I held a small video camera in my other hand and was recording close-ups that went from his expressive facial reactions to the root of my cock and the mingling of my black pubic curlies with the hair of his reddish-blond bush as I stroked him with all seven and a half inches. I felt like it was more—that's what the sexy young man did for me.

It was the second time I'd brought Ethan home to the bungalow at Fiddler's Cove in Beaufort and worked him over, teaching him how better to take cock and the nuances of giving pleasure to his partner. He'd even improved his sucking technique and had become completely open in taking big cock.

One of his hands went to his own cock and I photographed him masturbating himself to completion. I continued stroking him deep until he'd shot off onto the lens of the camera in a close shot and then I dropped my load too and went down on the bed, dragging him with me to where we were fully on the bed and I was stretched behind him and holding him close.

"Did you get some good close-ups?" he asked in a whisper.

"I'm sure I did. And video too. We'll have a great portfolio for you in no time." I'd volunteered to do a photo portfolio up for him to share with clients and prospects. It would up his rates considerably, I thought. Until now, though, he admitted that he'd only gone with me for pay. I still hadn't gotten him to admit that I'd been the first one to fuck his ass, but it was fine with me just to think that I probably was.

"I don't want to go with anyone else for pay until you've shown me more," he whispered. "I'm so embarrassed I didn't do well the first time."

"You did great the first time," I said. "There's a whole line of men who want to feel they are taking a virgin. If you get the idea you're with one who does, remember how you were that first time with me. Embellish a bit on that in innocence and reluctance and they'll pay you anything you want. And you're ready to go more public now. I'm going to up your rates for me myself. You're a great lay."

"Please. I'm learning so much from you," he murmured. "I'm not going to charge you anything. And I don't know if I even want anyone else to—"

"No, don't say that," I said. "You can't fall for the first john you pick up and give it to him for free. Or don't you need the money?"

"Yes, I need the money. My father foots my college bill and expenses, but I want a car too. And I want nice clothes. And, to tell the truth, there's an extra kick of taking it from someone who will pay me for it."

"Paying you for it is arousing for me too. And I know what you mean about the rest. I did my time as a rent-boy. I valued the stuff I bought from the money I earned on my back more than I did the stuff anyone gave me—anyone other than sugar daddies, of course. What they gave me was what I was earning on my back too."

"Speaking of earning on my back," Ethan whispered. "You were going to show me the position you called the 'rent-boy missionary.'"

I crouched between his legs, Ethan on his back, his back arched and me with one hand buried in the hair on the back of his head and arching his head back. I held the cleaned small video camera in the other hand, taking close-ups. I was elevated a bit on my knees between his bent legs and holding steady, as, his pelvis rolled up with a pillow under the small of his back, he moved his pelvis, fucking his passage from his own stroking motion on my held-steady cock.

I had told him that a successful rent-boy had to know how to gauge his john. Some wanted to control and make the moves. Others wanted the same kind of fuck, but they wanted the rent-boy to do the work. In this missionary position, the rent-boy was doing the work. Ethan was doing it well, but I was of the type who liked to control, if it was my cock being used in the fuck, which was another aspect of this. A successful rent-boy was versatile. To get the maximum money he had to be prepared to both take and give cock. I'd done that. There still were men I looked at and could think of both giving and taking with or just taking. My thoughts went to Mr. Wonderful. He was the sort of man I'd let make all of the decisions, including which of us was going to take cock.

Needing to control when I ejaculated, I turned him on his belly, with the pillow under his belly and his buttocks raised a bit with him on his knees, slid inside him and covered him close from above, my hands grasping his wrists, raising his arms above his head, and my face buried in the hollow of his neck. I fucked him in long, slow, deep strokes. This was another lesson in being a rent-boy that he was catching on to swiftly—to go with whatever the john wanted.

Later, I was sitting in a chair facing the side of the bed, watching him, and clicking off close-up photos. He lay there, exhausted—whether actually or not, I didn't know. I'd told him that johns liked to think they'd worn out the rent-boy and he should cultivate the look of being totally spent. He had the look down perfectly now. He lay there on his belly, an arm draped over the side of the bed, his knuckles scraping the floor beside the bed. He had a beatific, well-fucked expression on his face. I was sure the photos would be great.

"After you've rested, I'll take you over to the Beaufort waterfront and feed you dinner. Then I'll drive you back to Charleston."

"Bring me back here and fuck me again before driving me back to college," he begged.

"We'll see. I'd like to walk you around Beaufort and show the place to you. It's quite an atmospheric place. They make movies here."

"I know all about Beaufort," he answered. "I've lived here."

"You have?" I asked, in surprise. I asked him more about that, but he said he didn't want to talk about it. He wanted dinner and another fuck before he was driven back to Charleston.

"I want you to drive it in me before we go back. You say some guys will want to be rough and drive hard. I want you to drive me hard after dinner."

Sounded good to me, so that's what we did.

When I returned to Beaufort from Charleston that evening, I went immediately to the darkroom and processed the still shots from that third day with Ethan and hung them up to dry. I took the photos from the second session and looked them over. The progress he was making toward being comfortable and proficient as a rent-boy were evident. He wasn't as good the second day as he'd been earlier today. But the second-day photos were sexy too. I took them out to the sunroom and posted them in an array behind the computer monitor.

I already had switched from the teen novel I had been struggling with. For the past two days, my Muse had wanted me to write a "training of a young rent-boy" novel. Ethan, of course, was who was in my mind while I wrote this. I sat down at the computer, opened a new chapter, and the vision of Ethan and of my own training to be a rent-boy nearly two decades earlier merged in my mind. I closed my mind to all other matters and let my finger race on the keypad.

* * * *

I couldn't turn Kate Hamilton down. I hadn't been going to the Beaufort Christian Academy pool for a morning swim for over a week, but I had gone and intended to go again regularly when this infatuation with training Ethan settled down, so I owed her for arranging for my use of the school's pool. When we'd agreed to the arrangement I had promised to visit the English classes at the academy to discuss my Christian coming-of-age novels. She had a class that now had read one of the novels and was primed to discuss it with me. I was invited to the class. And, so, naturally I went—after, of course, I reviewed the book they were talking about. I wrote enough that, after a while, they all seemed to run together. I knew I'd embarrass myself some day when I was in a book discussion like this and started talking about a young guy getting fucked, mixing up what I'd written for the young Christian market and what I'd written for the dirty old man market.

I went and became petrified immediately. I have no idea how I made it through the class or even what I said to the students. I dearly hope we discussed one of my Christian teen novels and not one of my coming-out-gay novels. Kate was all smiles at the end of the class, so I guess I didn't get that muddled.

I felt I was completely tongue-tied, though. When she brought me into the classroom and started the introductions of the faculty members sitting in before starting the discussion, I almost went catatonic.

"First, I'd like you to meet our headmaster, Nathan Sheldon," Kate said. "He's read several of your books and said he wouldn't miss your visit for the world." As she said that, the head master, who was sitting directly in front of me in the first row in the classroom, stood up and flashed a brilliant smile. Mr. Wonderful put his hand out to shake mine, and I limply let him hold my hand for several seconds longer than necessary. It wasn't really discovering that Mr. Wonderful, the man I'd salivated over at the academy swimming pool was Nathan Sheldon, the school headmaster. That was logical enough—that the headmaster also would take in a swim in the mornings before school started to keep in the marvelous shape he was in.

I already had gone catatonic, because after introducing Mr. Wonderful to me, Kate said, "And this is his son, visiting from Charleston College, Ethan."

And it *was* Ethan. It was my Ethan. He looked as shocked as I was, but he seemed to be hiding it better than I did. He may even have gotten an inkling of who Christopher Collins was in his world before I had come in. Now that I saw the two, I understood why I kept thinking of Ethan as a younger Mr. Wonderful—and why I was attracted to Ethan in the first place when I was in heat for Nathan. What I hadn't caught, though, was that Nathan Sheldon was in an even better state of preservation than I originally had thought. He had to be more like forty than thirty-five to be Ethan's father.

Now I understood what Ethan had meant when he said that he knew Beaufort—that he had lived here. He had lived with his father. And presumably there was a mother and other siblings as well. My visions of Mr. Wonderful evaporated. He was Nathan Sheldon, a man with a family, a man who was the headmaster of a Christian school.

A man who was the father of the young man I was fucking and training to be a first-rate rent-boy.

Somehow I got through the class. But when it was done, Ethan had disappeared. I had every reason to believe he had now disappeared from my life altogether.

It wasn't until now that I realized how much Ethan meant to me—that the relationship, in my emotions, had gone beyond fucking or training—or considering—him as a rent-boy. I was dominating him and he had been melding himself to me. He had been completely compliant and submissive. His body melted into mine, and now when we fucked, we fucked as one, coordinated movement of need, desire, cooperative give and take—affectionate, emotionally unified. Could I say it? Perhaps now, when I felt I had lost him, I could think of it more than just as like and desire. I could possibly consider that I had been on my way toward a deeper bond.

I dragged home. I punished myself by taking the dried photos of my third session with Ethan out of the darkroom and pinning them up on the board behind my computer. What I had thought was true. The melding had been quickly progressive. We were as one in the photos of the third session. He was mine. I was his.

I tried to work on the rent-boy training novel I had started. Ethan did run through my mind, just as he had when I'd been so productive, so sure of what to write, previously. But now I couldn't see an end to the novel. I didn't want it to be a bitter one—or even realistic. It needed to be a happy one. My publisher would have said that it needed to be a happy ending to sell and receive good reviews—not that gay male erotica got reviewed much, even though it sold well. But I knew it was more than that. This novel had to have a happy ending, or my own life would be destroyed. I couldn't face life without a happy ending with Ethan.

But Ethan had left the classroom before I had finished. He had walked out. I was terrified that he had walked out of my life.

The horror that suddenly hit me was that the photos of him in coitus and afterward that I had pinned up around the room and was collecting for a portfolio for him weren't the only photos I had pinned up in here. Before Ethan, I had other photos I had taken—photos that I surreptitiously had taken of Mr. Wonderful—Nathan Sheldon—Ethan's father. They had included head shots. Ethan couldn't have missed seeing them when he was looking at the photos I took of him. They must have still been pinned to the boards here. I looked around the room. They weren't here now.

I was mortified. I tried to convince myself that I had taken them down before Ethan had come here, but it was a hard sell—

and, although I looked, I couldn't find where I might have put them. I knew I hadn't thrown them out. I had been obsessed with Mr. Wonderful—so obsessed that I had gravitated immediately to the son who was the spitting image of him at nineteen.

Thoroughly depressed, I turned out the lights, went to the bedroom, took a long shower, and climbed under the sheets of the bed. I reached for my cock to provide me solace. But I was so upset, churning inside, that I couldn't get it up to give myself relief.

Later in the night, though, I felt the sheets being lifted, and Ethan slipped into bed with me. I had no trouble getting it up then. He put all that I taught him a rent-boy need do to conquer a reticent john to full use, moving down my body, making love to me from mouth to cock and balls with his kisses and tonguing and sucking. When I was about to explode, he saddled himself on my cock, hugging my bent knees, holding, fully skewered until I was calming, and then starting to ride me, slowly, sensually.

I could only take that so long before I encircled his lithe torso in my arms, arched his shoulder blades back into my chest, laced my arms under his pits and locked my fists behind his neck, putting him into a full nelson. I laced my legs between his spread thighs, placed my feet on the surface of the bed for leverage, and, with him completely incapacitated, I took over the stroking, thrusting hard, long, and deep up into him, as he moaned, groaned, and sighed.

He gave himself entirely to me. I moved him into various positions that demanded flexibility and total submission and he denied me nothing. I brought him to release and beyond repeatedly. He took it all with no more than a groan and a moan. I exhausted him. We slept. I woke and woke him up fucking him again. We dozed off. I fucked him again when we woke up.

The next morning, with the sun up, he lay, totally spent on the bed, his eyes glazed over, a small smile on his face, drool running out of his mouth, and I moved around the bed, taking close-up shots of his beautiful, bruised, totally used body.

At breakfast, I said, "I'll drive you back to Charleston this morning."

"No need," he answered. "That's why I had come back to Beaufort yesterday. My father bought me a car. I have my own wheels now."

The dominator in me sounded an alarm. It was nonsense, of course, but what was ringing in my head now was the knowledge that Ethan had independence now that he hadn't had before. I had taken on the notion that the money I was giving him for use of his tail was going to what he'd said he wanted—a car. As long as he didn't have enough from our fucking to buy a car, he was dependent on me, in my mind. I was dominant; he was completely submissive.

I became panicked, idiotically so, I know—but panicked nonetheless. I remained outwardly calm as I stood at my door and watched him pat the hood of a small, but sporty Subaru, all shiny and new, get in, and drive off. In my mind I was the one buying him a car. His father, Mr. Wonderful—Nathan Sheldon—had beat me to the punch.

And now, if Ethan carried through on his plans to be a rent-boy, it was because he enjoyed being fucked by men—multiple men—and not just by me. He no longer was all mine. And I hardly could consider myself his master now—I hadn't managed to muster up the courage to ask him about the photos I had of his father.

* * * *

"4:00 p.m. Tuesday, as I know you don't have a class then. Not at Dudley's. New location, closer for you. North from the corner of Montagu and Rutledge, north on Rutledge. Two doors up from the corner. The brick carriage house with the arches in front."

Ethan arrived on time, all questions.

"Later. Afterward," I said, hustling him up to the larger of the two bedrooms, both under the eaves of a half second story. The massive bed took up nearly the whole room. I bent him over the foot of the bed and fucked him. I put him on his back on the bed and fucked him. I fucked him with him slouched in a chair, his legs hanging over the arms, his butt on the front edge of the cushion, and me hovered over him. I fucked him on the bureau against the wall, with his legs stretched out in either direction on the top of the bureau and me holding him from behind and fucking him. I fucked him on the carpeted floor, with him taking his weight on his shoulders, his head tucked in, and his tail waving in the air. His legs were in the splits and I stood over him, holding his hips between my hands, and jackhammering down into his passage.

He denied me nothing. He did it all. He gave me whatever I wanted. I wanted it all. I wanted to enslave him. He told me whatever I wanted I could have.

"I want you full time. My dedicated lover. Not anyone's rent-boy," I said later—after the close-up photos were taken of his debauched, ravished body. "I know I told you to avoid that, but now I'm begging you to do otherwise. I've moved here, to Charleston, three blocks from your college. I want you to live here with me—to go to college from here. But to come home to me. Here."

"Your boy toy?" he asked.

"No, my partner," I said. "My lover . . . my love."

"I would have agreed even if you had said as your boy toy," he answered.

I watched him leave, to return to his dorm room at the college, to pack up his things and return the next day.

As I watched him turn the corner on Montague and was about to turn, I looked up—to see Mr. Wonderful, Nathan Sheldon, approaching.

"Mr. Sheldon," I said. "If this is about Ethan."

"It's not about Ethan. He's enjoying you. This is about you and me." He was holding the photos I'd taken of him at the swimming pool in his hand. I didn't know what to say, and he didn't wait for me to say anything. "Perhaps I should come inside."

He fucked me on the tussled bed in the master bedroom, completely mastering me. I was totally submissive to him, letting him fuck me in a doggie fuck on the bed, me on all fours and him crouched over my hips, giving me more than eight inches. Giving me more than I gave his son. Giving it to me hard and longer. And I melted to it, wanting it, taking it, begging for it, and begging for more after we'd both come.

Then he gave it to me the same way I'd given it to Ethan that night he'd come to me in Beaufort—me stretched on top of him, trapped in a full nelson, my legs spread around his bent legs, him thrusting up into me, moaning and groaning.

Afterward, totally exhausted, I lay on my belly on the bed, an arm draped over the side, knuckles dragging on the floor, eyes glazed over, and a silly grin on my face. My buttocks was slightly raised by the pillow under my belly from the last position he'd taken me in, stretched out on top of me close, holding my arms over my head with hands grasping my wrists, swabbing my ear cavity with his tongue, and slowly, deeply, thickly, mining my ass, nearly the only movement discernible having been the rise and fall of his pelvis. I was drooling into the sheets, but I didn't care. His cum was slathered on the small of my back; mine was puddled on the sheets under me. I hadn't let men fuck me for years. Nathan fucked me without asking for permission, and he dominated me.

If he had wanted to fuck me again, I would have turned on my back and opened my legs to him. I felt the loss that he had stopped fucking me.

He sat across from the bed, in the chair I'd fucked his son in, magnificently naked, one foot casually raised to the cushion, snapping off photos of me in my debauched, ravished state with my own camera.

"Ethan gave me the photos," he said. "I remember when you took them—and then when you followed me into the shower to see me naked. I would have fucked you then, if you'd asked me to. Then, after I asked around and found out who you were and discovered your books—not the young adult ones, the becoming actively gay ones—I knew we would fuck one day."

I said nothing; just lay there, panting. I hadn't had a man inside me for years and even then few were as big as he was.

Nathan continued. "Neither of us minds sharing you—as long as it's you fucking him and me fucking you. He knows I'm here. He's the one who forwarded your e-mail to me to let me know you were here. I have his class schedule. I'll e-mail you when it's convenient for me to drive into Charleston and when I know he's in class. I know someone at your publisher's, by the way. When I said I'd read some of your books, it wasn't the Christian teen book drivel. It was your coming-of-age gay books. Quite some energetic scenes in those. We'll have to try some of those positions out. You described being a submissive so well that I assumed that you let men fuck you. Was I correct?"

"Yes," I answered.

"And that you would continue to let a man dominate you even when you were dominating others yourself."

"Yes." It was a bit late to ask for confirmation of that. The man had just fucked me every way from Sunday and I'd opened my legs for him.

The commanding voice of a dominator. He took it for granted that I'd let him fuck me again. He was right. With him I had been and would be the total submissive.

I couldn't process this now, though. I was too totally fucked. Tomorrow. I'd think about this tomorrow.

~

And I Will Be Yours

You ask what the secret is to my lying down for you, opening my legs to you, pulling your cock inside me, moving my core with the rhythm of you—what the key is to receiving the height of passion, the depth of service, the ultimate pleasure of total surrender to you from me? I don't ask for much; just a few minutes of homage and restraint and total merging of you and me that one time—the first time we fuck.

Just give me ten minutes of your hard, motionless cock deep inside me, shafting me to the bed, floor, countertop, or shower wall, and I will be yours forever. When you have given me that, I will give you whatever you want. I will be your lover. I will be your slut. I will be your slave. I will crawl across the room for you. I will bark like a bitch in heat for you. Whatever you want. You can have your way with me—again and again and again. I will die on the thrusts of your sword, as you wish. Just ten minutes of the shaft of steel sunk motionless inside me for me to build and wrap my passion around. Pay me that homage to the two of us being one. That is all I require, all that I ask. All I want is to be one with my lover for a solid ten minutes.

If you want me to jack you or suck you before that, I will do so, as long as I know you will give me ten minutes of hard, motionless cock deep inside my channel to release and feed my passion, to forge our connection.

When you are in heat from hand or mouth service, with a groan signaling your readiness, brush my hand away from your cock or raise me from where I am kneeling between your knees, fisting the base of your shaft and running my tongue down the side of it and back up the underside and then opening my lips over it, pulling it inside the warmth of my mouth, holding it close inside me, and flicking the slit with my tongue.

Lay me on my back on the bed, floor, tabletop, or grass and then lay me. Stretch out on top of me, like you're doing pushups, hovering over me supported on the heels of your hands and on your toes, our only connections being the flesh of the underside of my knees brushing on your shoulders as I keep my legs elevated, straight, trapped on your shoulders and my pelvis rolled up and your hard cock inside me, deep, throbbing but not moving, my claws clutching your biceps, opening and closing to the slow-motion beat of the throbbing of your motionless cock, the rhythm of my pants, and the beating of our hearts.

Remain there for ten minutes like that, your body rigid, unmoving, your eyes focused on mine as you watch me melt to you and feel the muscles of my passage walls ripple over your shaft. When I tear my gaze away from yours, my pupils have gone opaque; I am moaning in a low, sustained tone; and I roll my head up, lifting my chin and exposing my throat to you, tell me what you want, whatever you want from me. You will have it. If you want to turn into a vampire and sink your teeth into my throat, I am yours for the taking. I will lay there, docilely, moaning low as my blood pumps out of me and into you but your shaft stays hard, unyielding inside me. If you want to plunge up into my intestines then, do so. If you want to shred my passage walls with your cruelty, do so. I will be totally open to you, vulnerable. I will have gone soft and spongy, deep at the center, for you. Do what you will with me. We have been one. We are one.

Having granted me those moments of total, controlled merger and commitment, do whatever you wish of me. You will have freed me to be your slave. I am soft, yielding at the center. Take your pleasure of me. Give me pleasure too, or not. Whatever is *your* pleasure. Start to pump me in long, slow slides, withdrawing entirely to hear my groan at the loss of you. Then plunge to the depths, punishing me deep. Withdraw and plunge. Then again . . . and again, building up speed, and I will give you all the writhing under you, counterthrusting, and cries of passion that you can handle.

Use me, abuse me, beat me, flood me with your cum or deny me your cum. Conquer me as and how you wish. I will surrender all. All I plead for in return for ultimate submission is that ten minutes of hard, unmoving, even if throbbing, shaft deep inside me to make me feel as one with you.

Tell me you want us to come together and then tell me when you are coming, and I'll give you that too. Or deny me permission to come, and I will not. I am at your command. Then, if you dive deep and hold it, still with some steel in it, hard and motionless deep inside me, buried to the root, the curly hair of your bush mingling with mine, I will be yours and will lie under you like this whenever you command me to go onto my back or belly for you or to slither like a snake across the room to you.

Just say the word, give the command. All for just ten minutes of motionless, filling, flesh-enveloped steel shafting me to the bed, forging our bond as one.

~

Shared Crisps

Andy was in a visible huff as he sidled up to the news and snacks rack at the bus station kiosk. He'd left Reggie's apartment in such a rush of packing and throwing insults and recriminations at each other that he hadn't even thought about the long bus ride to York. Now he needed something to read and something to calm his nerves and unruffle his feathers while he was waiting for the bus to pull in to the station.

What was it that Reggie had said? That he rushed to judgments and ran hot and cold all the time? OK, so maybe Reggie *had* brought him Valentine's Day flowers and chocolates and he'd flown off the handle thinking he hadn't. But Reggie had just had to tease him by not bringing them in right away, pretending he hadn't even known it was Valentine's Day, and not saying anything about the sexy red shirt that was so filmy Andy's nipple bars Reggie said he liked so much could be seen and the tight white trousers he'd paid a day's salary for and was wearing on purpose, just for Reggie.

Maybe it was the way he'd said Andy made wild assumptions that made him unload his long-held resentment of Reggie's insensitivity and take-take-take attitude. Anyhow, he'd known the relationship was coming to an end for some time. He suspected that Reggie had known it too—that he hadn't been unaware of how Andy had been paring down what he had in Reggie's apartment to what he could fit into one suitcase. It had been a mistake to move in with Reggie in his flat to begin with. They should have kept separate places or Reggie should have moved in with Andy. No, he thought, that wouldn't have been good. Reggie wouldn't even have noticed that someone needed to move on. Andy wouldn't have been able to get rid of him. Reggie seemed to be a bit thick about Andy's feelings. Well, more than a bit thick.

No, it was better that Andy go camp out with his sister Abbie in York for awhile. It was a good thing that a hospital emergency department nurse could get work on short notice almost anywhere. Andy had had enough of "here." It wasn't just Reggie. Andy needed to burn these bridges down to the waterline. What was it that someone said to him the other day—that he'd gotten to be boring when he once was so spontaneous and fun easy? Whatever "fun easy" was to that guy. The guy, Dennis, had said, "You did it so naturally that sometimes I wondered if you realized you were doing it at all." "You fell right into bed and opened your legs when I no more than touched your dick," he'd added, leaving no question what he'd meant by "doing it naturally."

Andy wasn't about to go there, though. His "easy" days—if he'd ever had them—were over. He and that guy had had a whirlwind thing going for a while that was best not delved into. The guy had "just" touched Andy's dick a lot. Is that what eight months with old boring Reggie had done to Andy—made him as boring as Reggie was?

Andy pulled a book off the stand with such angry force that it and three others hit the floor together. A young man stooped and picked them up. He gave Andy a smile, which Andy only half returned, and put the books back in the shelf for him. They'd been in alphabetic order by author, though, and, as if to prove how ordered and pedantic Andy had become, he rearranged them with a "Marian the Librarian" show of irritation that couldn't have been lost on the young man, who shrank away from Andy and gave a hurt puppy dog flash of a reaction. This was quickly covered with one of apology on his part and another smile.

To Andy, the young man was being forward without reason. There were times—before Reggie, when Andy was in what that old boyfriend had called a "fun easy" state—that Andy had put out signals to a cute stranger. This wasn't one of those times.

So, there was nothing in return signaling from Andy. But the young man was still looking at him with a silly grin on his face. Andy was about to ask, "What are you looking at, Bub?" when he realized he'd left the flat in such a rush that he was still wearing the sexy shirt and trousers he'd donned for Reggie's benefit. Well, we'll just let someone else's tongue hang out in appreciation for those, good ole' Reggie, Andy thought. But he did give a tug to the lapels of his jacket to cover himself a bit better.

That the guy would apologize for helping to straighten up Andy's book toss in a snit of irritation irritated him further, and he blindly pulled one of the books out of the rack—reaching a new level of irritation when he saw the guy smile again—grabbed at a snack package of potato crisps, and flounced off to the sales counter with them. Andy didn't look around to see what the young man was doing, but the image of him flashed in his mind again: nice looking, irritatingly engaging smile and pale-blue eyes under a blond mop with a lock falling down into his face, good build—not bodybuilder good like Reggie's was . . . but why the hell did he care? All men were scum.

Andy found a seat facing the arrivals board, which would keep him informed on the change in arrival time for the bus to York. There would always be a rolling delay in the arrival of a bus one needed to get on—just like for trains and airplanes. There was an attached table in the seating unit on his left, with a seat on the other side. He pulled the paperback novel he'd just bought out of the floppy bag he'd brought to carry his incidentals for the trip and slapped it down on the table, only now looking at the title, which gave him pause and made him chuckle. He hadn't thought they'd carry gay erotica in a bus station. He could tell this one was just from the cover art and because he was familiar with the author. It was *Shores of Tripoli* by Dirk Hessian—randy pirates and such. Andy had read a few by this author and enjoyed them, but he wouldn't have bought a book like this to read on a bus where anyone sitting next to you could see the gay sex leap off the page.

He reached in the open bag of potato crisps on the table, took one out, and plopped it in his mouth. Only now did he realize that the young man from the news kiosk had sat down in the chair on the other side of the table.

The nerve of him, Andy thought. Coming on to me in a public place like this. He could have sat anywhere. But, looking around now, Andy saw there wasn't much of anywhere else he could have sat. Several buses were scheduled to leave in the next hour, and the waiting room was buzzing with other people.

Andy was about to calm down and tell himself that the young man wasn't following him when he looked at the guy's face and realized that he was looking at the book he had put on the table—the gay erotica book that was pretty well known to be that by anyone familiar with the author. The young man seemed to recognize the author's name—which told Andy something about the preferences of the young man and confirmed that he had been coming on to Andy at the news kiosk.

Blushing—and irritated—Andy turned the book over to hide the cover. Worse, as he did so, he saw that the young man had his hand in the bag of potato crisps. He pulled a chip out, and in doing so, their hands brushed against each other. He plopped the chip in his mouth, smacking his lips slightly at the pleasure of the taste.

Andy shrank away from him. The nerve of him, he thought. Taking one of Andy's potato crisps. It's something Reggie would have done without a thought, as well—the familiarity and signaling of dominance and possession in it. A stranger in a bus waiting room. And that little tingle Andy felt when their hands had brushed against each other. What was up with that? Such conflicted sensations he was having. Andy had felt aroused by the touch. To be honest, he had felt aroused by the feeling of submissiveness flowing into him by the dominance the young man reflected in freely taking of Andy's potato crisps. The thoughts he was having were of that "fun easy" period one of his formers had spoken of.

Still, the brashness of the young man without provocation. They were, after all, *Andy's* potato crisps. This was *his* territory the young man was invading. Making a big to do to rustle the bag, Andy extracted two potato crisps and gave them a noisy chomp. There, that would show him.

But what was he doing now? The other bloke was in the potato crisp packet again and had pulled a couple of them out . . . and he was eating them! And the bastard was giving Andy a sly little smile!

The challenge was on. Andy attacked the potato crisps again. A whole handful now. Maybe all of them. He'd taken too many out to eat all at once, so he ate them individually, slowly, making a production of it, savoring each one, making sounds of sheer pleasure as, one by one, they passed his lips and met their grinding fate. He did a sensual job of it—purposefully—moaning his pleasure, teasing the presumptive young man. He'd give the guy a hint of what he wasn't going to get by stealing and ravishing his potato crisps. But then Andy was gripped with the realization that he was being turned on by all of this himself—and not just the tug of war over the potato crisps but also at how cute and arousing the young man was, despite his forwardness and crass possessiveness with Andy's crisps.

He looked out of the corner of his eyes to see how the selfish thief would react to this. The cheeky bastard was smiling at him. Damn it, why did he have such an inviting, impish smile? Andy intentionally had a pout on—the whole thing with Reggie and the impetuous way he was running away. He wasn't in the mood for flirtation with another Reggie. Why didn't he just go away and leave Andy to wallow in his pout? Why didn't he take his cute butt somewhere else? Andy did a double take in realizing that he had, in fact, previously observed and unconsciously absorbed that the young man tormenting him had a cute butt.

The young man had discovered that there was one potato crisp left in the bag, a big one. He pulled it out, and they looked at each other for a moment like they were going to have a showdown over who would get it. He smiled again, though, broke the chip in two and handed Andy the bigger half.

They chewed together, eyeing each other. Then the man smiled provocatively at Andy, saluted him, rose, and left.

Andy slumped back in his chair, overwhelmed by a feeling of exhaustion and completion. It felt almost like having had sex. But he also was feeling a sense of loss. Why did he feel a sudden loss? The forward guy had been just another Reggie. A flirt and a taker. But why did Andy feel deflated as he picked up the paperback book, turned, and slipped it into his bag? . . . only to find, still nestled in his bag, the packet of potato crisps he'd bought at the kiosk. The unopened package of potato crisps.

The bag of potato crisps Andy and the young man had dueled over hadn't been Andy's potato crisps at all—as he had assumed. They'd been *his* potato chips.

Aghast and burning with embarrassment, Andy looked around the waiting room, both wanting to see the young man so he could apologize and not wanting to see him because of the depth of his embarrassment in having run with a misassumption. He wasn't to be seen.

Andy still hadn't seen him when they called the boarding for his bus. He was still feeling a sense of loss when he climbed up into the bus and found a window seat. As he settled in, he sensed someone sit in the aisle seat next to him.

It was, of course, the young man from the waiting room. He turned and smiled at Andy. He was holding his hand out, extending an opened potato crisp packet to Andy.

"Would you like to share these crisps with me?" he asked. "My name is Jack. I think we should know each others' names if we are going to share crisps intimately."

Blushing, Andy answered, "Hi, Jack, I'm Andy. Yes, I'd love to share crisps with you, thanks."

"Where are you bound to?" he asked.

"York," Andy answered.

"I'm glad," he said, "That's my destination too. Do you have someone waiting for you at the station in York? I don't."

"I don't either," Andy said.

Andy, of course, realized that Jack had a hand on his knee. He didn't mind that at all. As the bus pulled out into the road, Andy widened the stance of his legs and gave Jack a smile, showing he didn't mind at all as Jack turned his body to block the view from the aisle and slid a hand up Andy's thigh and to his core. No, thinking of the term "fun easy," Andy decided he didn't mind that at all. After all they'd already intimately shared a crisp.

* * * *

Jack pulled his right arm from under Andy's neck, where he'd been holding the young man to him in an embrace and his right hand from Andy's lower belly, slowly withdrew his cock from

194

Andy's hole to the sound of a deep sigh from Andy, and, picking the package of his cigarettes up from the nightstand after pulling the used condom off his cock, turned from Andy and stood up from the hotel room bed. As he did so, he knocked the packet containing the next condom onto the floor from the nightstand. Leaving it there, he walked over to the window of the small room overlooking the narrow street of the small hotel in old York. He leaned into the window, lit up his cigarette, and peered, reflectively, down into the street.

Andy rolled over onto his back, spread and bent his legs, and played with his cock. He looked across the room to where his sexy red shirt and white pants were neatly folded on a straight chair. Jack must have done that, he thought—while he was in the toilet after the first time Jack had fucked him. Andy was neat and appreciated that in a man—god knows Reggie had been a slob about taking care of his clothes. But Andy hadn't folded the red shirt and white pants. He'd been lost in how good Jack had fucked him.

It had been just as Dennis said it was. Once he and Jack had gotten beyond the misunderstanding about the potato crisps—Andy's misunderstanding—and Jack had touched him intimately in the bus and said he wanted to fuck him when they got to York, Andy had been easy. Jack was cute and had a nice cock, which made it all the easier.

He looked at the nightstand, hoping to see another condom packet there and was disappointed in not seeing one. The potato crisp bag was there—Andy's potato crisp bag—but it was empty now. They'd eaten the crisps after Andy came back from the toilet and Jack had fucked him the second time, taking him up to dance on the clouds just as Jack had done the first time. Nobody had done it better—not Reggie, and certainly not Dennis.

Andy then looked over at the window, where Jack's slim, yet muscular body lounged in the frame of the window highlighted by late-afternoon light streaming into the room. He thought he should warn the young man to come away from the window, as he was naked and someone down in the street surely would be able to see him. But Andy didn't want Jack to move away from the window just yet. His body was perfect and the pose was perfect—

sexy. Andy could hardly believe that such a perfect body had held him close and that such a perfect cock had penetrated him twice and taken him to heaven.

Jack turned his head toward Andy and smiled.

"You look perfect; so sexy, lying like that, fondling your dick," he said.

"Come back to the bed," Andy said, reluctant to give up his view of Jack in the window, but needing him again.

"In a minute, love," Jack said. He finished smoking his cigarette, still lounging in the window, his back to the frame and his hips jutting out, his left knee raised to the side of the frame opposite. His free hand had taken his cock and was slow stroking it back to hard. Andy shivered—they'd fuck again if Jack had another condom packet somewhere. Andy had come away from Reggie's unprepared, not giving any thought that, on the same day, he'd be in bed in a York hotel with a stranger.

The cigarette finished and his cock erect, Jack stubbed his cigarette butt out in an ashtray on the bureau next to the window, came back to the bed, picked the condom packet up from the floor by the nightstand, and slit it open.

Andy smiled as he saw that there was another condom after all.

"Is that the last one?" Andy asked, teasingly.

Jack reached over to the nightstand and brushed the empty crisps packet off the top of his toilet kit. He opened the kit, took out another condom packet, and placed it on the nightstand.

"For next time," he said. "Can you do four in one day?"

"Are there others in that kit?"

"Yes, as many as you'd like."

"I'd like as many times as you want," Andy said. "You fuck amazing."

"You take it amazing," Jack said. "You make love to it while I'm inside. It makes me want to live inside you."

Andy watched as Jack rolled the condom on his cock. "Come to me quickly," Andy murmured. "Take me fast and hard."

Jack came onto the bed, sliding his knees under Andy's buttocks, lifting the young man's pelvis. He took Andy's legs up and hooked the young man's ankles on his shoulders. Andy was flexible and could raise and maintain his legs raised with ease. He was whimpering, "Yes, yes. Do it, fuck me hard."

Running an arm under Andy's waist, Jack raised Andy's torso. Andy arched back, letting his arms dangle to the side and his head arch back as well, exposing his throat to his lover if he wanted to tear his teeth into him and devour him. He gasped and gave a little cry as Jack entered him strongly, moved deep inside him, and began to fuck him hard—just as Andy had requested.

Afterward as they lay side by side, resting for the next condom, Andy played his fingers through Jack's chest hair and kissed his nipple.

"Tell me, Jack, do you find me fun easy?"

"I don't know what 'fun easy' is," Jack murmured. "But I'm glad I found you."

"I could be convinced that I'm hungry," Andy said. "I think we need another packet of crisps."

"Later," Jack muttered. He had a hand between Andy's thighs, stroking Andy's legs there. Getting the hint, Andy spread his legs to Jack's touch, which went up to Andy's cock.

Andy moaned. "Screw the crisps. Fuck me," he murmured. Dennis had been right, he thought. All a man had to do was touch his cock and he'd open his legs. Of course Jack wasn't just any man. He spread his legs wider, bent them, and put his feet flat on the mattress, ready to use the leverage of his feet to move his pelvis with the action of the fuck.

Jack reached over to the nightstand for another condom packet.

~

Honey Tom

It were Franny's idea that we oughta keep bees, so, in the end, whatever the joke is, it be on Franny more'n on me.

"We need more than what we can grown on this land now that we have another mouth to feed," she had said. Her sayin' "we" struck me hard at the time, as it had done ever since I'd asked her pa for her hand over in Pearisburg, where we'd both been at school, she bein' from the flatland and me from the mountain. She'd gotten herself in a bad way and people were talking about me too, and it seemed the right answer to two problems at the one time. It seemed the right thing for us to take up the old Tolbert place too, abandoned since my Uncle Eddie died two years before that, up Sugar Tree Holler on Sugar Run Mountain. Everything around here seemed to be somethingorother sugar, like you could make somethin' sweet out of these mountains. I shouda knowed that takin' on honey bees would be trouble, honey bein' a form of sugar, as we all know.

"We can talk about it if you be wantin' more work, Franny," I said. "I got my hands full adding to the cleared land. But you be right that we need more out of the land than we are gettin' this growing season. We're still beholden to family for gettin' by, and we won't want to be in that way any longer than he have to."

I were watching her feed Billy Junior with her tittie, looking at his little screwed up face again, tryin' not to see the red hair. There was no red hair in the Tolbert family, or Franny's Gleason family neither, as far as I knowed. I couldn't see how people couldn't see it right off. The redheads around in the Blue Ridge Mountain section of Giles County, Virginia, were the Previes. And it had been Jamie Previe who'd been at Franny that fall. Folks should tell how things were right off, I would think. But I guess not, if folks don't see the baby. That's why Franny had said yes to comin' up here in Sugar Tree Holler, high up on the mountain. Franny was a flatland girl by raisin' and she knowed how flatland folks could gossip and criticize. Mountain folk are more for keepin' their mouths shut and lettin' be what be and knowin' that, in most cases, folks are just getting' by as best they can.

Still, *I* could see the red hair every day, and I knowed what was what, and I couldn't feel a family or a daddy much at all—at least not yet. Franny had said that would come in time. I'd said somethin' to my pa, Michael Tolbert, about it when he was helping me figure what to do about the rumors—and what were behind them. He told me not to be a fool about it. He tole me to take it as a lesson and to fight the urge and to make peace with it. He'd seen Franny's problem as a chance for me.

"Make a family," he'd said. "Forget what else you been up to."

"Easier to say than to do," I told him, "under the situation." He'd been forgiving but not understanding. But in telling me that there was Uncle Eddie's abandoned spread we could have—the old, original Tolbert place—he'd told me that I was being given a second chance, a second chance not to be a fool. I couldn't say he were wrong. Somethin' was tellin' me, though, that I could maybe deny myself if I tried real hard and temptation didn't come my way, but was I bein' fair to Franny? Could I ever be enough for her? Would she ever be enough for me?

"She'll have the baby," pa had said. "She'll be a damn sight better with a Tolbert than lettin' those Previes take the child." I couldn't say he was wrong about that either—or that I should expect better from him in understandin'. Some pas would have taken me out in the woods and shot me fer bein' unnatural. And nobody on the mountain would have blamed him.

"Bees don't take much care," Franny had said. "All you need do is make boxes; I'll take care of the bees. Two boxes. I got the directions for that. I already put in an order down at the general store in Thessalia when I met my folks down there for them to give us staples to tide us over."

"You've already put in an order?" I asked. "For what?"

"I asked that the bee man bring us bees for the first hive. Will Lambert down at the store told me we should make two boxes, but only put one out. The bee man would bring bees when he got around to us for the first box. We're not to put the second box out until that one fills with comb. Then the bee man will bring us another colony. And so on. One box will meet our own needs. If we can fill more, we can be making cash money off it. Will told me what to do to bottle comb what's above our own needs and that we can bring it down to him to sell."

"We can bring honey down to Will to sell in Thessalia?" I guess Franny didn't know. She knew I married her out of more than the goodness of my heart, but she didn't know it all. She didn't know that I wouldn't want to be goin' to Will Lambert down at the Thessalia general store for anything. And the bee man. "What bee man would this be?" I asked.

"Why Honey Tom," she answered, all innocent and unknowing. "It's already done. He'll be bringing bees in another couple of weeks, Will says. We need a box by then. You best make two off the bat. We won't know how fast the first swarm will fill a box with comb."

I couldn't look at her direct. She weren't in the know of it. It weren't her fault. But it were her doin' if the temptation of it got to me. She'd be the fool of the piece. She will have done fooled herself.

"I might be out working the field when he comes," I said, lookin' out of the window of the two-over-two wood house my grandpappy had built with his own hands, with the help of a few neighbors. There weren't many around here close enough to call neighbors anymore, not that there ever were. The black hermit, Rufus Jefferson, up beyond the Sugar Holler pools at the top of the holler were the nearest neighbor, I guess. But I ain't seed him for years. After Uncle Eddie passed on, I hadn't come up here at all—not until we needed to hide our shame and from the gossips, Franny and me both. "You might be the only one here at the house when Honey Tom comes in with a swarm."

"That would be OK with me," Franny said. "I do hope it's soon, though. The directions for the boxes are over there on your grandfather's desk. Sooner is better to build them than later, I think, Billy Ray."

"I'll get right on that," I answered. "And then I'll go look for someplace to put down the boxes."

"In sight of the house, I think, but not too near that we'll worry about getting stung when we're workin' in the yard. Will said in a cleared area of milkweed, dandelions, clover, and goldenrod—that's what they like to gather from, he says. As much as they can have near if we want them to fill the box fast."

"I guess up at the top of the meadow, by the sycamore stand, will do," I said. "Just be knowin' that I can't stand around waitin' for Honey Tom to show up. I'll probably be off in the field when he comes and goes. He comes and goes as he likes—and does what he likes too. Always has."

"He's a wild man for sure," Franny said. "But he's a fine looking man too, a golden man, a man standing in the sunshine. Half the ladies up the mountain swarm over him no different than those bees of his do."

"That they do," I said, "that there's a fact." And some of the men too, was my thought—but no way in hell I was gonna say that. I decided there and then that I damn well would make sure I were off in the field and would miss him comin' and goin'. 'Stead of fightin' her on this and makin' her curious, I picked up the paper Franny had writ the directions for the bee boxes on and went out to the wood shed to get to work on them boxes.

* * * *

It were the last day of June and it were hotter than normal for this day. I'd been weeding in the new field south of the house all morning and was right tired and hotter than blazes. Franny was down on the flatland at Staffordsville, with her kin, sayin' it were just too hot and close up here in the holler for her and the baby. I didn't expect her back in the pickup before sundown.

It were too hot to work and nobody were there to say otherwise, so I took myself off to the pools up at the top of the holler. This was where we came, whenever the season allowed, to do our bathin'. The stream that came down near the house came from a spring up here. When the rains were good, as they'd been this year, water ran down the rock walls up there from one pool into the next before it ran out into a steady stream and by our house. The pools were deep and there was room to stretch out and dry on the rocky ledges around them.

I was doin' that—stretchin' out on a ledge after bathing in the cool water—and, I admit, I was naked and takin' care of myself. I did that whenever I come up here alone, as a way to find relief. Franny was of a mind that we could do it—she said she wanted to do it—but I'd been puttin' that off. That seemed just a might too far of this pretendin'. I supposed we'd have to do it eventually, though. I kept thinkin' of my pa's advice to just be normal now—to forget all of that other stuff and foolishness.

Well, I was layin' there, stretched out, pulling on myself, gettin' hot and bothered and real big—I was sort of prideful that way, although there were men around who were bigger than me—not that Will Lambert, but Honey Tom, most certain—and comin' real close to flaring off when I heard rustling in the bushes off the trail leading up to here. Well, I curled into a ball right quick then and looked t'ward where I'd heard the noise comin' from. There had been something out there, I was sure, but it wasn't there now.

For some reason the name Rufus stuck in my mind—probably because the only other one living this high up in the holler now was the black hermit, Rufus Jefferson. He had a cabin not more than a mile from here on the rim of the holler, near the top of Sugar Run Mountain. I don't know what Rufus did to keep himself goin'. He came down to Lambert's store in Thessalia now and again for supplies, but I never seed him workin' anywhere down there, and folks gave him a wide berth, as big and hulking as he was—and black. More of a chocolate brown, of course, but a black is a black. I admit when I *did* see him, it gave me pause, standin' there and lookin' at him with a funny feeling coming on me. It probably was because of what I heard about him from one of the men at the mill. At one time he was a trapper, I heard, but I didn't rightly know if there was a market for skins anymore.

I lay back, but I couldn't get my mind off Rufus. The last I knew, he was one fine figure of a man—big, massively big, but not fat. Muscular. A man there was once at the mill who asked if I'd ever lain under him or seen the size of him, sayin' that when I remarked about Honey Tom. I never did, but it got me to thinkin'

202

'bout him now and again. Whatever he had been doin' for a living, he was built strong. Now that I think about it, I think I heard he was doin' some blacksmithing or at least workin' with bending iron to how he wanted it. If so, he had the muscles to show for it.

As I thought about him—the chocolate brown of his skin, the size of him, and that muscular torso, as I recalled it, my hand went back to my dick, and I lazily stroked myself off again. This time I went to completion, and then I just laid back and took myself a snooze.

When I woke, it was a good hour past noon. I slapped my canvas shirt over my shoulder, it being too hot to put it on and nobody around to care at me not wearin' no shirt. I pulled on my worn jeans, noticing that they were gettin' a might small for me and pulled down at the waist until it was almost indecent wearing them. 'Course it might be too that I was toughening up and trimming down more from working the fields than I had down at the lumber mill in Pearisburg in those after-school hours. My chest was expanding and my waist narrowing and my biceps brought Rufus Jefferson back to mind—or Honey Tom, although I didn't want to be thinkin' of him. He hadn't come yet with the bees, and I'd had the box sittin' up there at the top of the meadow and waitin' on them for nigh on to three weeks.

But just thinkin' about him when I'd promised to keep him out of mind is probably what conjured Honey Tom up in the flesh. I'd gotten almost all the way back to the house when I heard whistlin' and I turned and looked up into the meadow, and there he was. Honey Tom, blond and muscular and wild and untamed and golden looking, was stridin' out of the tree line near where I'd set out the bee box and into the sunshine, which made him glow. He was carrying a cut from a tree, one with a hollowed-out section in it, and he was carrying it right gingerly. I could tell the hollow had a bee hive in it, because the bees was swarming all around him and buzzin' something fierce. He was walking steady like, like he knew exactly what he was doin' and could get away with it with them bees—and he was, in fact, doin' that. The bees was all over him— in his tossed blond curls and his close-cropped beard and crawlin' all up his naked, tanned, and muscular torso. But nary a one was stinging him. It was like they knowed he was taking them to a better home than where he'd found them. Everyone said it was a gift he had, and I guess it was, because that's what he'd become—a honey man.

The gift weren't just with bees either, I could tell a person. He had a way of calming a person and getting them to go where he wanted them to be and doing what he wanted them to do.

Even though he didn't look my way at first, he knowed I was here, stopped in my tracks near the house, just in my low-riding jeans. I had the thought that I should pull my shirt off my shoulder and put it on and cover myself. I knew how he sometimes before got when he saw me all naked. But I was mesmerized in watching him get that there tree section put nicely into the box I'd built and settling those bees—all without getting stung. Then he looked my way, and Honey Tom were watchin' me more than he were watchin' what he was doin' in putting those bees to bed. It was like he could do the bee work in his sleep, and he probably could. But it gave me chills that he was watchin' me while he worked—giving me more attention than he were giving them bees.

He didn't call out or nothing, but I knowed from the way he were looking at me that he wanted me to come to him. So I did. When I got there, he put a hand on the small of my back and said, "Billy Ray."

I answered with a "Honey Tom."

It took no more than that to bring us back together as before. Even with all the changes—me marryin', Franny having what was called our baby, the move up the mountain to here—all he'd needed to do was come out of that there tree line, will me to come to him, and, when I did, say my name, and I would let him do what he wanted to me. He did say my name, and then he did do it all to me.

"I brought you your bees. When you see hive through the slit near the top of the box, you put out another box and I'll bring you more. They get confused if they have more than one choice of box unless another colony is in the other box."

"How will we let you know that—?" I said, my voice shaky—not because of the bees buzzing around us both but because of that hand he had palmed on the small of my back—on the flesh of my spine, running fingers below the dip in my waistband at my butt. He had the tip of a finger on the rim of my asshole and I couldn't think of nothin' but it pushin' inside me— and when he'd get to doin' that.

"I will know when to come," he said. "Now—"

"I meant for Franny to be here when you came," I said. "I didn't mean to be here to meet you. This was Franny's idea and arrangement. This weren't my doing. Franny's—"

"Franny's down at her folks in Staffordsville till at least dark, I know," he said.

I didn't ask how he knew. I didn't want to follow that line of discussion.

"I don't know what we owe you for this or when we can pay you," I said.

"You know what I want in payment," he said, and his finger did push inside me then, and the heel of his hand was pressing on my back, turning me toward the house, showing me what was next.

"You know we can't, Honey Tom. That ship has sailed. I'm a married man now. No more of that foolishness for me."

"You say that, but your body tells me different," Honey Tom said. His other hand was on my crotch, feeling me up, finding me hard. Hard for him. "We can sail that ship again anytime I come here and have the notion. Come on down to the house with me."

And so I did. I didn't see no other choice. I didn't see no other choice from the first time Franny said Honey Tom would be coming up here on the mountain to us. Seems my mind and body couldn't agree on wantin' the choice or not.

I knelt between his spread thighs as he sat on the corncob mattress in the bed Franny and the baby slept in. I slept on a pallet in the other room upstairs. The light in the room was splotchy, bright on the floor where the windows let the sun in, but dim over here by the bed. His dick tasted sweet, the first of the essence coming out of it as I sucked it even sweeter. That's what I'd remembered the most about Honey Tom—the sweet taste of his dick, leaving the idea that that was what he mostly ate—the honey that he dealt in. As I sucked him, he leaned over my back, his fingers pushing under the waistband of my jeans in back again and

205

reaching all the way to my hole—entering me and opening me to him, rubbing on that nub there inside that made my juices rise.

When he wanted it, he pulled me up, upending me, till I were streaming down between his legs to my head bein' on the floor, lookin' up the line of my trembling body at him, my arms above my head, fingernails clawin' at rough floorboards. My legs were bent on either side of his torso, feet pushin' into the mattress, as he held my crotch up to his face by cupping and spreading my ass cheeks, the smooth blondness of his beard tickling my tender ass flesh, and, taking his time as he pleased, he done everything he wanted to do with my dick, balls, and asshole with his mouth.

When I were moaning and beggin' for everything, wantin' and needin' his dicking, he done everything with me, givin' me the dick, deep. Pushin' in hard, stretchin', and puttin' me full of both pain and pleasure, the first time with me upended that way, body arching back t'ward the floorboards. Him grabbing me at the waist and pullin' me on and off the dick, on and off the dick, on and off the dick. Diggin' deeper, throbbing thicker, and me bein' wild, cryin' because of the pain and filling of it, but cryin' out for it like I was possessed, like he couldn't dig deep enough, couldn't fill out thick enough inside me. As always before I gave him all he wanted of me, and were beggin' for more. And he took more and then took more again.

"Remember this, Billy Ray?" he muttered.

"Shit yes, I remember it all," I cried out.

"You been missin' this, Billy Ray?"

"Fuck, yes, don't stop. Give it to me hard, Honey Tom!"

Plowin' me hard, deep, long, lickety-split fast, then slow, then fast again. The two of us workin' together as one, groanin', gruntin', rutting animals of the wild. No, after him getting' goin' good, like angels dancing on the clouds, golden Honey Tom the angel Gabriel, playin' me like a harp. Me singin' with the angels, releasing my seed with a cry of passion, "Fuck! Shit yes!" Honey Tom goin' so deep inside me with a growl deep in his throat and then a long, drawn-out sigh as he flowed in spurts.

Fuckin' me real good.

"You are the sweetest lay," Honey Tom murmured when he stopped jerking jism out and his muscles relaxed into a calmness.

It weren't true that what I remembered most about Honey Tom was the sweet taste of his dick. What I remember most is that he had the biggest, longest, thickest dick I'd ever taken inside me before. And he put it to me directly, makin' no bones nor nicety 'bout it. And I just lay back there on Franny's corncob mattress when he done me the second time and spread and bent my legs for him and moaned as he slid it all inside me, me all open to him this time. Like we'd done this forever and were meant to be doin' it for that long. He held there deep inside me until I begged him to do it to me. And then he started his hips moving and he did it to me, and did it to me, and did it to me.

We dozed a might and I woke to knowing that Honey Tom had the need again. He were hard and he were pulling on my dick, which were what woke me.

"You are one sweet lay, Billy Ray Tolbert," he whispered to me, like he couldn't say it enough. "You always was. You take it better than any lad on the mountain. This is your nature. This is what you were put on earth for—to give men the pleasure of putting it in you. You can set up family up here in the nowhere holler—that be very nice—but don't you go denying your calling."

"My pappy says it's for a fool—to be drawn to it. 'Don't you go bein' no fool no more,' he tells me."

"How do you feel with it inside you, deep in your sweet passage? Do you feel like a fool when I put it inside you, deep?"

"You know how I feel, Honey Tom. I feel like the most golden man on earth wants me, and I feel like one with him when he's inside me. You gonna put it to me again? You done me for hours, it seems like."

"You're gonna put it to yourself, Billy Ray Tolbert. You're gonna declare it as your nature—something natural for you that you won't fight. You get that sweet body of yours on top of me now. Fuck yourself silly."

I did as he demanded, him turning onto his back, his hands helping me get settled on his shaft, me swinging a leg over his hips and laying my palms on his chest as he held himself in position.

207

With a big sigh and a groan, I came down on him, taking him all the way inside me, hard and thick and throbbing. Me being measured to size of him now, sliding down easy on the dick with the help of the honey cum he'd put inside me earlier—and then put inside me again and again.

I rose and fell on the staff, taking him deep, with him workin' my dick with one hand and rolling and squeezing my balls with the other. When I had released on his flat belly, he took over the fuck. He grabbed my hips 'tween his hands and slammed me up and down on his cock, with me writhing on top of him, leaning back against his raised thighs, his feet flat on the mattress, pushing off his feet to thrust hard up inside me. Again he gave me a blast of his honey and we both collapsed, me on top of him, both of us breathing hard and sighing deeply.

"Woowie, you was hungry for it, Billy Ray," he murmured in my ear.

"It's been so long, Honey Tom. So long since I been laid out good like that. I tried to put it behind me. I surely did."

"It don't need to be that long. This is your nature. This is what you was meant for, Billy Ray Tolbert," he murmured. "To bring pleasure to men like this. If it makes you a fool, as your pappy says it do, why then be the best fool in Giles County. Just don't go on foolin' yourself by trying to deny who you are and what you want and need."

The sunlight through the windows had dimmed and moved together until both slices of light was picking us out—Honey Tom and me—on Franny's bed before he was finished moving inside me. He had seeded me again and again, and I had laid there and taken it and asked for more, moving from gripping his buttocks to hold him inside me as he convulsed and released his seed, to digging my fingernails into his shoulder blades as he dug deep and fast inside me. I were filled to the brim with his honey and humming for it.

He left, whistling, before dark, not long before I heard the motor of the pickup returning. It was like Honey Tom was in tune with the whole world in ways that others were not. He knew when to come. He knew I would lay down for him. He knew how to work my body up to beggin' for him. He knew when to come inside me. And he knew when to leave.

I walked to the door of the house, naked, and watched him melt back into the tree line.

As he passed by me in the doorway, he turned and gave me a kiss on the lips. He tasted of clover-fed honey, which were natural, but I said what needed to be sayin'. "That's got to be the end of it, Honey Tom. Give some warning next time when you come and I'll be away in the field. That were nice, it were, but I got to stop playin' the fool."

He gave me a knowing little smile and said, "I'll be back, and you'll be here for me when I come."

I lowered my head at that, not wanting him to look into my eyes—into my soul. After he'd disappeared into the trees, and as I turned to enter the house and to fix up the signs of Franny's bed having been used, a bee stung me on the ass. He had left me something to remember him by.

I should have been satisfied, completed. But I wasn't. I was keyed up. I hadn't had it since before Franny and I had gotten married. It was like Honey Tom had pulled me back into the need for it after I had dulled my senses and needed nothing more than to pull on myself for my own release. Now I needed more. I had got some. Honey Tom had fucked me for more than an hour and had tired me out for then—but he'd keyed me up for now, when Franny was back home, all smiles because of her time with her family.

"Put the baby in the cradle tonight, not in the bed," I whispered to her as she was preparing Billy Junior for the night. She turned to me with a questioning look, but when I ran my fingers into her hair and brought her face close to mine, she was as much into the kiss as I was—our first kiss since the one we done during the ceremony because those watching expected it of us.

"You must have missed me today," she murmured after we kissed. She was smiling. She'd been sayin' that she wanted this— that we might as well, since we was married.

"I did. I missed you in the worst way," I answered, almost choking on the words. I hadn't meant it as some sort of joke, but I knew it had a meaning that she wouldn't know—or, probably, appreciate.

But then maybe she would have, because she certainly showed that she appreciated me coming to her bed, to the mattress stuffed with corn cobs, for the first time. And that I covered and fucked her for the first time as well. And then, before the light of day, fucked her again.

I didn't tell Franny about the bee sting or tend to it myself—I could not have reached it and I could not explain to her how I would have been bare assed to be stung there. It did bother me as I fucked her, but I think it also helped me through the awkwardness of fucking a woman—feeling the sting kept me thinking of moving with Honey Tom in a fuck and I could fantasize about him doing me while I were moving on top of and inside Franny in the dark. So much did I feel the presence of Honey Tom in the fuck—and, I don't know, his approval and encouragement, I guess—that I imagined I felt him next to us, his hand on the small of my back, pushing me forward when I was thrustin' inside Franny.

"That's it. That's it. Oh, Sweet Jezzusss, I think you done it, Billy Ray," Franny cried out as I let loose inside her and she dug her fingernails into my shoulder blades.

* * * *

Our daughter—*our* daughter, not Franny's and someone else's daughter—was born in the early morning of April 1st. I'd managed to get Franny down to Staffordsville in time—and to her people—to help Franny in the birthing. God knows there twern't nothin' I coulda done to help her with that up there in Sugar Tree Holler. Billy Junior was down there as well. It were a long night, and, after the birthing, I came on home, as there were planting to do and I'd noted that the top of the bee box was bein' lifted up by the overflow of the hive. I'd put the second box out and, after I'd had a rest, was fixin' to go down to Thessalia to ask Will Lambert at the store to let Honey Tom know we was ready for another swarm of bees. I hadn't wanted to eyeball Will direct in case the old yearnings hit, but there wasn't any way out of it. Franny weren't gonna be goin' anywhere anytime soon, not while she was being tied down with two younguns. I'd go back in four days to get Franny and our little ones—our boy and girl—to bring them back home.

As I pulled into the yard in the pickup, though, there, comin' outa the trees up by the bee boxes, gingerly carrying a hollowed out section of tree and with bees swarming all over his head and bare torso, was Honey Tom. Just as he said he would, he knew when we'd be ready for another hive.

He also knew when Franny wouldn't be home.

I was exhausted from the panicked ride down the mountain and the hours of fretting as Franny was giving birth. There was nothing more I wanted than a cold beer from the house and to fall into the sack. Instead, I got out of the truck and walked to Honey Tom and stood there, submissively, beside him, as he settled the new bees in the second box. 'Course I went hard for him, and 'course, he knowed I was hard for him.

After he bedded the bees, he turned to me, put a hand on the small of my back, and pulled me into him. He kissed me, all out in the open like that, and I returned the kiss, hungrily.

"Come into the house with me," I murmured, in resignation and want, not bein' able to help myself from being a fool for him.

"Walk up to the pools with me," he said. His hand on the small of my back guided me which way he wanted me to go, and I found we was walking up the path in woods, to the top of the Sugar Tree Holler, where the spring-fed pools was, the water falling from one rock-carved pool to the next lower one, on the stream's way down past the house.

We weren't alone when we got to the pool. I could hear him hummin' and movin' around in the pool as we approached— Rufus Jefferson, the big black hermit who lived in the log cabin up here abouts.

"Maybe we should go back down to the house," I said, as we drew near. "Someone's already at the pool."

"I know," Honey Tom said. "It's Rufus, who lives up here. I told him to meet us here. Rufus takes pleasure in men too. Me and Rufus are gonna do you together."

And so they did.

Upon hearing us approach, Rufus rose up out of the pool water, naked, all chocolate brown and hard bodied—and with a big ole erect thick and long cock, a cock to rival Honey Tom's and any man's in Giles County, and a big ole grin on his face. I couldn't stop myself from stoppin' and lookin' and shudderin'. He were chocolate brown across his big, muscular body, exceptin' that for his dick and balls. They was black, black, black, and huge. He were hard and standin' proud, the head of his dick pushed out all pinkish and purplish. I started to tremblin' then and there, knowin' that he were gonna put that black snake inside me.

With a moan, I turned, thinkin' of getting' away, goin' on down the mountain as fast as I could move my bare feet. But Honey Tom held me fast and then pushed me to my knees, holding me fast, as Rufus took up his place in front of me and held my head as I took that old black snake of his in my throat. He tasted tangy, not honey sweet, like Honey Tom did, but I moaned a moan of want for him as I took it all inside my mouth.

They lay me out on my back on a rock ledge hangin' over the pool, Honey Tom saddled over my chest and me sucking his sweet-tasting dick and Rufus crouched in the pool between my spread thighs, sucking on my dick until he wanted more and stood up in the pool, hooked my ankles on his shoulders, fed that big ole black snake of his inside me, and fucked me good. I didn't fight him any; I bucked against him in rhythm to his thrusts as I got all het up in the dicking. After Rufus done plowed me good, Honey Tom turned me on my belly and stood where Rufus had been and fucked me with his big shaft while Rufus sat, legs folded under him at my head, with my head in his lap, and his dick down my throat.

Through it all, I was cooperative and willing and giving them anything they wanted—and they wanted it all. I wanted it all done to me, and they obliged. They did it all but one thing—one thing I kept thinkin' of them doin' since there were two of them at me up here.

That big black cock really did me. Rufus filled me to full stretch and he knew just what to do to get my wall muscles to shimmerin' and clutchin' at the thick black snake, making love to it as it made love to me—and filled me with its cum, the tangy taste

212

of it mixing with the sweet honey of Honey Tom's seed inside me, creating a rich slick for the men to take turns slip slidin' away inside me, me jacking off nearly as often as they done together. Completely drained, fully satisfied, moaning for them and clutching at their asses and their shoulder blades, beggin' them to do it again.

There for some minutes, I thought as how they'd really do me together—that other thing I'd been thinkin' about—both pushing inside me at once, but they didn't do that then. They saved that for later, in Rufus's cabin, when I was a full slave to them, opened up to them completely, and wantin' everythin' they could do to a man.

"You are such a little whore," Honey Tom said, with a laugh, and that I couldn't deny.

Afterward, Honey Tom said, "I know you'll be wanting it more often than I can come by and give it to you. That's why I talked it over with Rufus here. You can have as much as you want from Rufus—and from me when I'm here. You can have whatever you want, as much as you want. We are going up to Rufus's cabin now, where we are gonna do you again—and again. You can stay as long as you want. Forever, if you want. As long as you stay, though, you will be a slave to Rufus's cock, and mine when I am there."

He was good to his word. They held me there in Rufus's cabin for the next two days, doin' me in turn—in all positions and all places: In Rufus's bed, on the cabin floor, on his eating table, and bent over the railing on his front porch. And then, as I had been thinkin' as soon as they was two, workin' on me in the pools, they did me together, havin' theyselves a Billy Ray sandwich. And I liked it that way too.

I loved it all. Honey Tom had been right. I had been made for this—to serve the pleasure of men, and both Honey Tom and Rufus knew how to give pleasure as well as how to take it.

Increasingly as time went by, though, the words of my pa rang in my ears those first days of April, while I was stretched out up here in Rufus's cabin on my back with my legs open and Honey Tom lying on me, working his dick inside me, and then Rufus at me, stretching my passage with his big black dick, and then Honey Tom inside me . . . and then me between them, Rufus at my back, Honey Tom at my front, both of them sticking it inside me together, all of us gruntin' at the effort and strain of it. I heard my pa sayin' I would just be a fool to abandon what had been given me to pursue fleeting, sinful pleasure—to be used by other men's lust. What I could give a man and be to a man would only be for a few years, while I was young and supple, and good-lookin'. Family, with a grateful wife and children to blossom into grandchildren, and so forth, down through the ages would be a forever pleasure.

On the morning of the third day, I got up sore from the bed, pulling myself out of the entangling arms of a hunk of a man on either side of me. Honey Tom woke up and smiled at me. Rufus continued to snore. He had been the one to fuck me hardest and longest in the night, and now was enjoyin' the reward of a deep sleep.

As I was pullin' my jeans on—the first time in two days, Honey Tom said, "You're goin' back down to the house, ain't you?"

"Yes, Honey Tom, I got to. I took on responsibilities. I can't be a fool forever."

"There are ways of having your pie and eating it too, Billy Ray," he said. "You can have what you have there and here as well. I do believe you'll find all will be more content if you do—even Franny. You'll be wantin' to add hives, and I'll be bringing bees to you ever once in a while. I'll know when to come. I'll know with Franny ain't here. And you know you'll lie down for me on those times. But there's Rufus too. Anytime you need it, you can come to Rufus. Rufus will give it to you good. So, you go on now, and you raise your family. But you get your pleasures otherwise too. It's in your nature. And it's in Rufus's and my natures to want to git inside you when we can and the chance is there. Can't none of us escape or fight that."

Then he turned over on his stomach, put an arm over Rufus's chest, and looked away from me. I didn't look back as I walked out of the cabin.

* * * *

"You were supposed to come tomorrow," Franny said when she came out on the porch of her parents' house, baby held against her shoulder, as I got out of the pickup. "Did you forget the day?"

"I couldn't stay away from our family a day longer," I said as I climbed up on the porch and Franny turned her shoulder to give me a good look at the baby. I could see it hadn't been missed on her that I'd said 'our family' rather than 'your son.' It might have been the first time I'd done that—made all three of them my family. Nothing that happened on the mountain with Honey Tom and Rufus Jefferson changed what havin' this baby Franny and me shared meant to me. I was a daddy now in my own right and a husband too. And I were feelin' I needed to be Billy Junior's daddy too. I knew he looked up to me as his daddy, and it 'twernt his fault I weren't his natural pa. Honey Tom had made a point to tell me that I could run my life on two separate tracks and that, in fact, it would be better for everybody if I did.

For a while I'd thought that wouldn't be fair to Franny. But me and Franny had been sittin' better with each other after Honey Tom came back and got to me. We'd been havin' at it off and on too. I were comfortable doin' it with Franny now. I got hard fine with her now, and the plowin' of her were easy and pleasurable enough. She sure as hell wanted it whenever I hankered to do it.

We'd created this baby together. Somehow havin' Honey Tom on the side—and now the offer of Rufus when I needed it that way—had calmed me down and made me more of a family man than before. And if goin' back with men occasionally made me a fool, like my daddy said it would, at least I was a fool who knew it. Talkin' about April fools, that would be Franny, not me. She had brought it on—what led to Honey Tom getting his prick inside me again and now Rufus as well. She's the one who brought Honey Tom back into my life and jammed up my ass. Franny was the one playin' the trick that she didn't know were a trick and that bounced back at her. And it more than likely was gonna work out to her benefit anyhow. Better she never know what an April Fool's joke it had been.

"I can stay the night and we'll go home tomorrow as planned," I told her. 'Home.' Sayin' that meant something had changed in our life, and Franny had picked up on that too.

"There's just the bed I'm in at my parents' house," she said, lookin' at me real hard. I'd been in her bed for fuckin' off and on since that last day in June when Honey Tom visited and I fucked her after—the night when we probably made this baby, the night she kept sayin' it happened and did her countin' of time from—but I hadn't moved in on her completely. Franny had made clear that I was welcome to, though.

"Well, I figure we need other space for the younguns from now on, so I'll move to your bed when we get home. I understand we can't do nothing for a while, but you might—if you want to—tell me when we can."

"I'll be sure to do that," Fanny said, with a deep smile. "It won't be long," she added, holding that smile. Then she went on. "Good thing we're here. Me and my parents have been talking names for the baby. You have any ideas on that? You get a big vote on that."

I thought for a minute, and a little mischief came into my head, something April foolish in keeping with the baby having popped out on that date. I bet she'd grow up to be a mischievous little spitfire too. "She were born on the first day of April. How about we name her April? Maybe April Marie. April for havin' the gumption to come out on April Fool's day and Marie for your mother. I always liked that name."

"Sounds like a possibility to me," Franny said. I could tell she was please that I'd thought of using her momma's name.

I didn't care one way or other because I knew I'd call her something else altogether. I knew I'd always be calling her Honey—so's I wouldn't forget those two tracks I was on.

"By the way," I said, as if it had only now come to me and was incidental like, "soons we get back to Sugar Tree Holler, I guess I'll be goin' back into makin' those bee boxes."

"Oh, somethin' happen to the spare you made?"

"It ain't a spare no more. The bee man has been by and brought another swarm. He tells me we have a real good place for raisin' bees and we can really go into the business—that he could be bringing us new bee swarms as steady as we can put boxes out for them."

"That sounds good," Franny said. "With the adding of mouths to feed, it will be good to have a business bringing in money."

"Oh, and you talked about having an iron fence built to go around your kitchen garden to keep the deer out," I said, pushing my luck. "I hear tell that black hermit up on the ridge, Rufus Jefferson, is blacksmithing. I reckon I could go up there now and again and get him to do work for us."

Franny bought that one too. Them two tracks were well on their way.

~

Indisposed

Gavin had arrived from Geneva earlier in the day, but he wanted a breather and had a lot of paper work to go through before the Cyprus reunification talks he was moderating for the UN began on April 1st. Therefore, he'd booked for the night into a five-star beach resort, the Four Seasons, west of the airport on the southern coast, at Limassol. He would go up to Nicosia, the country's capital, located in the center of the island, the next day. These negotiations were his big chance to move ahead in the UN Secretariat. He knew it was a test of his ability and diplomatic dexterity. There was little hope of the Greeks and Turks coming to a reunification settlement, although the need for inclusion in the EU was a stronger incentive to reunify now than ever before and the two sides had been inching toward each other ever so imperceptibly over the last decade.

His job—like that of the representatives of the divided communities sharing the island—was to show some progress and to make anyone but his own side responsible for any lack of progress. If he were lucky enough to have been involved in forging any form of greater agreement in the process, his career as an international negotiator would take off.

He'd been told that both the Greeks and the Turks were masters at these turf wars and he'd have to be masterful himself to remain above and balanced in the fray. The talks would start in a week at the old Ledra Palace Hotel, which had gotten locked in the no-man's land between the Greek and Turkish sectors of the island, where the armed dividing line ran through the center of the capital city of Nicosia, in 1974. This line had been softening for a few years and the movement from one sector to the other was becoming easier.

It had been particularly hard for Gavin Collins to develop his career in the UN Secretariat, as he was known to be actively gay. It was all discreetly handled, but it still was a worry to his superiors and as much a question of what might upset the balance of his objectivity as having holdings in international corporations would be in any international economic negotiations he might be involved in as a moderator. It was just an added issue in his suitability to rise in the Secretariat. In this case, his situation was exacerbated because an up-and-comer Brazilian, Eduardo Alvarez, had been assigned as assistant moderator and already was here and on the job in Nicosia. Gavin had never before seen the younger Eduardo as competition, but it lately had dawned on him that he should be seeing him as competition.

It didn't mean, by any means, that Gavin was remaining celibate to counter worries about his sexual preferences and practices, however. Just his arrival at the Larnaka airport and the drive west to the Four Seasons resort had been enough to whet his sexual appetite, as all of the Greek men he observed and encountered were alluring hunks. He'd only come from Geneva, but it was snowing in Geneva, and all the men were bundled up and had been for several months. Cyprus was a land of sun, sea, and Speedos. He had checked out the weather on the island and knew that, even though it was only late March, he could swim in the sea and lay out in the sun. But he also could ogle and be ogled—he was sure he was objective in believing he was presentable enough to be ogled—and he had dreams of hooking up with a Greek hunk.

And, speaking of Greek hunks, one rose up—literally, from the Mediterranean Sea in front of him—early that afternoon as he was stretched out on a beach lounge bed, in a Speedo and an unbuttoned and flared cotton shirt and was going through background papers for the coming Cypriot negotiations.

The man was relatively young, at least ten years younger than Gavin's thirty-eight, with a man's muscular body, but he was in splendid shape. He was olive skinned, enhanced probably by being tanned by the Mediterranean sun, had black curly hair—not just on his head, but also swirling around a bit on his pecs and flat stomach and on his forearms and thighs—long, curly lashes, without appearing the least bit effeminate; pale blue eyes; and a glorious smile. He was beautiful, but he also was rugged-jawed all man.

As he emerged from the sea in a skimpy black, shiny Speedo, he leaned down, scooped up a beach towel, leather sandals, a couple of magazines, and a pair of sunglasses from the sand, and walked, in confident strides, but like a male model on the catwalk, toward where Gavin was stretched out on his lounge bed.

Gavin's eyes went from the man's face to his magnificent torso to his basket, and he sighed. Then he almost hyperventilated when the man picked out the lounge bed next to his to lie on. There were more empty ones than occupied ones fanned out where the grass met the sand across the hotel's seafront, but the man picked the one next to Gavin's to stretch out on.

When he was settled on it, on his back, the back of the lounge bed raised, he put his sunglasses on, turned his head to Gavin and smiled, and then lit up a cigarette from a pack, matchbox nestled between cellophane and pack, blew a couple of puffs with a sigh of satisfaction, and opened one of the magazines.

The magazine was a gay male skin magazine, and the man made no attempt to hide that fact.

Was he putting a make on Gavin, the UN diplomat wondered. If so, it was working. Gavin, always discreet when he could be, ran the risk factors over in his mind. He couldn't discern a single problem. He wasn't expected in Nicosia until tomorrow. No one had met him at the plane; his itinerary indicated he was arriving tomorrow. And he hadn't prebooked the hotel. He'd checked the beach resorts out earlier and had come here by rental car from the airport, taking his chances a room would be available, and one was. They'd taken and copied his passport, but that wasn't something that was going to be reported to the UN High Commission office in Nicosia.

He had a free day on a Greek island—or an island that was half Greek, and he'd heard good things about the Turkish men on the Turkish side of the island as well. He had plans to go over there for a discreet hookup or two, just as he'd had in the back of his mind the possibility of a hookup on this side—today. Well, not in the back of his mind—in the front of his mind. He wouldn't have taken the trouble to establish a free, out-of-sight, day on the Greek Cypriot coast if he hadn't planned on spending part of that day being laid by a Greek Cypriot.

"Is that a good magazine?" he asked, deciding there was no time like the moment to check out possibilities.

"A very good magazine, yes," the man said. His English was good, albeit accented. "I needed to check out something," he added.

"Checking out if you're in there?" Gavin asked in a playful tone. "Because you could be," he added.

"Nice of you to say so, but did you see what kind of magazine this is? Maybe you would not mean what you say if you knew what was in this magazine."

"Yes, I saw what kind of magazine it is," Gavin said. "I got the impression you wanted me to see it and wanted to know something about me."

The man shrugged and smiled, lifting his sunglasses so that Gavin could see the sparkle in his eyes.

"I will agree to that point. My name is Niko," he said. "Niko Constandinos. I am Greek, from Athens." He looked at Gavin expectantly.

"I'm Craig Smith. Canadian," Gavin answered. Of course he wasn't going to give his real name. He was happy to say he was Canadian, though. That was neutral enough and didn't have the problem of whether or not the other man liked Americans or Brits. Canadian also, for some reason, helped in establishing preferred position. It was taken as a good possibility of a submissive; just as saying you were Australian left the impression you'd be a dominating top.

"Are you here in Cyprus for business or pleasure—or do you live here?" Niko asked and then immediately filled in those blanks on himself. "I'm down from Athens for both business and pleasure. I am here alone."

"Me as well," Gavin answered. "Business . . . and pleasure . . . and alone. It's my first time on island. You too?"

"Oh, no. I have been here many, many times. I think I could be a guide for the island—and for some of its forbidden pleasures."

"You think so? I've heard that there's a lot to see and experience. I was hoping to see some castles. I understand there are some crusader castles here and fortresses of earlier and later periods. It's sort of an interest of mine, since I traveled in China and Japan and found that castles there had similar designs to Western castles without the two cultures having met before—an important difference being that Western castles are designed from the outside in, while Japanese castles are set on the edge of a cliff and designed from the entry back to the cliff drop . . . but, sorry, I've rambled on."

While he'd rambled on, though, he'd noticed that Niko had been running his fingers down his body and hadn't neglected brushing them across his crotch. The bulge there had become noticeably bulgier.

"I can't help but notice that you are a very handsome and well-built man," Niko said. "I love to hear your enthusiasm for places like castles. There is one near here—Kolossi Castle—which is very unusual. It's just a thick square tower really. But it has history. When Richard the Lionhearted's betrothed woman was shipwrecked here and captured and imprisoned, it is said by many that it was in Kolossi Castle, and the Knights of Templar occupied the castle at one time. They made wine and also served as the bank for the island's nobles. I would love to be your guide there—perhaps this afternoon? Now, maybe?"

"I don't usually think of Richard the Lionhearted as being married," Gavin said, "but I guess he was."

"Ah, you think of him as being with men."

"Yes, I do," Gavin answered.

"And this being with men—"

"Yes, I do," Gavin said, and smiled. "As I said, I got the impression that you were checking something by letting me see that magazine."

"Yes, I was. And you are telling me that I was right to assume?"

"Yes, you were right. And, in case you wonder, I am a submissive. Men cover me. I think that you might be—"

"Yes, I am. I, as you say, cover, men. It is a good fit, no? You say you are here for pleasure as well as business. I specialize in pleasure."

"Yes, pleasure is important to me—both getting it and giving it."

"I don't have a lot of time to meet with a man during this trip to Cyprus," Niko said, looking at Gavin expectantly. "I am a straightforward man. I offer myself to another man and move on if the offer isn't completely accepted."

"I too can be straightforward and am available only for the day. Do you want to fuck me?"

"Yes." He looked a bit surprised at the bald question, but he responded immediately. "So, would you like to see Kolossi Castle and perhaps a club or two before we return to the hotel and I fuck you? You are staying here, at the Four Seasons, are you not?"

"Yes, I am staying here." he didn't ask if Niko was staying here as well, or establish with him what Niko's business was in coming to Cyprus. In the latter case, he didn't want to reveal what his own business here was.

They found themselves alone at the top of Kolossi Castle, and Gavin was over standing by a crenellated wall and looking at a slit opening in a punched-out section.

"Is this like the Blarney Stone?" he asked, bending over and looking down through the slit. "Do I kiss something here?"

"Look down. What do you see?" Niko asked.

"The drawbridge. We're over the entrance to the keep."

"Yes. That opening is for pouring boiling tar or whatever you have on hand on the heads of anyone trying to force the front gate. But if you want it to be for kissing . . ." He pulled Gavin up and turned him and took his mouth in a long, dueling-tongues kiss.

"I want to fuck you now," he murmured when they'd come up for air. "I want to drive you somewhere private and fuck you in my automobile. I don't want to wait for tonight."

And that's what he did. They got back in his car and he drove toward the sea from the castle on a sandy road, pulling off behind a sand dune in a small stand of trees. They sucked each other hard in the front seat, one leaning over to the lap of the other, and then they moved to the backseat and Niko sat in the middle of the seat, gripping a now-naked Gavin's waist between his hands, while, facing him, Gavin straddled the Greek's lap and rose and fell on his cock until both had ejaculated.

Niko took Gavin to a series of gay clubs in Limassol, where they danced and drank beer, and then to an outdoor restaurant on the waterfront. They had arrived more than an hour before the usual 10:00 p.m. opening for dinner in Cypriot restaurants, but they were served anyway, dining on a meze—a progression of small dishes of Greek food—and drinking Palomino wine.

"We're the only ones dining in this restaurant," Gavin observed.

"It's a popular restaurant. It just hasn't really opened for supper yet," Niko answered. And then to forestall the next question, he added. "It won't open for two more hours, but this is a tourist area so they are always ready to serve those who don't know the Cypriot way. It's a pleasure to eat in a Greek restaurant with others—everyone becomes friends. But you say you must leave tomorrow, and we both have said we are here for pleasure. In two hours I want to be in your bed in the hotel with you, with both of us taking our pleasure. Is that not what you want?"

"Yes, that's what I want," Gavin answered.

And that's what transpired. Both of them naked, and having worshipped each other's bodies, Niko was sitting on the side of the bed again, as he had done in the backseat of the car, and Gavin was saddled in his lap, facing him, legs bent, fists locked behind Niko's neck, and feet leveraging off the mattress as he rose and fell on Niko's cock. Before either came, Niko took over the fucking, pressing Gavin to arch back, head on the floor, arms extended in a cruciform position, ankles on Niko's shoulders, as the Greek pulled the Canadian on and off the cock to a mutual ejaculation. Afterward they lay, stretched out against each other and entwined in each other's arms and legs embrace, moving and writhing against each other, as Niko entered and pumped Gavin from the front, from the back, and from the sides, each coming again and again and again.

In the morning, when Gavin woke, Niko was gone. It struck the diplomat that, other than a name, which no doubt was as false as the one he'd given the Greek—if, indeed, the man had been Greek—Gavin knew nothing about Niko. Most important, he didn't know how to get in touch with Niko to continue their glorious fuck.

By the time he was in the Mercedes he'd rented and was driving north toward Nicosia, though, he had decided that that was just as it should be. It was exactly the hookup he'd been looking forward to having the previous day—one of complete anonymity and compartmented duration. There surely would be other opportunities like that while he was in Cyprus. Friends of his had told him he didn't even need to seek them out in Cyprus. As long as he looked as fit as he did, they said, the hookups would come to him.

* * * *

Gavin was booked in one of the newer Nicosia hotels, the Park Hilton, but the offices assigned to the UN administrators of the Cyprus reunification talks were in the old, once-luxurious, British colonial hotel, the Ledra Palace. The grand old hotel was locked in the Green Zone between the Greek and Turkish sectors at the major checkpoint for those who could go between the zones, primarily diplomats, but increasingly tourists and even Greeks and Turks as the relationship between the two sides improved. Its position in the neutral zone was a factor that had permitted the reunification talks to resume—it was where all meetings between the two ethnic groups had occurred since the 1974 Turkish invasion of the island.

Besides Gavin, the UN delegation included Eduardo Alvarez, his second, a couple of secretaries, three bodyguards, and an equipment technician. Appreciable setup work and coordination with the Greek and Turkish delegations had had to be done, but Eduardo and the staff had come two weeks ahead of the talks and Eduardo was so efficient that nearly all of the preparation work was done before Gavin arrived. Gavin felt like a fifth wheel, but he did what he could to pose as the senior official and chief moderator. That still left him with considerable time to spend at the Park Hilton swimming pool, gathering a tan and trying to be good. It

225

wouldn't do for him to pursue Greek men while he was on public display in Nicosia.

Sensing that he was restless and knowing there wasn't much for him to do until the talks actually started on April 1st, Eduardo suggested, "Why don't you take a few days and go over to the Turkish side? The UN has a guesthouse by Five-Mile Beach to the west of Kyrenia, and I know you have an interest in castles. You could explore the seventh-century Byzantine one in Kyrenia Harbor and the castles built by the crusaders in the eleventh and twelfth centuries along the tops of the Kyrenia Mountains."

"That sounds like a good idea," Gavin said. Two days checking out Turkish men on the Turkish side of Cyprus, away from the prying eyes of his staff in Nicosia. What could go wrong?

And so he took a UN car, because his rented Mercedes couldn't go into the Turkish zone, crossed through the checkpoints in Nicosia, and drove the sixty miles north to Kyrenia and then the five miles west to the UN guesthouse at Five-Mile Beach, notable in Cyprus as having been the beachhead for the Turkish invasion of Cyprus in 1974.

After being settled in the strong fence-enclosed UN guest house a few steps up a rocky hillside from the Mediterranean Sea and just west of Five-Mile Beach, Gavin drove to the picturesque harbor town of Kyrenia, or, as the Turks called it, Girni, to explore the harbor castle there that dominated the eastern end of the waterfront. He found the castle fascinating, as it had originally been built in the seventh century by the Byzantines and, in the sixteenth century, the Venetians enclosed it in a thick-walled fortress of later design. In the interim period it had been besieged and conquered by Richard the Lionhearted, whose crusaders occupied and reinforced the mountaintop St. Hilarion Castle in the Kyrenia range dominating Kyrenia to the south and overlooking both the town and the mountain pass to the interior of the island and its capital, Nicosia.

It was while he was looking around in the castle, being nearly the only one doing so that afternoon, that Gavin saw the young man he later would call Erol. The first sighting was from the ramparts of the castle across the large training ground to the top of the fortress' seawall. The young Turkish Cypriot was only seen from a distance, but even at a remove Gavin was struck by the man's athletic build and his ability to scramble over the stone ruins. He was dark—in both complexion and hair coloring—and, even from here, Gavin could see that he had a ready and dazzling smile. He was strongly built without being noticeably tall. Gavin enjoyed watching the young man—he evidently was at least fifteen years younger than Gavin was—moving around. And Gavin wondered what he was doing in the castle alone. In his observation of Turkish men when he had visited the Turkish mainland, they liked to move in groups. He'd found that they liked to fuck in groups too, which he had enjoyed.

Without giving the young man much more thought—he was too far away for Gavin to do more than develop a sensation of hardening, which he did for quite a few young men—Gavin left the castle and stopped for lunch at the outdoor section of one of the many restaurants that had set tables out directly at the edge of the stone walkway between the buildings arcing around the inner harbor and the water, where an assortment of working and pleasure boats were tied up.

The young man who served him lunch at the harborside café said that his name was Sami. He was lithe and moved like a dancer. He was all smiles and youthful beauty and curly black hair and great body and eagerness to please and touched anyone he was engaging in conversation with animated hands—and obviously was available. Sami couldn't be away from the restaurant very long, so instead of driving him all the way back to the UN guest house, Gavin checked into the Dome Hotel at the western end of the inner harbor, having no difficulty booking only for two hours that afternoon. As Sami lay on his back on the bed, Gavin rode his cock, slowly moving around to all aspects of the compass that was Sami's hard body to feel the young man's cock kissing all angles of his channel walls. Gavin was delighted to find that Sami's cock was the most formidable aspect of his body, being long and thin and ever erect. The young man just lay there, nervous and in awe in the initial fuck with the older, but movie-star handsome, Western man. Gavin had the sense that there would be more fire in him with added familiarity. For the first time, though, Sami gave his cock over to Gavin's complete use.

After a brief rest, there was a second fucking. As anticipated, Sami now was more sure of himself, bending Gavin over the bed and fucking him from the rear, egged on to increased physicality when Gavin gasped and begged for more when Sami slapped him on the bare buttocks and cruelly twisted an arm high up onto his shoulder blades while he pounded him with vigor.

"What time do you stop working at the restaurant and do you wish to earn more money?" Gavin asked, as they dressed.

"It's my uncle's restaurant. That means I won't be off until near midnight tonight. I'm sorry, I would have liked to—"

"I will come for you at the restaurant shortly after midnight. Don't plan on sleeping in your bed tonight."

When they returned to the restaurant, Gavin almost regretted having made the assignation with Sami, because the other man was there, at a table of the adjacent restaurant, drinking beer and looking around. He watched Gavin intently as Gavin and Sami approached, and he made no effort to hide that he was giving Gavin assessing stares. For his part, Gavin could hardly take his eyes off the young man. He was sultry and sensuous while having a commanding, cocky, and self-confident air about him. He was far more alluring close up than he had been from across the inner-wall ramparts of the harbor castle. He was dark and impossibly handsome and sexy, and, as was obvious by his forearms and the deep-cut V of his muscle T-shirt, hirsute.

His look at Gavin was one of already being inside Gavin and cruelly using him, and it was all Gavin could do not to hyperventilate.

But Gavin had already made a hookup for the night with Sami. Perhaps this man would still be in evidence the next day and would be available. Gavin loved Turkish men. They were universally well equipped and fun loving. And most of them were forceful, dominating, and a bit brutish. There was nothing in that combination that Gavin didn't like. Sami had not been completely what Gavin melted too, but he was young and virile and showed every sign of being able to hold an erection through the night. Gavin hoped that that was enough to build on.

And then maybe this other man—or a man like him, there being so many possibilities among Turkish men—for the next day, or the day after that.

* * * *

Gavin woke up on his bed in the UN guest house, lying between Cemal and Tamer, each with an arm over his chest and turned to Gavin, each eying the Canadian diplomat like it had been he who awakened the three of them with his snoring. Sami was standing by the bedroom door, pulling his jeans on.

"I'll see what there is for breakfast," Sami said. "I could use some help."

Cemal and Tamer went up on their elbows and looked at each other across Gavin's bare chest. Tamer said something in Turkish that sounded like he was making a forceful point. He was the bigger of the two young Turks, and Cemal sighed, rolled over to the side of the bed, sat up, and reached down to retrieve his briefs. Gavin watched him stand, pull them on, and pad out of the bedroom. As Cemal hit the door, though, Gavin's line of sight was obstructed by the beefy and muscle-bound Tamer, who rolled over on top of him, forcing his knees between Gavin's thighs. Gavin groaned and Tamer grunted as he hovered over Gavin. Gavin arched his back as the Turk's hard cock split his ass cheeks and moved up into his channel. Tamer reached up, grabbed Gavin's wrists, and held the Canadian's arms over Gavin's head. He looked down into Gavin's face with a half smile and half sneer, as he started the rhythm of the fuck.

When Gavin had gone back to the Kyrenia harborside restaurant at midnight the previous night, he'd found that Sami's friends had shown up and wanted Sami to go carousing with them on their motorcycles. Gavin hadn't formed any alternative plan, though, and hadn't taken into account how loose young Turkish Cypriot men could be in their entertainment plans.

He had money in abundance, and they were given the choice of spending money or receiving money for essentially the same result in entertainment. They followed him back to the UN guest house on their motorbikes, being duly impressed at being

229

admitted to a compound that all of the locals knew about but none but the gardeners and caretakers were permitted to enter. There they triangulated on Gavin and each other through the night.

And all had a good time.

Sami was doing turns in the kitchen of his uncle's restaurant in Kyrenia harbor, so breakfast was good—and so plentiful that Gavin would have to go to the market again sometime that day or eat the rest of his meals out during this vacation on the Turkish side of the island.

After breakfast, all four of them went to the shower for a suck and fuck session, with Gavin doing most of the sucking and receiving most of the fucking under the cascading water of the shower. Now clean, the three chattering and laughing Turks took off in a cloud of dust, smoke, and rumbling motorbike engines, leaving Gavin sitting on the floor of the shower, moaning and smiling.

That didn't stop him from going out on a castle hunt, this time driving up into the Kyrenia range at the pass between Kyrenia and Nicosia, parking in what had once been a jousting field, and then climbing up by foot to the entrance in the Crusader-period St. Hilarion Castle. From there he climbed again in a purposefully twisting stone passage, up, up, and up into the fastness of the castle ruins.

It was here that he got a fleeting glimpse once more of the dark, sultry young Turk he'd seen on the Kyrenia Castle walls and then later in the harborside restaurant area. Seeing each other at some difference with a chasm of ruins between each other, they both stopped, stared, and smiled. The young Turk saluted Gavin and then disappeared behind a stone wall. Gavin worked his way in that direction, but by the time he got there, the young man had vanished.

Despite the workout Gavin had gotten the previous night and that morning, he felt himself go hard and fresh desire build inside him. He continued to look around the castle for another hour, figuring out in his mind how the plan of the structure had originally meant to function, and he almost convinced himself that he was exploring the castle and not trying to find the young man . . . almost.

230

He had lunch at the Kyrenia harbor, half expecting to see the young Turk there, but he didn't. Keyed up, slightly disappointed, and more than slightly tired, he drove back to the UN guest house and fell into the local custom of taking an early afternoon nap.

* * * *

The young Turk's name was Erol—or at least that's the name he gave to Gavin after the first time he fucked the Canadian diplomat.

After resting, Gavin went to the beach at Five-Mile Beach, which was close to the UN guest house and ran in a horseshoe shape around a cove of the Mediterranean where the water was shallow and the bottom was sandy. He had been lying on his back on a beach towel on the sand after having taken a dip and swim in the sea and was dozing and half listening to the cavorting of a group of young Turkish men, who were playing a form of beach soccer not far from him. He'd spent considerable time ogling the young men as their ranks gathered for the game and was pleasantly aroused and hard as he lay there dreaming about them.

The soccer ball rolled up against his side. He opened his eyes to see the elusive sultry Turkish man—*his* elusive Turkish man—looking down at him, with the soccer ball in his hands and a smile on his face. They looked at each other for the longest couple of seconds, conveying all that needed to transpire between them— they found each other attractive and arousing, they were sexually interested in each other, the Turk was a power top and Gavin was a submissive bottom, and that they would fuck.

The young Turk—Erol—took the ball then and returned to the game. But after establishing that he was in command and that Gavin, who followed his every movement with his eyes, was at his beck and call, Erol left the game, with many smiles and hand waving, and returned to Gavin's side. He extended an arm to motion that Gavin should stand and follow him, which Gavin did. They walked down the beach and into the sea and out to where they could stand with the water coming up only to their nipples. They were a good way off of the beach. Erol reached down and tugged on Gavin's Speedo. Gavin got the hint and pulled his Speedo off. Erol had done the same with his.

"Hang it on your arm so that it doesn't float away," the Turk said. "Like I'm doing."

"You speak English," Gavin said, as he pushed his forearm through the Speedo and let it hang on his arm. The two were close together, facing each other. He gave a little jerk and groan as the Turk grasped their cocks together—both of them already in erection—and frotted them.

"Naturally. My name is Erol."

"I'm Gavin."

"Climb my hips with your knees, Gavin, and be open for me when I enter you. I am going to fuck you."

Gavin hooked his legs on Erol's hips and locked his fists behind Erol's neck. Erol grasped Gavin's waist between his hands and lifted Gavin's body in the water. Gavin cried out and began to pant as his body was pulled down on the cock. And then up and down, up and down, As Erol fucked him to a mutual ejaculation.

Gavin took Erol back to the UN guest house, and Erol fucked him for two days. On the third day, Gavin's last before he had to get back to Nicosia to check up on whether Eduardo and his staff had made the talks ready for Gavin to conduct, Gavin woke up alone in the bed. Erol was gone. Gavin hadn't told him he had to return to the Greek side that day. The best he could do was pin a note to the outside gate to the UN guest house compound. He couldn't give a Turk who didn't work there free access to the compound.

As he drove the eighty miles back to Nicosia he realized that all he had was a name—and that might not be a real one. He had given Erol his real first name, but he hadn't given him his last name or told him where he came from or why he was able to use the UN guest house on the Turkish side. He was lost to Erol sexually. He would just have to try to find him again the next time he came over to the Turkish side.

* * * *

232

"I think it would set the right tone if you entered the Treaty Room last," Eduardo said on the morning of April 1st as the delegations were gathering for the start of yet another attempt at Cyprus reunification talks. The Treaty Room, once the VIP parlor for the Ledra Palace Hotel, containing an imposing Tudor-style stone fireplace with the coat of Richard the Lionhearted on it, had been the venue for all talks on Greek and Turkish Cypriot differences through history. Indeed, it was where the British had drawn the Green Line that separated the Greek and Turkish sectors of the island, called that because a green grease pencil had been used to draw the line on the map. It had also been the venue of several border demarcation negotiations in the greater Middle East world. "Let me get the delegations in and settled at the table first."

Gavin tersely nodded. He'd left so much of the work to Eduardo, who seemed to know what he was doing and who had established rapport with all sides—not just the separate Greek and Turkish Cypriot contingents but also the observers that Greece, Turkey, the Americans, and the British had sent.

Left alone in his office while Eduardo was getting the meeting set up, he noticed for the first time the red folder laying on the blotter in the center of his desk. He flipped the folder open and blanched. There were two sets of photos, one was of Niko Constandinos fucking him in his hotel room at the Four Seasons Hotel outside of Limassol the day he'd arrived on the island. The other set was of Erol fucking him at the UN guest house near Five-Mile Beach on the Turkish side. He slammed the folder shut in fear and shock.

"Mr. Alvarez says they are ready for you to make your entrance," one of the staff secretaries called to him from the corridor. Still disconcerted, he opened the center drawer and slipped the folder inside. He had no idea what it meant or what he could or should do about it.

Entering the Treaty Room, Gavin received his second and third shocks. There standing in the second row of the Greek delegation, in a suit, stood Niko Constandinos. Not being able to look the man in the eye, Gavin swiveled his face toward the Turkish delegation, only to spy Erol, in a suit, standing in the ranks of the Turkish delegation.

Gavin knew he was going to be sick. Rather than taking his position in the room, where Eduardo currently was standing, he muttered, "Excuse me, I'm sorry," and turned and fled the room. He stumbled to the nearby men's room and vomited in a toilet.

Eduardo entered the men's room. "Are you all right, Gavin?" he asked solicitously. "Are you ill?"

"No, no . . . I'll—"

"You look ghastly, sir. You are ill, aren't you? Here, I'll go call up the chauffeur and we'll get you back to your hotel right away. You rest. I'll manage somehow here without you until you feel better."

Eduardo wouldn't listen to all of Gavin's protestations that he'd be fine, and Gavin's response grew weaker and weaker as he realized that in some greater dimension he wouldn't be fine. Both delegations out there seemed to have thought they had compromised him in their favor. How could he possibly continue as moderator of these talks? Eduardo was being so masterful with this crisis and Gavin, after all, was a submissive. In no time he was in the UN staff car and being motored back to the Park Hilton Hotel.

As soon as he left, Eduardo went back to the Treaty Room. "I'm sorry, gentlemen and ladies, Mr. Collins is indisposed. We will proceed, however. I will do what I can to step in and manage without him. We will take a short break now and then get started."

He motioned to two men in the room, and the Greek who had given Gavin the name of Niko Constandinos but who, actually, was one of the Greek checkpoint guards here at the Ledra Palace border crossing, and the Turk who had given Gavin the name of Erol but who, actually worked in the kitchen here at the Ledra Palace joined Eduardo outside of the Treaty Room to receive their packets of money from him and to return to their respective jobs.

Eduardo paused for moment to settle himself and to wipe the self-satisfied smile off his face and replace it with one of concern, competence, and confidence. He then returned to the Treaty Room to take up the moderator's position that he had trained hard to be able to handle and to manage "somehow" without the man, Gavin Collins, who he had seen as competition to upper administrative posts in the UN Secretariat.

~

Final Turn of the Wheel

I don't know what draws me to the dining room window at the front of the house, but when I look out I see him—David—walking up the dirt drive from the county road, past my house, to his house farther up the mountain. Where has he been? He never goes out anymore. I hadn't seen him walking the road all winter, which only now was turning into spring. Someone must have given him a lift this far. Why didn't he ask me to take him wherever he's been? He's dressed up in a suit, but it hangs on him like he's lost fifty pounds. He's walking so wearily, hunched over on himself. He's lost weight; there doesn't seem to be much left of him. He was once so robust . . . we were essentially the same size. I feel guilty that I've stayed the same . . . through it all.

As always, I feel the clutch of seeing him. I haven't seen him for two months and five days now, not since the funeral for his Amy—and the only time before that in a long time was at the funeral for my Helen. Both times we'd been standing away from each other, not being able to chance more than a glance or two for each other.

Seeing him stirs something in me. I move around the house nervously, unable to concentrate on any task for long or to settle. It's a good thing it's only me now and there's nothing much to do anyway.

I anticipate the phone call. I have no idea why I do. Nobody calls me anymore. It was Helen who had been the social one. Within two weeks of her passing I'd become an "Oh, does he still live around here?" someone people once had known. That is all right with me. It means the phone doesn't ring and I can melt into the silence of the house, with only my memories for company. For some reason, though, I keep walking by the phone, looking at it,

236

expecting it to ring. And when it does, I nearly jump out of my skin and don't pick it up until the third ring.

"Please come up," is all he says, and then I hear the click as the line goes dead. I don't have to ask who it was. I knew who it would be—even though it has been nearly fifteen years since he last called me. Fourteen years, seven months, and six days, actually. He doesn't give me time to respond. He knows I'll come. He's always been the one in control, even from a submissive position. And I do go, after I shower and shave and brush my teeth and carefully pick out my clothes—nothing worn, nothing needing mending. I couldn't do that to Helen. I couldn't go in anything that hadn't been kept up and ironed nicely. It isn't she who failed at anything.

The front door is open to his house. I don't knock; I just walk on in. All the time I was showering, I was dreaming about where I'd find him—how I'd find him, and it made me go hot. That's just where I find him, in his bedroom, stretched out on his bed, naked, propped up on his elbow with his eyes trained to the doorway.

The look he gives me when I appear in the doorway is worth it all—all the years of agreeing that "We can't do this. Amy and Helen, both of them, are too good for us to continue doing this to them."

He doesn't have to tell me to take my clothes off. He doesn't have to tell me anything. I am already half hard when I come onto the bed behind him and pull him into my chest. He is too frail for me to lie on top of him—God how frail he's gotten and how quickly. He hadn't been this frail at the funerals. And he is too proud to admit the effort to be on top of me would be too taxing, so we do it with me behind him, spooning him into my body.

We kiss and I cup and squeeze his cock and balls as he reaches back and strokes me harder. He is the one who puts me in position and juts his buttocks back to take me inside him. I would never be the one to take that responsibility. He had always been the one to take on the greater guilt. Leaving one hand to work his chest and nipples, I move the other one down to run my fingers through his pubic bush and down the sides of his engorged cock and work him there while we move our hips in rhythm, harmonizing our sighs, and taking our pleasure of each other.

It has been so long, but it seems otherwise. We still fit together perfectly, despite him having diminished in frame and me as solid as ever, and have all of the same moves to pleasure the other that we ever did. I come in a peaceful flow and shared sighs. Then we sleep, me withering inside him and stroking his chest, cock, and balls until I have drifted off listening to his soft breathing, soft breathing with a bit of a ragged edge to it that I don't remember it having before.

When I wake it is to see him sitting in a chair, facing me and looking at me while he fondles himself. Seeing me awake, he smiles and says, "I want you to help me with something. Come with me. No, as you are, please."

David takes my hand and guides me to the back of the house, to his inner sanctum, his pottery room. The pottery room was where he has always retreated when he is tense or anxious or melancholy. It's where I had envisioned him living the hours away after Amy's death. It's where we first fucked, the tension of not doing so having gotten to us when our wives were out shopping.

"Please. Over in that bin," he says, "A large handful of clay, please." He keeps telling me to add clay until the ball is the size he wants. He sits me on the stool in front of the wheel after pulling the stool away from it. "There, put it on the wheel," he says.

As I lean over and put the ball of clay on the wheel, he kneels in front of me, spreading my thighs, moving his frail body between my knees, and takes me inside his mouth, cupping my balls in one of his hands and gently distending them. I sit there, leaning over, the ball of clay resting on the wheel but also cupped in my hands, as he works my cock with his mouth, engorging me, and making me tremble and moan for him.

He does not let me come, though. Rising, he tells me to do so also long enough to pull the stool closer to the wheel. "Sit," he says, and when I do, he turns and comes down into my lap, positioning himself on my erection and then taking me deep inside him, coming down until his buttocks nestle in my crotch.

Then, at his direction and guidance, with him sitting in my lap, both of us facing the wheel, which is now positioned between our spread thighs, we start working the clay together on the wheel, my hands on the clay and his hands, trembling, on mine, guiding my hands as the wheel turns and the clay begins to take form. I am deep inside him, pulsing. He is rising and falling, almost imperceptibly, on my shaft, but enough so that we both know we are fucking. We have become one, joined at the core but also at the clay with our hands. I kiss him on the back of his neck, and he begins to hum.

We were never happier, connected as one, than we are at this moment. This fleeting moment.

We are making something with the clay, but I know not what. So I ask. Years later I wonder if life would have taken another turn at this point if I had not asked. Of course it wouldn't have, but I fantasize that it might have.

"What are we making?"

"An urn," he answers.

That probably would have satisfied me. An urn was something I sort of knew—enough not to have to ask further. But David doesn't leave it there.

"A funeral urn," he says.

"Ah." I can't say more for several moments. I'm too choked up. But I understand it all now—not having contacted me after Helen and Amy had passed until now; his walking in from the main road so wearily in a suit, no doubt returning from that decisive trip to the doctor's office; his having become so frail so fast; his "at long last" telephone call early today; our also "at long last" sex; his wish and need for my help in forming this urn.

I direct my attention to the urn we are making. It's important now that I don't screw this up, that nothing I do in working it on the wheel under his hands causes it to collapse into itself—not like my world is collapsing into itself at this moment.

At length I have myself under control. I have come inside him again and the urn is taking shape. I'm not fucking that up like I helped fuck everything else up in life so far. So I ask.

"How long?"

"Not long now," he says in a small, resigned voice.

"Well," I answer.

He takes our hands away from the wheel, but I entwine my fingers in his and won't let him go. I can't let him go. The urn is formed, its shape perfect. He smiles, and I know he is pleased with it. I feel a loss at it being completed, though. Maybe if we could just continue turning the wheel . . .

The smile turns to a slight grimace and becomes wistful.

"What?" I ask.

"I'm afraid. The way it was with Amy . . . I don't think I could endure that."

"We'll just have to see what comes," I answer after a moment of silence.

"We?" he murmurs and the smile strengthens a bit, but then he sighs and looks around the room. The light in the room is dimming. "It's getting dark," he says. "You'll be needing to go home."

"I think I'm home now," I answer, impulsively, but as certain as I can be about anything at this moment.

We pause, each concentrating on the breathing of the other. "Are you sure? It will be difficult." I can hear the catch in his voice, a glimmer of hope maybe.

"Everything worth having in life is difficult," I respond. My mind is working on what, if anything, I will ever need enough to leave his side again. He and I were much the same size once. If it doesn't disturb him, I can just fit into his clothes—fit right into his life. All I can think of that's there, in my house, and not here—in our house—is my gun case . . . if . . . well, if. I'm not taking lightly what he has asked of me without forming the words.

But I wouldn't think of that now—and thank God it never came to that. Now was time for living, not for dying.

~

240

About the Author

Habu is one of the pen names of a former supersonic spy jet pilot, intelligence agent, male model, movie actor, and diplomat. A wild youth in Southeast Asia was spent enjoying whatever sexual opportunities came his way, and much of his gay male writing is about recalling incidents from those days and inventing ones he'd perhaps have liked to experience. He now leads a very quiet and ordinary happily married family life.

An American, he is a published mainstream novelist and short story writer under another name and in another dimension of his life. He has written or cowritten (with Sabb) approaching 1,000 published short stories and over 100 published erotica e-books, primarily of gay fiction but also memoir, straight fiction and ménage fiction. His hand and creative writing can be seen in stories and books by habu, sr71plt, Dirk Hessian, Shabbu, and Stephen Kessel—among unrevealed others that might surprise readers. The fictionalized GM memoir *Flying High, Diving Deep* is loosely based on his life experiences. He can be found at the adults only gay male site BarbarianSpy, which he shares with Sabb and Dirk Hessian.

Our authors always like to receive feedback, and appreciate it when readers post reviews at distributors and other sites

BarbarianSpy

FOR LITERARY HEAT

BarbarianSpy Books

Not all books listed below may currently be on release.
* indicates the book is available in paperback and e-book.

BOOKS BY CHRIS CROSS
Multisexual Adult Romance
Pulaski Square
Chocolate in Vanilla (MF)2
Christmas with Chris (MMF) (MM) (MF)

BOOKS BY ALEX LOCKHEED
Transgender Romance
Meeting Jenna
Transgender Other
Being Sarah

BOOKS BY DIRK HESSIAN
Xtreme Historical Erotica
Dirk's Ancient Times Collection (Print only Bundle)*
The King's Men
Shores of Tripoli*
Prophecy of Noto
Pretender's Fate

General Historical Erotic Romance
Dirk's America's Founding Collection (Print only Bundle)*
Soldier,Spy
Ridden West
Deliver a Virgin
Clouds and Rain
Confederate Gold
Puttin on the Ritz
To the Hessian Hills
Fire Down the Valley*
Constantinople*
The Beautiful Way*
Blue and Gray
Colonel's Treasure
Beginning of Time
Labyrinth

BOOKS BY HABU

Gay Erotica

Memoir Faction

Flying High, Diving Deep*

Xtreme Erotica

Fist of Gold

Liaisons

Chain Gang Banged (Short Story)

Tramp Steaming*

Escape to Girne

Silas' Choice*

Last Call

Choke Hold

Apyko: The Greek Pimp

Visits of the Schlange

Second Coming: Emile La Cour Unleashed*

Vortex: Sacrificed by Curiosity*

Dark Angel Sounding *(in e-book & included in Sounding:Ultimate Control paperback)*

Sounding: Ultimate Control (*Print Only*)*

Sounding Five *(in e-book & included in Sounding:Ultimate Control paperback)*

Romance

Big Sky Country

Gift from the Sea

Shore Leave

The Aviators

Poison Pen

Need to be Needed

Key Westing (short)

Finding a New Sam

Bangkok Summer Seduction

The Photograph

Inevitable Case

Turn to Love

Rain Check

Built for Pleasure (Sci Fi)

Danny's Choice*

Pull of the Groove

Sugar n Spice Christmas

Friday Nights with Lenny (Christmas Romance)

Snowy, Snowy Nights (Christmas Romance)

Tank n Bull

Sail to the Sun

War Letters

Ravens Roost
Caribbean Cruise Top to Bottom
Arena Stage
Trading Partners (Valentine's Day)
Four Coins
Lower Than the Heart (Valentine's Day)
Brambleton
Finding Amnad
Platres Conclave
Other Novels/Novellas
Also Want to Thank
Ranger Guided
Key Westing
Syrian Ram
Temptation's Clutches*
Descent into Chaos
Escape to Girne
Journey Through Abilene
Harmony and Dissonance
Stallion Station
Racing With the Devil (espionage suspense)
Prepared in Cape Verdi
Gilded Cage
House on Park*
Anything for Ambition
Dance of the Ravishers
Hard Knocks U*
My Neighbor's Spa*
Man's Man: Tales of a High Priced Gay Hooker*
Trip Money
The Indian Doctor
Sailorboy
Home to Fire Island
Switching Sides*
Big Sky Country*
Murder Mysteries
Retribution (Hardesty)
Snitches (Hardesty
Gotta Keep Trying (Hardesty)
All Fools Day Foolery (Mike Kavanagh)
Inevitable Case (Mike Kavanagh)
Vanishing Laura
Death on a Ping Pong Table
Clint Folsom Mysteries Compendium Volume 1*
Death to Blonds - Stolen Judgment (Clint Folsom Mystery)*

Clint Folsom Mysteries Compendium Volume 2*
Gay Erotica Anthologies
A Hell of a War*
Earth Cry*
Shunga
Habu's Christmas Balls
Eight in D*
DevilMENt
Silas' Choices*
Stallion Station (A Novella in Parts)
Eleven to the Dogs*
Fifty Seventy*
Spy Tails 001*
Spy Tails 002*
Doubled*
Doubled Again*
Tails in the Tropics*
Tails in the Med*
Tails in the West*
Rough Riders*
Grab Bag 1*
Grab Bag 2*
Grab Bag 3*
Grab Bag 4*
Grab Bag 5*
Grab Bag 6*
Grab Bag 7*
Grab Bag 8*
Grab Bag 9*
Grab Bag 10*
Grab Bag 11*
Grab Bag 12*
Grab Bag 13*
Beyond the Beaded Curtain*
The Sporting Life*
Fetish Galore!*
Literary Gay Erotica
Cairo Surrender*
The Handyman*
Homeward Bound
Journey to Mirage*
Bisexual/Menage/Multisexual Erotica
And Eat it Too
Two Men, One Woman*
Every Which Way

Summer of Denial
Death on a Ping Pong Table
Cruising Gigolo
13 Ways for Halloween
Luther*
The Indian Prince*
BOOKS BY SABB
Spanish Lovers
Driver Reliever
Hiring in Hollywood
The Legend of Holleystone Grange
Surprise Encounters*
She is He
Wrong Man
Loyal to his King
Barbarian Tales - Book One - Traveler's Tales*
Barbarian Tales - Book Two - Journeys Begin*
Barbarian Tales - Book Three - The Inheritance*
Barbarian Tales - Book Four - Road to Persepolis*
BOOKS BY SHABBU
A Season in Galicia*
Blind Dates*
Velvet Interrogation
Finding Jason
Dirty Pool
Operation Black Jade
Cigars!*
Angel in the Barn
Gayly Complicated*
Despoiling David
The Tree of Idleness*
I Met a Man
Rough Road to Happiness
BOOKS BY STEPHEN KESSEL
Gay Romance
The Forever Man
Two Chances
BOOKS BY KIM BLACK
Lesbian Romance
Transfixed on Tammie (F/T lesbian)
~

www.ingramcontent.com/pod-product-compliance
Lightning Source LLC
Chambersburg PA
CBHW020756250626
47155CB00003B/1107

* 9 7 8 1 9 2 5 5 6 8 2 6 4 *